continued . . .

LOST ON THE DARKSIDE

VOICES FROM THE EDGE OF HORROR

Edited by John Pelan

A ROC BOOK

ROC

Published by New American Library, a division of
Penguin Group (USA) Inc., 375 Hudson Street,
New York, New York 10014, USA
Penguin Group (Canada), 90 Eglinton Avenue East, Suite 700, Toronto,
Ontario M4P 2Y3, Canada (a division of Pearson Penguin Canada Inc.)
Penguin Books Ltd., 80 Strand, London WC2R 0RL, England
Penguin Ireland, 25 St. Stephen's Green, Dublin 2,
Ireland (a division of Penguin Books Ltd.)
Penguin Group (Australia), 250 Camberwell Road, Camberwell, Victoria 3124,
Australia (a division of Pearson Australia Group Pty. Ltd.)
Penguin Books India Pvt. Ltd., 11 Community Centre, Panchsheel Park,
New Delhi - 110 017, India
Penguin Group (NZ), Cnr Airborne and Rosedale Roads, Albany,
Auckland 1310, New Zealand (a division of Pearson New Zealand Ltd.)
Penguin Books (South Africa) (Pty.) Ltd., 24 Sturdee Avenue,
Rosebank, Johannesburg 2196, South Africa

Penguin Books Ltd, Registered Offices:
80 Strand, London WC2R 0RL, England

First published by Roc, an imprint of New American Library,
a division of Penguin Group (USA) Inc.

First Printing, September 2005
10 9 8 7 6 5 4 3 2 1

CONTENTS

At The Circus of the Dead

Tony Richards

We had just watched the lion tamer being torn to shreds. Danny was sitting next to me, my wife was sitting beyond him, and if I was a good father at all I would have gotten them out of there, right then. It was the first of the five acts and things were going to get much worse—but, right then, my stomach was boiling like dry ice, shooting splinters of pain through me. As though *I* were being mauled, from the inside out. I was frozen. I sat there in that brown and battered tent. And watched.

The tamer was conscious right to the end. The lions had pinned down his chest and arms, and while they worked at him he struggled like a damaged butterfly. His scream! It went on and on and never seemed to stop—and when at last it did, when his legs gave one final sharp thrash and were still, the ensuing silence was featureless and unscalable. The night was hot. The smell of cats and blood and spilled guts choked me.

No one moved.

Not even to turn away.

And the cats let their victim lie, and went back to their stools. They waited, calm now, unblinking. As though the killing might have been part of the act: the greatest show on Earth.

The corpse: no longer anything remotely human. Dead meat. Viscera and exposed bones, swaddled in shreds of a coat which had been a far lesser red. Impossible angles. Just lying there, steaming obscenely. *Lying there*.

The cats would not touch it.

And neither did anyone else.

A sense of time vaguely impinged my consciousness. I could not be sure, but . . . at least a minute had passed since the man had died. By now, the circus staff should have been moving, driving the cats back to their enclosure, trying to retrieve the body. Trying, for the audience's sake, to conceal the scene.

Still no one moved.

The blood glistened, brighter than it should have been. There were strange shadows folding from the corpse. I realized, for the first time, that there was a spotlight on it.

What kind of circus *was* this?

*   *   *

It had arrived early that morning. We had been the first to see it come. Danny, my seven-year-old son, spotted it first of all.

We were returning from the general store, weighed down with brown paper bags of Saturday shopping. Christine and I were struggling with imbalances of potatoes, escapes of cans, while Danny raced ahead testing his brand-new balsa glider. It was a gaudy locust of a thing, and he hadn't gotten the knack right yet. He would throw it too hard, making it hurtle upward several yards only to nosedive on the dusty street. It was annoying him, so he invented a new game. The moment the glider began to plunge, he would leap forward, catch it before it hit the ground.

"Danny, you'll break it! I'm not buying another one!"

He did not listen to me, kept on playing at his kamikaze game, each throw and dive taking him a few yards closer to our cottage just beyond the edge of town; by hops, by fits and starts and stops, at one with the locust motion of his toy.

"Danny!" Christine dropped a can and, stooping to pick it up, dropped two more. "You're going too fast. Come here and help your daddy and me."

"Make me!"

He was passing the third to last cottage. He threw the glider extra hard, flying it wild and jagged. It stopped in midair, plunged. Danny was after it, about to catch it.

When he let it go.

The glider impacted on a stone, lost its nose and half of its left wing.

I expected my son to start crying, but he just stared obliviously down the road. His body was set at a curious angle, his hands still raised where they had missed the wooden plane. Reaching him, I saw what he was looking at.

Around the bend of the main road, passing the village limits sign—HOPE'S HATCH; POP. 214—the circus was coming. It emerged from the shadows of the flanking trees like a funeral procession for some tragic clown. The color brown was very much in evidence, that and the color gray.

Christine struggled to my side. "Aren't you going to . . . ?" She forgot the glider suddenly, just as Danny, just as I, had done. "My God, what a *mangy*-looking circus."

Mangy and small, for only eight drab wagons trundled into view. The first, by far the largest, carried the big top, the poles and generator, and the heavy equipment. The legend KNIGHT'S TRAVELING CIRCUS was faded into its side. After that came the road-borne cage, bars giving onto a fetid dark, and animal moanings which scared the cattle off in the adjacent fields. The six other wagons were smaller still. Each bore the name of the resident act and a poor illustration of the performer in action. SIMBATA THE LION TAMER; FERROS, MAN OF IRON; THE HUMAN TORCH; THE AMAZING DANDINI; THE FLYING RAMONES.

Each, that was, except the sixth and final wagon, which was featureless. I had no idea what that last one was for.

Huge brutes of horses, dirty gray and dirty brown, drew the strange procession on; ugly beasts that sweated as they pulled and flicked their tails at the surrounding cloud of flies. Their harnesses vanished into the thick shadows at the front of each wagon. I simply could not see the drivers—not a living soul.

The first wagon turned off the road and headed for the tree-ringed village green. And the others followed, keeping pace.

"Looks like they're stopping here," said Christine. "Just like that?"

There had been no advance publicity, no posters, no handbills. We'd heard no news of any circus from the townships further up the road. We were, it seemed, being uniquely graced by their presence.

"Just like that," I nodded.

A crowd had gathered near us now. A lot of children, some small dogs. Both types of creature, true to form, would have been chasing the tail of the procession by now, driving it on with barks and shouts. They remained immobile, silent though. Like Danny. Like all of us.

The final caravan was swallowed up behind the trees. Faintly, there was the sound of loosed activity as unseen people began setting up their show. Some while later, a banner appeared through a gap in the branches.

KNIGHT'S TRAVELING CIRCUS. ONE NIGHT ONLY. SHOW STARTS 8:36.

"Why not 8:45?" asked Christine. "Or 8:30?"

I shook my head, and then said, "Sunset."

We lingered a while more. There was nothing further to see. The crowd broke up by increasing degrees until we found ourselves the first to come and last to go. The shopping bags were turning our arms to softened lead.

"Can we go to the circus?" Danny asked.

His eyes were wide.

"Of course." Christine put one of her bags on the ground and fished two cartons of eggs out of it. "First though, you give me a hand. Take these, Danny. I don't want to break them."

He held out both hands for them, seemed about to take them. Just as Christine released her grip, though, he pulled back. Both boxes joined the glider on the ground, discharging yolk.

"Danny!"

But he was already gone, running for home like a quarterback with the ball, moving on wings of dust. We hurried after him as best we could, stumbled in through the back door and dumped the groceries on the kitchen floor.

"Where are you? Come here!"

"Make me!"

He was not even trying to hide. Just standing in the hallway, refusing to come to us like some prophet-sought mountain. Seven years old and small for his age—a mountain.

Christine rushed to him, gripped his arms too tightly, shook him.

"What's the meaning of this, young man? *What? Are you crazy?*"

His lips were compressed. He returned her gaze directly, defiantly.

"Well?" Christine shouted.

Nothing. At least, nothing in words.

"Okay, if that's the way you want it, I can play rough too. Forget the circus tonight, Danny. You've had it."

He broke free of her grip in an instant, ran up the stairs to his room. On the landing, he turned.

"Go to hell, both of you!"

His bedroom door slammed shortly after that.

Christine stared after him bewilderedly, then turned to me. Bright spots of color marked her cheeks. She had found a new target for her anger.

"That's your fault, Rich. He learns that kind of language from you.

She was right, of course. A dozen times, while arguing long-distance with TV producers, creative department heads, other damned fools, my fury had erased the memory of Danny's presence in the room. *No, I won't rewrite it, go to hell! Scrap the thing, find someone else, just go to hell!* Now, it had rebounded on me.

"I'll talk to him," I said. "I'll try to calm him down."

"Do that."

She went back into the kitchen, leaving me to face my son. My stomach tightened. When I was a boy, my father had filled me with a fear far worse than God. Now, I was a father myself—and my own son scared me.

I listened at his door before knocking. There was no sound of movement. When I entered, I found him lying facedown on his bed. He would not turn around. I had to kneel right down beside him, hold his chin, and work to move his face toward me. Like turning over a large, soft stone.

His face was puffy and his eyes were wet. There was a damp patch on the bedspread where he had been crying. He tried to jerk his head away to hide the tears. I held him fast though.

"Danny, you can talk to me."

He sniffed, wiped his nose, regarding me sullenly.

"Come on, kiddo. I'm not going to punish you.

But why keep behaving like this? You're driving your mom crazy."

"Well this place drives *me* crazy," Danny said. "I *hate* it."

"But you hated the big city too. You can't have it both ways."

"I'm bored." As if none of what I had just said had registered.

"There are other kids to play with."

"They're all dumb. Why do we have to stay in this dumb place?"

I sat beside him on the bed, one arm around his shoulder. "Well, Danny, lots of reasons. It's cheap here. And Mom and I really like it. And then there's my work. I've been writing better here than I ever did in the city. Which means I sell more of what I write. Which means that pretty soon I won't have to work for TV anymore—you know how much I hate that."

I trailed off, aware of how selfish I must have been sounding. Danny was bored, and that was that. My own artistic sensibilities meant nothing. Who was it said, "There is nothing so bourgeois as children"?

"Danny," I said, hugging him, "let's forget all this. Okay? You apologize to your mom and help her put the groceries away, and I *promise* we'll take you to the circus tonight. Deal?"

It was. I left him to dry his eyes and clean his face

up, certain that everything was going to be all right. My study waited, and a brand-new project: a segment of an afternoon soap opera which had been running for fifteen years. Written by bored scenarists for the amusement of bored housewives —but it paid the bills. Thirty pages later, it was growing dim outside and Christine was announcing dinner. I typed one final line, then hurried downstairs guiltily.

Christine met me in the hall, a plate of rib roast in each hand. Her eyes contained anything but love, though.

"You've been up there all day. Christ, Rich, when do we get a weekend to ourselves?"

"I've got to get it done, haven't I? How's Danny been acting?"

"Quiet, like he's bottling things up." She shot me a fierce glance as she made for the dining room door. "You could have at least played with him today. Christ, but you can be a rotten father."

And that set the whole tone of the meal. Afterward, I went upstairs, got washed and shaved. Sunset approached. Christine and Danny were waiting for me in the hallway when I reappeared.

We went. To the circus.

The evening was as still as a becalmed ship. Nebulous clouds of midges filled the air, and Danny swatted at them as he hurried onward. We had to keep calling him back, reining him in and forcing him to rein in his high spirits. Every nerve and sinew of his body spoke of some rich, hardly bearable excitement. He seemed happier than we'd seen him in quite a time.

We were far from alone on the main street. Almost all of Hope's Hatch appeared to be there. The Corlays and the Madisons each had a new baby, so would not venture out late. And old Smithson was too blind and deaf to appreciate this kind of show. But everyone else had turned out. The whole village. We walked toward the green like an ambling herd.

"Look!" And Danny pointed.

The pinnacle of the big top was now visible above the fringe of the trees. Black against the dimming sky, its sharp tip seemed to pierce the sun, and the sun seemed to bleed. The western horizon was smeared vermilion, the clouds were stained like bandages. Then, as the minutes progressed, even that color was drained away. A residue of burnished gold remained out on the very edge. The grayness above that was deepening.

We moved on.

The trees rustled softly as we passed through them.

Somewhere out in the fields, crickets began to sing.

Ahead, lights glowed. Drawn, we moved toward

them. I noticed that we were leading the crowd now. We stopped, and so did they. Gazing.

The big top lay before us. And surrounding it, half a dozen smaller tents that might have sprung out of the ground like mushrooms. I had expected candy colors, fairy lights. Instead, a few storm lanterns hung on poles, and the canvas on display was uniformly dried-earth brown. Holes were sealed up with crude patches. Big edges hung frayed and loose.

Christine let out a nervous laugh at the sight of all this lack of splendor. "Heavens, what a fleapit!"

Danny, though, seemed transfixed. As if this were the grandest place in the whole world. His eyes glowed, reflecting far more than the lanterns.

At the entrance, there was a small booth where we paid our fee. An old woman, her face half lost in shadow, dispensed tickets for a few small coins. Inside, the lion cage had already been set up. Three rows of battered seats surrounded the ring. The audience began to fill them . . . and when we had all sat down, I realized that there was not a spare seat left. How had the owners of this place known . . . ?

They'd gotten it *exactly right*.

And yes, our population could be read about on the way in. But the two young couples with the babies? And the deaf and half-blind man?

There was a generator humming somewhere near, subliminally quiet. The lights dimmed. When they came back up again, the ringmaster was revealed before us. Mr. Knight. Medium of height and build, and very plain looking. He wore the traditional costume, top hat, tails, except—instead of red, his coat was black. A diamond stickpin glittered in his lapel like some solitary star. In place of a whip, he held a leather leash in his right hand. A huge and vicious-looking mandrill squatted at the other end—his pet?

Knight raised his free arm in an extravagant salute.

"Ladies and gentlemen! Welcome to the greatest circus show on Earth!"

Christine snorted with mirth. Danny shushed her.

"Tonight, you will see five wondrous and highly dangerous displays! Five acts performed by the very bravest men and women! Gasp as they risk life and limb! Marvel as they stare death squarely in the face!"

His patter went on for a while. I shuffled in my seat, unimpressed, wondering how literally the term "fleapit" applied to this place. At least they were not selling refreshments. I wouldn't want to buy them, and it would be hard explaining why to Danny.

Knight had just announced Simbata, and he disappeared into the wings with another wide flourish. The lions were let into the cage through a trapdoor at the back. The tamer, a painfully skinny, rather sad-looking man, entered.

He stood dead center. Spread his arms in a messianic pose.

The lions moved. They smothered him in rich gold fur and tawny manes.

And red. And red. And red.

Still no one moved.

The mutilated corpse lay untouched in its pool of gore and spotlight.

Danny nudged me in the ribs. My mind unfroze, my body felt a little more like solid flesh. I looked down at my son. And he was smiling.

"Wow!" he breathed. "They really, *really* killed him, didn't they?"

Christine had not even heard. She was gazing at the cage, mesmerized, her mouth a slack oval of shock. Her eyes showed—nothing. Nothing at all. Like a fixated bird before a snake. The whole audience was like that.

I wondered how long it would be before they snapped out of it, began to scream.

They were not given time. Theatrically precise, the spotlight flickered off right then. We were plunged into breathless darkness. Mere seconds later, when the lights came back, the cage and cats and corpse were gone. Knight was standing in the ring again. Opposite him was a huge archery target board, concentric circles, black on white.

No one could have moved the animals and bars that silently, that fast. But they *had* vanished. As though I had blinked my eyes and. . .

There was still blood on the sawdust. Mr. Knight was standing right by it. His mandrill sniffed the damp patch curiously, began to lick it.

Knight was smiling.

Just like Danny.

Smiling.

"Thank you, ladies and gentlemen! And now, for the next act of the evening, we have brought you at great—"

Next act. As though nothing untoward had happened. No grief, no concern, no apologies. Next act.

"—all the way from the mysterious mountains of the East. Reared by a tribe of abominable snowmen. Trained by arcane Buddhist monks in their wild mountain retreat. I give you Ferros, Man of Iron!"

And he looked around, as though expecting applause. I sat there thinking, *This has to be some kind of stunt—some sick, revolting, awful joke. Please?*

The Man of Iron stepped into the ring, olive-skinned and massive, shaggy hair cascading down his back. From beneath his moustache, he displayed the whitest set of teeth. Knight began explaining what was to come. Ferros was a man of extraordinary strength and lightning reactions. He would—Knight produced a silver pistol from the depths of his black coat—catch a bullet between his teeth. That simple. Except, there would be no tricks, no dud slugs or sleight of hand. Carefully, so that everyone could see, Knight inserted one shining bullet into a chamber, snapped the chamber shut and turned it, cocked the hammer. Ready.

Christine was only just beginning to come back alive.

She leant toward me, whispered in a shaky voice, "What about the lion tamer? What's happened to *him*?"

"I don't know."

There was the flat, unmistakable crack of a pistol shot. Everybody stared at Ferros. Who stood there, and opened his mouth, and . . . a thick stream of blood spurted out.

The Man of Iron toppled like a tree, revealing that the bullseye behind him had turned to red, textured with shattered flecks of gray. A hole the size of a fist showed through Ferros' mane of hair.

As the man hit the ground, part of his skull came clean away.

Mercifully, the lights went out once more.

Panic should have been the order of the day; yells, and a stampede for the exit. Danny ought to have been horrified by now, Christine hysterical. Yet they were not, and neither were the people all around me. Good folk, people I thought I knew. It was as though some unseen force were holding them in place. In the surrounding gloom, there were small shufflings and nervous coughs. That was all.

As my eyes adjusted, I could just make out Knight's silhouette. Within the shadowed mask of his face, his eyes glittered. He seemed to be staring right at me. I looked away, and saw that the big target board was gone. Ferros, I guessed, had also been removed. His *corpse* had been removed. This was no trick, no joke. Just like the lion tamer, he was dead.

What was this, a circus full of suicidal lunatics?

Knight was announcing the third act.

The lights stayed down this time as a man dressed all in silver stepped into the ring. He held a flaming torch in each hand. Casually, he drew them both toward his mouth.

"If he catches fire," Christine muttered weakly, "I'm going to be sick."

And he did. Immolated himself.

But she wasn't.

Just sat there, weird lights dappling her face, as the Human Torch still writhed across the ground.

In the darkness, with the flickering light, it might have been on television.

Watching. We were all just watching. None of us did anything to stop it.

I might have never moved, except I looked again

at my young son. There was no shock on Danny's face, just that same smile. He was no longer bored, I realized.

Jumping up, I clambered past the front row, leapt over the barrier. I landed unsteadily in the dark, moved toward the burning man, wondering how I was going to help him.

Knight laughed. Gently, he let go of the leash, and before it had touched the ground the mandrill was in front of me. Barring my way, snarling, its vulpine fangs set in a picket fence of razor white. One step closer, it would have my throat.

The Human Torch was motionless by now, although smoke still rose from him. Angry and frightened, I turned on the ringmaster.

"You've got to stop this!"

"Why?" asked Knight. And then, "Return to your seat if you please, sir."

"And let this go on? Who the hell *are* you people? What *is* this?"

"Entertainment."

"There are children in this audience. *Children!* We didn't pay to see *this!*"

"Oh, but I must disagree," came the reply. "This is precisely what you paid to see."

His eyes held mine.

The diamond stickpin glittered.

The lights came up again and I stumbled back to the edge of the ring. The fourth act commenced. A

replica of the Iron Maiden of Nuremberg domi-
nated the ring this time, a forest of spikes protruding from its coffinlike interior. The Amazing
Dandini would be strapped inside, and the doors
slowly closed. He would, of course, said Mr.
Knight, escape.

He did not escape, of course.

And as the Maiden's gutters filled and over-
flowed, I gazed on, sick with myself. Not one member of the audience had the decency to turn away,
not even when Knight reopened the doors.

And as the Flying Ramones looped and spiraled
high above our heads, and as they tried to link
hands, failed, and tumbled screaming to their
deaths, that single truth that Knight had told me
rang ever more true. *Entertainment.* A dozen cir-
cuses I'd seen over the years, not counting
sideshows nor televized displays. I'd watched hundreds of dangerous acts. And they had always held
me—held everyone around me—rapt for just one
reason: something might go wrong.

Had we, without knowing it, been waiting for
that to happen? A slip, a mistake, death? To see
somebody defy the darkness, lose?

Well then, this was our lucky day, wasn't it?
We'd had our fill, five times over. The ghoul in each
of us . . . had been entertained.

There was a drumroll, thunderous and sharp.

Knight stood alone in a clear disc of light. He

gestured to the wings, and silhouettes began moving toward him through the gloom. Slow shadows, shambling and bent. I could not see their faces, but I knew who they were. Simbata, torn to ragged meat; Ferros, with half a head; the charred Human Torch; Dandini, moving on severed, loosely swinging limbs. And the Ramones, ultimately fallen. I could hear shattered bones and torn flesh dragging across the sawdust.

They entered the spotlight.

And a cymbal crashed.

They were whole. For the next performance, further down whatever road they took. For the next entertainment, whole.

Danny went wild with applause, and I couldn't take that. It was too much. I rushed across to him and slapped him hard across his face. But he didn't cry, and when his eyes opened again, he gazed at me accusingly. He understood. He was seven years old, and I—I was just a hypocrite.

By rights, I should have slapped myself.

The crickets had stopped singing when we emerged from the big top. The moon was hidden behind dense clouds. We did not speak, nor did any of our neighbors. There were not the words.

Christine and I walked either side of Danny, holding him rather too tightly as we made our way back home. When we had got him safely into bed, Christine undressed in the darkness of our room.

She slipped on her nightdress and got in between the sheets. I caught a glimpse of her face as she settled down. It was expressionless as ice. Then, she turned away from me. I was alone.

I'd never hit Danny like that before.

Somehow, despite the grief and shame and guilt, I managed to fall asleep some hours later.

The noise which woke me was a delicate tapping. It was coming from Danny's room. I sat bolt upright on the bed, still fully clothed. Then got up, blinking against the rising dawn, and went into the upstairs hallway.

The tapping went on, insistent.

What was happening now?

A pause. Then I pushed Danny's door wide open. The bed was empty, the sheets pushed back into an untidy heap.

I stared round stupidly as a light-dazzled owl. "*Danny?*"

The window was wide open. And a breeze was making the curtain cord tap against the sill.

Christine was up by now. I could hear her moving around. But above that noise, there was another, much louder, from the street below. I hurried to the window and leant out.

Knight's Traveling Circus, the circus of the dead, was disappearing down the road. The wagons were in the same order. Except . . . the final one had now been painted on. KIMO THE SNAKE BOY, read the inscription. Below it, there was an illustration of my own son struggling in the thick coils of a python.

I bolted downstairs and out through the front door.

But by the time I reached the street, the circus of the dead was gone.

THIS BODY OF DEATH

Maria Alexander

Pretty, pretty, that one. I must find out who she is. You go. I don't give a fuck. She's just another bird. We shall insinuate ourselves. Oh . . . what a wretched man am I. Who will save us from this body of death . . . ?

"I'm canvassing for the Satanglicans. Are you currently a member of our church?"

He was 6'4", a slick tower of Eurosex in his late 20s, wearing leather pants, a dress shirt and tie, and a black woolen fedora. One inhalation of his skin as he stood close, his London accent snaking in my head, and ringlets of smoke slipped from my burning sex. Some people verbally reach between your legs, as if sexually bilocating from where they stand. Englishmen do this to me, using nothing more than words to turn blackened keys in the lock of my Pandora's box. Because I'd had such bad experiences with them in the past, everything said to run—*Run!*—don't walk back into the club. But instead I stood outside with my cigarette-pinching friends in the Los Angeles smog, lifting the long hair from my sweating neck to cool in the night air.

He'd stolen the bit about the Satanglicans from a website by the Van Gogh-Goghs. I didn't know at the time.

I laughed. "No, but I am president of the Neo-Anglicans of America. Do you think if I wrote a letter to Tony Blair apologizing for the tea debacle that he'd take us back?" As he chuckled, the smoke of him roiled behind my eyes and under my tongue. "I promise to learn how to drink real tea, boil vegetables, and drive a Citroën."

The blue flames of his eyes coolly flickered as he examined me. He wiped long black bangs from them as he continued with a reel of charming banter. He didn't know if The Queen would take me back, but all sinners would be welcomed back by His Majesty Satan, for all are welcome in Satan's house. Frankly, I don't remember much else of what he said now. I just remember the feeling of him, and how the delicate skin between my legs grew slick. I wanted him badly, but . . .

The lovely Dahlia stood beside me, large green eyes and ashy blond hair tucked immaculately under a short black wig. Her black velvet corset molded her already statuesque figure into a slick hourglass as she dragged on a cigarette. Dahlia was a SAG actor; we'd met when she starred in a low-budget horror film I wrote that was produced last year during a strike. She rapidly became one of my closest friends, bringing me to Carpe Noctem a few months ago after my absence of three years from the club scene. I'd had a horrid relationship with a popular dominant and had to leave when we split because he was so ubiquitous. But Dahlia assured me that Master Whatsit had vanished and that it was safe to return. "Oh! I'm sorry, Blazes. This is Ezra. Ezra, Blazes."

Ezra took my hand and kissed it. "You will play with me tonight, Blazes?" He then crossed his arms and slumped playfully against me. "I'm rather hoping you will," he said.

I had seen Ezra before. He looked right through me that night as he leaned over the bar and spoke to the bartender. Dahlia had told me about Ezra—I had seen his many posts in the club guest book. I also noticed from the guest book entries that he was engaged to a woman named Leah who liked to talk about TV shows, but for my life I could not guess who the woman could be from what I'd seen of Ezra so far that night. Anyway, I've often thought there's a reason and timing for all things. This was no exception.

"How could I refuse?" I replied. If nothing else,

this would be a good way to determine if I still liked it.

Inside the narrow club, the diminutive DJ with smudgy eyes spun Velvet Acid Christ's "Slut." Dahlia leaned in to my ear. "I don't know, Blazes," she said. "Ezra hasn't much control."

I shrugged. "It's not a big club, Dahlia. I'll just say something if it gets out of hand."

She eyed the stage worriedly, then smiled reluctantly. "You better get up there. Twenty drunken Goth chicks are about to charge that stage."

Ezra waited for me on the large stage crowded with band gear. He took my hand and led me like a princess to the red velvet-draped stool. As spectators gathered around, he removed my top hat, loosening my still damp, waist-length red hair. I was left in my short lavender silk skirt, a black leather corset, and my spiked corset boots.

As Ezra wrapped the soft white rope around my wrists, securing my hands in a clever knot, I thought, *I'm in trouble. Deep, deep trouble.* Ezra bent me over the stool. My smooth bottom blossomed just under the edge of the short skirt, the corset exaggerating the curves. My garters and the backs of my spiked corset boots turned to the audience, laced perfectly from heel to calf. Whistles pierced the crowd.

I never suffer stage fright. I'm an exhibitionist *par excellence.* The thrill of performing—not sadomasochism—is what attracted me to S and M in the first place. So as the series of blows came from Ezra's floggers, a fist-over-fist whirlwind of soft leather, I winced without pleasure.

When the strikes stopped, Ezra reappeared before me and lowered his face to mine. He wore the shiny black leather beak of Pulcinella, the mocking, lewd buffoon from the Italian *commedia dell'arte*. The blue flames of his eyes flashed from the openings and a dry burning for him singed my mouth. *Well met*, I thought. *And so the association of pain with pleasure.* He held my face in his hands and that's when I noticed the swelling erection in his leather pants. That long devil. The wicked, flirtatious nymph in me grinned. "It seems you are enjoying this as much as I am." His eyes widened, then he looked away as if I had surprised him.

Eventually the stings ceased and Ezra used his bare hand on my ass. I yelped with real pain, no longer for mere dramatics. Then, he turned me over and untied my hands, drawing my arms Christ-wide as he locked my wrists into fleece-lined cuffs suspended from the ceiling. I swooned backward, the bawling guitar of Rob Zombie battering the club walls. *Unholy just like you.* Below me, Ezra knelt out of my line of sight. When he turned to me, I inhaled sharply. . . .

Ezra twirled flaming fire sticks, a giant match in each hand. I shifted my weight involuntarily backward, endorphins carrying me an inch off the floor as I quavered.

He played my arms like a fire dulcimer. I gasped at every other strike—not from fear or pain, but rather the sensation that poison seeped under my skin at his every touch. When he finished, he picked up a straight razor and slowly traced my neck with its gleaming, sharp edge. My stomach Lindy Hopped with excitement and I clenched my jaw. Those eyes shined unsteadily again behind Pulcinella's lewd scowl as they skittered between mine and the movement of the blade.

The tension unraveled instantly as he then stepped back and extended his arm toward my pale chest where the neckline plunged. With a steady hand, Ezra dragged a dagger tip from collar bone to cleavage, leaving a long pink scratch in the blade's wake. I cursed him silently for marking me, however lightly.

When he released me, I wobbled with exhaustion. I bowed and he helped me off the stage, the voyeurs clapping and whistling. I had forgotten how much energy one expends in the power exchange as the body chemistry ebbs and flows with pain and pleasure. Dahlia walked me out to my car past where Ezra held court in a crowd outside as he smoked a pipe. I still could not tell who his fiancée was. He did not say good-bye.

* * *

Mistressss. Mistressss Blazessss. Her real name is Rachel. Besides, she won't hear you. She sleeps as a soul tortured, yessss. She's in REM, you dolts. The deepest of sleep. We have broken the Law of Moses! SHUT IT! The muscles of the body stiffen, the eyes move, the heart rate increases, breathing becomes more rapid and irregular, and the blood pressure rises. . . . Delta? She's a creative one. That means we can talk to her in her dreams. . . . Forgive us for we have sinned against thee, oh Lord. We look upon a woman with lust in our eyes. . . . I'm going to take every one of you wankers and peel off your sausage casings with a blunt knife if you don't shut it NOW. . . .

I awoke early the next morning, feeling as though my dreams had been broken under the footsteps of constant conversation. The dream people left only brushstrokes of meaning: insecurity, fear, astonishment, secrecy, and desire. So much desire. I am very much a believer in the Gestalt view of dreams. Everything in my dreams is a part of me speaking to myself. But this loose stream of words seemed utterly apart from my consciousness. Something foreign. Yet the feelings were mine.

I was doing a rewrite for a producer I hated. That morning I sat down at my home computer with a cup of tea, wondering how I was going to take this piece of crap action script and turn it into a gleaming Golden Globe contender. It wasn't going to happen with the notes the overly stupid development woman had given me, and I needed to email my agent all the complaints. As soon as I signed onto my ISP, my MSN Messenger notified me that "Lautreamont" had added me to his IM list. I wondered who that was as I clicked the box allowing this mysterious person to see me online. "Lautreamont" appeared online immediately and sent me an instant message.

It was Ezra. He must have searched the club guest book and gotten my email address from there.

"I have so many questions I want to ask you," he typed.

"Like what?"

"Well . . . like what were you thinking as you looked at my mask?" I hesitated, and he continued. "And what did you feel as I brought my razor close to your throat?"

"Those are very personal questions, Ezra," I told him. "I feel uncomfortable answering such things, especially online."

"Can we have tea today then? Meet in person?"

When he entered my apartment, I was sure he could smell me: my excitement, my fear. Sensing something animalistic about him from the beginning, I masked my scent with perfume to throw him off. I wanted so badly to touch him. He wore khaki slacks, a soft white dress shirt with sleeves rolled up at the elbow, and black Marc Jacobs shoes.

But as we drank tea on my black leather sofa, he dissolved into a buzzing swamp of tensions. Instead of asking me the questions he had asked online, he began to unravel a bizarre tale of growing up in London without a family. His parents were killed in a motoring accident when he was thirteen and he was taken in by members of the London Hellfire Club, an underground S and M community. (I couldn't help stroking his hand at this point as it lay on the back of the couch. His bare skin—I *had* to touch it. His speech faltered as I did so.) Living at the club and learning about bondage, he took his A levels by fifteen. By twenty-two, he had completed postdoctoral work in genetic research at Cambridge; had been in seminary but stopped short of his vows; took over the Hellfire Club from its aging leader; earned a second-degree black belt in Tang Soo Do; owned and ran his own mortuary; and served in the British military as SAS. . . .

I almost spewed tea out of my nose. And why do they always have to say they're spies? I had another English friend, Richard, who it turned out really *was* an ex-spy. As of last December when he retired, he'd been in the British military for more than twenty-five years. He was so addled from the Secret Air Service that he could not maintain a normal romantic relationship with a woman (i.e., me). I saw his SAS plaques, his paperwork. He was the genuine thing. But this young man on my couch . . .

"Ezra, you're awfully young to have accomplished so much. How old are you?"

"How old do you think I am?"

I bit my lip. "Twenty-nine."

"You flatter me," he said. "I'm twenty-six."

Eventually Ezra had to leave to meet Leah for dinner with friends. He asked me if I would consider playing with him privately. I gently explained that I could not play privately with someone who wasn't available. He was engaged. It was not going to happen. Ezra looked sheepish, then sighed. "All right then, luv. I understand," he said as he kissed my forehead like a brother.

But with his face that close to mine, I couldn't help it.

I kissed him.

I blocked him on IM for weeks after he continually asked to see me again for tea, and I only eventually returned to Carpe Noctem with Dahlia. Huddled on the red velvet couches in the shadows, I told Dahlia what happened with Ezra . . . although I did not tell her I kissed him. She once had a tremendous crush on him, but the spell soon dissipated for no reason she could articulate. What she wanted to know was his real name. No one knew. They only knew him as Ezra. And now he claimed to have directed three independent films, yet without his real name no one could verify if it was true.

Dahlia needed the work and contacts in the worst way. She brightened. "Let's dance!" She took my hand and lead me out to the dance floor.

The bells chimed, the tympani thundered, and the brush scratched the snare as Nick Cave's "Red Right Hand" played. As Dahlia and I danced, Ezra in a black suit and derby slinked onto the dance floor and put his arm around my waist.

He danced sublimely. I giggled as he spun me around and dipped me back. He smiled devilishly as I hung in his arms, utterly at his mercy, then he plucked me back up and swung me out. I caught Dahlia watching with a frown. She must have been puzzled by my dual behavior, to say the least.

When we finished, he picked up a gin and tonic off the bar and swilled it back. "I haven't seen you online in ages."

"I've been very busy." It was true. Sort of. "How are you?"

"Good, good," he said. "Have you reconsidered my proposition?"

"Ezra! You're still engaged!"

"Right." He looked distracted as he finished off his drink. He placed the glass on the bar, then turned to me. "How are *you*?" He gathered me in his arms for a hug.

Everything inside me teetered. "Fine . . . I think. . . ."

With all the evil that is Man, he licked my neck.

I closed my eyes, sick with lust. He pulled away slightly and his liquor breath warmed my face. I felt some kind of basic molecular shift, as if every atom in my body had just passed its half-life. Drunk with him, I pressed my lips to his. Thick shadows swam over us, yet I could see the spectral color of his eyes when I pulled away. I involuntarily stroked his smooth jaw.

Never in my life was even the most casual touch like 10,000 volts of sin. I touched him whenever I could that night. As my eyes followed him, I identified the woman who would be his wife: a short waif with glasses and wavy blond hair. Leah. A whisper in black. An afterthought of the scenery. The uncurled ribbon that ties the bouquet. If only a razor were stripped across her, then she would ripple and curl with life.

Pater noster, qui es in caelis . . . Oh, my brothers, slooshy what I have in store for her. A little of the old in-out, real savage. Would you quit talking like that stupid film? She's beautiful and sweet and lonely. . . . I can hear her heart thundering in the emptiness of her home . . . sanctificétur nomen tuum . . . Listen, I've been trained to go without sleep years longer than you can keep your sausage in your trousers . . . But you don't feel for her? Of course I do, you bloody sod. We all do. She's not like the rest. She's clever, courageous . . . Panem nostrum cotidiánum . . . But quite weak. . . .

*   *   *

I awoke in a heavy sweat at 3:18 A.M. The strange voices in my dreams grew louder, more insistent. As if someone was trying to get my attention. *Someones*. All distinctly male. Tonight a Latin prayer rambled through my dreams. I tore off the now soaking robe I'd fallen asleep in and rolled over, my fingers still remembering how the skin of his jaw felt.

I fell back to sleep.

At my usual time I awoke. And after making some tea, I sat at the computer and signed on to MSN. Immediately, "Lautreamont" appeared online but blocked. I sipped my tea, thinking. Feeling . . .

I unblocked him.

"Good morning."

"Good morning, Ezra."

"How are you?"

"Very well. You?"

"Good, good." A pause. "So, what is your day like?"

"Writing."

"Writing? What exactly?"

"That rewrite for Warner Bros."

"Dan Hurts, right?"

"LOL! You mean Hertz."

"No, Hurts Like Hell, Hertz."

"Right!" I was beyond surprised.

"Do you, in your busy writing schedule, have time for tea today?"

You will think me a terrible whore if I tell you that, when Ezra arrived, I peeled off his clothes as he wiped the bangs from his wild eyes. So I won't—mostly because it did not happen that way. Instead, we sat on the couch and I made him listen to a song on a CD I just bought. He had me sit back against him. I could hardly refuse. When the song was over, I turned to him to say something but was confronted by his soft lips after he had been heating my back with his irresistible warmth the last four minutes and twenty-two seconds. What a waste it would have been, to let that delicious mouth sit un-tasted. So I pulled him against me.

His breath was sour. I didn't care at all.

After a few moments he began to pull up my stretchy Donna Karan sports shirt, but I stopped him suddenly. "Right," he said, pulling down the shirt and sliding aside. But within a moment we were entwined again. As he sucked on my tongue, he pulled up my shirt, hooked my bra with his thumbs, and slipped them both up over my breasts. He licked my nipples until I went mad, unable to sit because of the powerful urge to straddle him. He then lifted me off the couch and laid me on the floor. He pulled off his shirt with one slick move-ment. A broad, perfectly smooth torso. I ran my hands over his pale chest, pinching and pulling on his nipples. He seemed to enjoy the pain. He devoured my mouth as I opened his khakis, all the while those eyes half-lidded and smoldering as he looked into mine. I reached inside his pants, the heat and the sweat engulfing my hand as I stroked his sweltering erection. His eyelids fluttered and his eyes rolled up in his head.

"Are you sure you want to do this?" he asked.

I nodded emphatically. He pulled off my jeans, pushed open my legs, and his warm tongue burrowed into my swelling cunt until I dug my fingers into the carpet, toes curling, and screamed. The brief detour to get condoms did not dampen the inferno for a moment. In fact, I'm not sure I ever stopped screaming.

It wasn't perfect. It's never perfect. But I knew something had been unleashed that I could never put away.

I needed his skin like my own.

We met whenever we could to sate ourselves. I let him tie me to my bed once with elaborate Japanese knots and draw my own knives over my body. He asked me questions about what I first thought when I saw him. About my most outrageous sexual acts. About my deepest fantasies. Fortunately, he talked so much I didn't have to answer most of his questions.

And he did tell me his name. Evan Blake. I told Dahlia, who could find nothing about him. I assured her that, just because he didn't appear in the International Movie Fucking Database, it didn't mean that he was automatically a fraud. She agreed.

Twice, he was horribly late. I realize that, since the invention of telephony, women have been trying to get men to use telephones, but Ezra seemed utterly incapable of calling to say he would be late. One time he was held up and I caught him online. He claimed he was having a contractual negotiation crisis for a film he was to direct, and was talking to his attorney. I almost blew up at him for not telling me, but my hunger was overpowering. When he requested that I come to his apartment, I came forthwith. We tangled on the soiled sheets and pillows of his and Leah's soon-to-be marriage bed. Their enormous white cockatoo, Beelze-Bob, strutted back and forth on the footboard railing as he squawked, "Make it so! Make it so!"

"Can't we put him in the other room?"

"Nope," Ezra responded breathlessly, kissing down my stomach as he rolled off my panties. "Or else he starts to make the Code Red alarm sound from the old *Star Trek*."

When I left, I walked past the carport and realized that he did not even have the car that day.

And I didn't care at all.

I was also having trysts with two other "unavailable" men who tempted me. I gave up on the idea that by being good I would be rewarded with a suitable lover. I had to make myself happy. And because of Ezra, I was a torch dragged over one hay bale after another, igniting everything I touched. I knew that I had always been like that—hence the nickname Blazes—but now I was more aware of it than ever.

I wondered if I could give him up when he was married.

I wondered if I would have to.

If only I could sleep. . . .

Do you think she likes me? You? The ugliest bastard to ever be consumed? You're all ugly bastards, every one of you. . . . Still . . . it's us she loves, not him. . . .

I decided to expose Ezra to my non-Goth friends. I had told all of them about him: his entertaining stories, his beauty, his treacherous effect on me. I wanted to show him off and Ezra wanted very much to meet Richard. So I invited him and Leah to a party to celebrate my ex-SAS friend's birthday. Although Richard and I had not been able to maintain a romantic relationship, he was a very close friend. We gathered at Richard's condo for wine, chili, and Dead Can Dance. Ezra's fiancée faded against the tile in the kitchen, chatting quietly with one of Richard's many ex-girlfriends—a scholar in musical anthropology. I could see the woman tiring of the tissue-thin discussion within a few moments, as Leah was a barely educated bank clerk. At first I wondered why Ezra stayed with her, but I soon realized that whatever inspired his bluster, his marvelously short temper, and his Machiavellian approach to relationships would certainly render him unable to operate within a normal work environment. If he wasn't doing whatever it was he did, he needed her to live.

I whispered into Ezra's ear that I wanted to introduce him to Richard now. Richard—strong, thick brows, black irises—received Ezra warmly. I sipped red wine on the couch and watched the two talk by the fireplace. After several moments of intense conversation, people gathered about as Ezra entertained an ever widening circle. Richard remained dark, and he fixed me with a look that pressed a cold edge of fear between my ribs.

"Rachel!" Richard said, the cell phone warbling from splotchy reception as I drove down Fairfax, the hands-free amplifier plugged into my ear. I was returning from the optometrist that morning, just after Richard's birthday party. "May I have a word with you about your friend? Buckaroo Banzai, is it?"

"You mean *Ezra*?" I couldn't believe the jealousy

in his voice. "He insisted on meeting you, you realize."

"Right. Are you having a 'thing' with this guy?"

"Richard!"

"Sorry. But I don't have to tell you he isn't remotely SAS or MI-5."

"Well, I didn't think you would."

"But there *was* something very strange about him . . ." His voice trailed off. "Many things, in fact."

"Well?"

"To start, his language . . . He used terms that haven't been used by the Agency in over seventy years. His ID number, as well. It's much too old for him."

"Really? Perhaps he got it from a book, then."

"Not so simple," Richard replied. "The descriptions he gave of places, they're real places only the operatives know. And he had details . . . yet . . . they all were very old. Things have changed drastically."

My eyes flitted over the wide lanes of Fairfax Avenue as I bit my lip. "What else?"

Richard fell silent.

"Richard?"

"He's not even English, Rachel." He fell silent again for a moment. "I can't place his accent. He's not . . . from anywhere."

I swerved to the curb and slammed on my brakes.

"Rachel, are you all right?"

I could not respond. I clutched the wheel as if I would tear it from the column.

"Listen to me. There is something very disturbing about this young man. If you are at all involved with him . . ." He hesitated.

"I'm listening."

"Just be careful," Richard said.

I fear for her, my darlings. They will find her body in her apartment, covered with flies. Blood will stain the carpet, the walls, her feet. Her soul? Nowhere to be found. Deep inside us will she be. Consumed. (Can you hear this, my sleeping beauty?) The devil is a roaring lion, seeking whom he may devour. . . .

The following week was filled with meetings and conference calls as my agent and I went back and forth with Hertz and his evil flying monkeys over a writing credit. They wanted another draft, above and beyond what was agreed upon, but they did not want to cut a check. By Thursday we had worked out most of the issues. I then had a particularly successful meeting with my inner muse and produced something better than I had hoped.

Richard's words had faded from my hearing and I was starving for Ezra. He IM'ed me.

"Do you miss me?" he asked.

"Very much. Do you miss me?"

"No."

"No?! LOL!"

"I crave you."

"I yearn for you."

"I burn everlasting . . ."

"What is your day like?"

"Open, but I don't have the Durango."

"The what?"

"The car. It's a reference to *A Clockwork Orange*."

"Ah. Well, damn." I remembered how the flames of hell licked the soles of my feet as we fucked in his bed. "I could come by."

"Better yet, why don't you pick me up?"

He climbed into my passenger seat with a black valise. After nearly eating off each other's lips, we took off from Culver City over the hill into the Valley. We drove clear up into Sunland where the roads ramble between hills gritty with sand and sage. We parked outside one of the white ranch-style houses nestled between two crests on some property surrounded by phallic cacti whose succulent pricks glistened in the brash sunlight. Ezra headed down the walkway lined with weeds to the garage, pulling keys from his pocket. He stepped to the side door, inserted the keys, and wiggled his eyebrows at me as he fussed with the lock. The door popped open with a whine to dusty darkness.

Ezra snapped on a light and closed the door behind us as I stepped into the cool garage crowded with boxes and furniture draped with drop cloths. He gripped one of the cloths covering a large piece of furniture and ripped it off dramatically.

A gynecological chair. Menacing wrought iron stirrups and dreary beige vinyl cushions. Ezra reached over to a workbench and flipped on a stereo. The Adagio from Vivaldi's violin concerto in D major sang soothingly from the speakers surrounding the interior. Then, with a flick of his wrist, a pair of leather handcuffs lined with black fur leapt over the top and landed squarely on the backrest. His eyes flashed as he watched for my reaction.

"Welcome to my office, Miss Blazes! Ready for your exam?"

"You are not serious."

He slithered up to me and unwrapped my Balinese skirt from my bare hips as he kissed me, exposing me from the waist down except for my spiked corset boots. My pubic hairs bristled against him. He lifted me onto the gynecological chair, spread open my blouse to expose my full breasts, and strapped my hands into the handcuffs. Another moment passed as he flipped the switch for the overhead fan, sat the valise by the massive garage basin, and ran the water. He whistled with the music. "I was once a concert cello player," he said as he turned back toward me, holding a very sharp-looking straight razor and a bowl of soapy water. "First held a bow in my hand at four years old in Vienna. Although, what I always wished I could do," he intimated, "was write. Like you." He approached the chair.

I gasped as he placed the razor close to my labia. "I don't know about this, Ezra."

"Trust me"—he winked—"I'm a professional."

He proceeded to gently scrape and dab at my vulnerable mound without raising even a pin-prick of blood as Vivaldi played Dolce largo. And when he finished, he pressed his thirsty mouth to my smooth, hairless flesh as his warm tongue licked away the dampness. After I writhed for several moments, his saline-smeared face lifted from between my legs. He unclasped the hand-cuffs and stripped off his clothes. As he climbed up on the table with me, he embraced me so pas-sionately that a storm raged in my blood for him. A storm that would never quiet, no matter what season.

I could not live without him.

When he left me to use the tiny bathroom in the garage, I started to dress. As I pulled on my blouse, I stopped cold when I saw his wallet lying on his pants. I had a split second to decide if I would be-tray him. . . .

I flipped open his wallet to his driver's license.

Evan T. Blake.

I trembled with guilt and closed it.

When Ezra invited me to the private play party at Master Corlois' house, I did not refuse, but I explained that I would not play with him publicly again. Everyone would know we were lovers. Ezra insisted that no one would have any idea. I knew better. I brought Dahlia as a sort of morality guard. I had not told her I was sleeping with Ezra, yet I could surely count on her to support me against his advances.

We entered Master Corlois' Victorian mansion, which he had converted to a full dungeon. With the corset boots, I wore a black PVC teddy with only a thong in the back, a black leather waist cincher, and black fishnets. Subtly, even though I knew I could never be with him, I wanted my long devil to know he *should* be with me. That I was the most beautiful thing in the place. Dahlia wore a long black satin gown that corset-tied up the back. Simple and elegant.

A bald male slave in his early fifties, naked save for a butler's jacket and a black leather thong, led us into the house. I asked if Master Ezra was there.

"Hurry upstairs, ladies," the butler replied. "I believe he is getting ready to play with Miss Natalie on the cross."

We ascended the narrow staircase flanked by

black-and-white framed photos of bound and gagged women. As we crested the second floor, a cement mixer of voices and low techno music churned in the big playroom above.

In one corner an obese woman straddled a bench, facing the wall as her Rubenesque mistress in a short latex dress painted long red welts on her bloated bottom with a thin cane. A lovely young man with a perfectly round ass was draped over a sawhorse in the middle of the room, black rope tying him in place. His burly master grabbed his curly blond hair and yanked his ear to his mouth as he spoke. I realized how much I had missed private play parties. The scenes were so much more intense than anything that could happen in those Goth clubs.

On the cross in the corner, a small crowd had gathered to watch Ezra. He wore a gorgeous azure dress shirt and a gray suit with his bowler. I noticed fully for the first time the delicate shape of his nose and lips from profile. The girl tied to the iron cross was overweight, with a ring piercing in her bottom lip and a stud in her nose. She wore only a bra and pair of black nylon panties. Leah sat nearby drinking a Diet Coke, monopolizing the attention of a reluctant listener as she obsessed about the TV show *Angel*. She said nothing when we entered, but Ezra's head jerked to attention. He abandoned the girl and stood before me, ignoring Dahlia entirely.

She rolled her eyes and wandered off to watch another scene. His hands wandered to my bare ass and he whistled, overjoyed at how the PVC barely contained me. He wrapped his arms around me like he did that night at the club when he licked my neck. But this time he said, "Play with me, Blazes. Please."

"I'll see you another time."

He pulled away and glowered. "I want you *now*."

"*Later*."

Was he going to cry? A sheen of sorrow wet those blue eyes, and his lower lip slackened. "You don't know what you mean to me, Blazes. You don't know what you are."

My heart started that familiar Lindy Hop. "I do, Ezra." I was actually shocked. I had no idea he had any real feelings for me. And if he did, I was in greater danger than I had imagined. "But you risk too much. That would be going too far. *We* have gone too far. And perhaps we should stop."

His cheeks flushed purple with rage. His arms dropped to his sides as he shuffled back to the cross. The young woman, Natalie, swooned backward slightly as he approached. He held her round face for a moment, as if trying to find something in her features. He then reached into his medical bag on the stool beside him and withdrew his straight razor. His expression was as empty as a government building on Christmas. Then, with a sudden flick of the wrist, he slashed the girl's chest. A long pink line across her breasts wept scarlet. The girl gasped in shock. He snarled and slashed her again, this time across the cheek, ripping into her upper lip. "*Stop!*" she cried. No one said anything, but I began to shake uncontrollably. This was not part of the scene. I knew it in my gut. Then he viciously struck the folds of her neck and her thick belly with the blade as she shrieked over and over: "*RED! STOP! RED!*" Blood dribbled from her lips and streaked her torso before two men surged forward and grabbed his arm from behind.

By the time they wrestled the straight razor from his grip, I had already began to run.

No one has ever stood up to him before. We must save her. . . . Yes, Lord! Save her soul. . . . SHUT IT, will you? We were mates once, right? Not all of us. Well, we can be mates if we try. For her. We can join together and stop this. . . . He's not exactly the brightest penny in Satan's pocket, is he . . . ? God help us all. . . .

Who are you?

(Shhhh! Let me talk to her.) Don't you know who we are by now, luv?

No. I don't. And why do you speak to me like this? In my dreams?

We're in the belly of the Beast. We are the swarming chaos of souls long since devoured by this body of death.

This servant of darkness you call Ezra has consumed us over the centuries and now indwells this flesh. We love you, Rachel. And we want to warn you.

Warn me?

You see . . . we're in him, luv. . . .

And he wants you to be in him, too. . . .

I stayed offline for days and then blocked him as soon as I could. I knew he would not call me. A terror of myself and my intense desires held me out of his reach. Every night the voices in my dreams grew increasingly desperate. Words of warning turned to pleading as someone would step forward and speak Ezra's case in a twisted discourse of desire, only to be shouted down by a strident chorus of bitter indictments.

My mind slipped away every night as my body inflamed with need. I masturbated all day and into the dark hours thinking of him. I thought perhaps by now he would be in jail, but Dahlia left a voice mail saying that Natalie did not press charges. She was probably ashamed of where she was and didn't feel anyone would believe her.

A week later, he knocked on my door. Someone had let him in downstairs, past the security door. I looked out the peephole and I could barely stand, that hot vein *flick-flicking* between my legs in frantic response to his proximity. He wore a tight red tank top and faded carpenter jeans with a fedora and long black leather jacket—in the dead of a balmy Los Angeles summer night.

"Rachel! Please. I don't know what you've been told, but it's not true. I have to speak to you."

I clawed at the door. He had never called me by my real name before.

"Rachel," he whispered. A brilliant blue eye filled the peephole. *Let me in.*

He stood forlorn in my living room. I had seen his brow kindled with rage, his eyes smoldering with passion, his lips upturned with bravado. But never sadness. I wondered if he had ever cried in his life. *In his lives.* . . . I inhaled sharply as he took my face in his cool hands.

"All I ever wanted since we first met was to feel my skin against yours," he said. "You are such a beautiful creature, Rachel." Distress smudged his forehead as he stroked my jaw.

I shuddered as if each stroke reached deep into my body and seized every nerve with fiery hands. I closed my eyes briefly and mottled desert sands stretched before me, a wasteland of blistering nothingness. Patchy images of a craggy mountain— *Masada*—burned behind my eyes, an ancient fortress that towered above the wasteland.

"I was there, you see, in the mountains of Moab," Ezra explained, his breath sour. *Sulfurous.* "I convinced the Jews at Masada in 73 AD to slit the throats of their women and children, and then one another to escape the Romans—all in the name of freedom. And I was one of the last inhabitants, with the monks who dwelt there in 486." He hesitated as I opened my heavy eyes, and he looked deeply into them the way he did so many times during our most intimate moments. "Yet I lived before that and since then, on and on through the millennia. And, like every living thing in creation, I must eat to survive."

"You . . . consumed . . . the souls of those people," I slurred. *My long devil.*

"Yes, Rachel. I did. And you know what I must do now?"

I nodded, sorrow blooming from my heart to dampness behind my eyes. Then, for whatever strange reason, I started mouthing the words *Dan Hertz. Dan Hurts. Dan . . . hurts . . . like . . . hell.*

"They warned me," I said at last.

Ezra's expression turned to bewilderment.

"But you cannot devour me . . . because you love me."

A blizzard of fury erupted in his eyes.

"And even if you do not love me—*they do.*"

Ezra's hands seared my cheeks. He yanked them away as his flesh seethed on the bone. He howled as his smoking clothes burned away like charred paper. Transfixed by the corruption of his body, I backed against the door, unable to move. His face melted to the bone, dark fluids seeping from his eyes as his skin boiled and his rib cage heaved. Blood and bile sluiced over his body in thick black rivulets and he reached heavenward to a pitiless deity, bellowing as his features contorted in a series of changes. Faces. Bodies. Every soul he had devoured came forth momentarily to reclaim his form from the demon. They were collectively rebelling against their captivity, against his atrocities, against his desire to destroy me—the woman they all loved—and in this newly found unity they stopped bickering and were now finally able to break free. There were far more of Them than him, after all. . . .

Ezra wailed from the excruciating pain and reached for me. "Rachel!" he cried, his voice now basso profundo. "Rachel!" he cried, his voice now tremulous. "Rachel!" he cried, his voice now ragged with age.

I watched him for an hour, my emotions thundering like a Michigan storm. The air in the apartment thickened, crackling with static. Delicate clouds formed briefly above Ezra's prone body, then dispersed like candle smoke as he convulsed on the carpet. Those thousands of trapped souls escaping the belly of the Beast. As they left en masse, I grieved to watch him stripped of everything I both loved and loathed about him. My long devil. Pulcinella. All of his masks torn away to leave me illusionless. I wept into my arms, then pressed my face against the door as the demon Ezra left both me and Evan's body, which he had used to show me such longing.

With no warning, Evan collapsed in a pool of gore and ash soaking the carpet at his feet. I waited a few minutes to see if he was dead, the demon having fled his body to chase his legion. I listened intently for his breath. As soon as I heard it, I crawled to him and gently touched his cheek. My fingers came away slick with gore, but they revealed a bare patch of shockingly normal skin on his face. Wiping tears from my eyes with the back of my wrist, I quickly got up and filled a portable basin with soap and water. I flung a towel over my arm and heaved the splashing basin to the living room, setting it beside him, where we first consummated our desires that day at tea. My hands and knees sticky with his gore, I tenderly washed away the congealing fluids covering that lovely face, that pale torso, those fingers—every part of him I had consumed myself in my own way—until he was clean. I kissed each eyelid. I then spread a blanket over the couch, with sheets and more blankets.

"Ezra, get up," I urged him. Nothing. "*Evan.*" He stirred and I got him to crawl onto the couch, where he lost consciousness entirely. I watched him sleep, but the shadows had fled with my Ezra forever, somewhere into the eternal.

I sighed and went to bed. I knew he would be all right.

Because, in the morning, he would be nothing. . . .

And I wouldn't care about him at all.

THE BLOOD OF INK

Joseph A. Ezzo

"Just what is it between the two of you, anyway?"

Lionel looked up, eyes hard. He certainly did not have time for this today. "As a secretary here, Diane, I'm not sure that really concerns you. Your job is—"

"Is to catch shit from both you and Trent constantly. Tell me about it. The two moodiest people in the world."

"If you value your job at all, you'll leave my office now. If memory serves me correctly, we got you from a secretarial pool. Hardly a hotbed of philosophers. And if Trent and I are moody, maybe there're very good reasons behind it. Reasons that do not have to be explained to the likes of you."

"Fine, I'm leaving. You call me in, you ask how I like it here, then you jump down my throat when I say something negative. If you don't want to know, don't ask." The buzzer on Lionel's phone rang.

"Is Diane in there, Lionel?" Trent asked. "Can you send her in here, please?"

Lionel saw Diane roll her eyes. "What? He wants to chew me out, too? Great. Maybe I can amuse myself by comparing which of you two is worse today. All the while twirling that damn, gold-embossed pen he has, or whatever." With that, she turned abruptly on her heel and left.

Lionel ground his teeth. He had far more than enough worries with the company in such a financial mess, he hardly needed the secretaries to begin ragging on him. How could these people, with such little minds, have such audacity? Of course he hated Trent—had for decades, ever since Shayla had chosen Trent over him. But the marriage had not worked out so well, and Trent had grown increasingly reclusive, difficult to deal with in the workplace. And now, with the tragedy of Shayla's death only four months before—killed in circumstances that suggested suicide—he had become morose to the point of vindictiveness.

And yes, there was that damned pen Diane had just mentioned. He seemed to be clutching it constantly, even while both hands were busy at his computer. Although Lionel had never held it or seen it up close, it appeared to be quite an exquisite implement, no doubt very expensive. Knowing Trent, it was probably purchased on a company account. And . . . strange to think of it, Lionel reflected, but he could not recall seeing the pen until after Shayla's death. Surely Trent had had it around before then, and he just had not noticed.

An hour and a half later, Lionel's thoughts still on Trent's pen, the supervisory staff convened for an office meeting. As always, it was Trent's job to chair the meeting, and Lionel watched him intently the entire time. Yes, the pen never left his right hand—constantly being twirled about, rubbed, caressed even. For some reason Lionel could not articulate, by the end of the meeting he was seething with rage over Trent and his pen, and now wanted to slap Diane for planting the image in his head.

Two days later, virtually crippled by the growing obsession, he resolved that in order to save his job and his sanity only one course of action was open to him: he had to steal Trent's gold-embossed pen. He spent the morning feebly concocting schemes to purloin the writing implement; came up dry. Then, upon returning from the men's room, he saw that Trent had left a stack of invoices in Diane's IN basket on her desk. A note stuck to them read: "These must go out today!!!" Diane had left for lunch a short time ago, and possibly had not seen them. Lionel coolly lifted the invoices from her basket and took them into his office. He bided his time during the afternoon, waited until he heard Diane being called into Trent's office. He immediately slipped out of his office and returned the invoices to her IN basket. Sure enough, Trent emerged a minute later, shouting at the nonplussed secretary.

"But they're right here!" he bawled. "How could you miss them? Now get them enveloped and out of here before you do anything else!" He stormed back into his office and slammed the door. Lionel hurried to her aid.

"I swear he didn't put them in there before," Diane cried. "I don't how they got there just now."

"It's okay," Lionel said soothingly. "Here, let me give you a hand to make sure you can get them all sealed and out before the last mail run's made today."

"Well, thanks. I could use the help."

As they were finishing up, she thanked Lionel again. "No problem," he replied warmly. "Say, was he twirling his pen around when he chewed you out?"

She thought for a few seconds. "No. I think it was sitting on his desk."

"You know what we should do? Just play a little joke on him. Get him to chill out a little. What we really ought to do . . . ?"

It worked like a charm. First, they whited out part of an address on an invoice. Then Lionel called Trent to his office to sign some documents. Just as he finished signing, Diane shrieked, "What happened to this invoice? And from our biggest account!" Trent went pale, rushed from Lionel's office so suddenly that indeed he left his pen lying innocently on Lionel's desk. Lionel scooped it up and slid it into his desk drawer. Trent reentered Lionel's office, searching his pockets.

"What else?" he asked.

"That's it, thank you much," Lionel said, stacking the documents. "I'll get Diane to file these for us."

"Uh-huh, okay. Well." Trent looked around Lionel's desk, still feeling his pockets.

"Everything okay with the invoices?" Lionel asked innocuously.

Trent shook his head, patted his forehead. He had begun to sweat. "Yeah, yeah," he said absently. Then he blew out air and slowly returned to his office.

Lionel drew open his desk drawer slowly, peered in. The pen, black with its ornate gold embossing near the base, stared back. "You're mine now," Lionel whispered, unable then to stifle a laugh.

He took the pen home that evening, and, shortly before retiring, decided to break it in by writing in his diary. He opened his diary and took up the pen, felt it between his fingers. Well balanced, comfortable to the touch, with a flexible tip that allowed one to write at almost any angle. Trent paid well for this, and was at the moment probably fretting at home, trying to figure out how he had misplaced it. Lionel chuckled at the thought, then set the pen to paper. He wrote about how he had gone out of his way to help Diane during the day, and how, for reasons not quite understood, he felt better about his position in the company that he had in months. He wrote effortlessly, the pen tip gliding over the page with remarkable smoothness. By the time he had finished his entry, the pen was warm in his hand, so pleasant that he hesitated putting it down. He raised it to his lips, lightly kissed the gold embossing, then laughed. After his shower, as he was preparing for bed, he felt so pleased at his last entry he decided to read it over. He smiled as he read what he had written; the ink color was surprisingly attractive. It was black, but with a twinge of something else, something he could not quite define, that gave it such a distinct and superior look from the ink of his other entries that he determined he would buy a new diary and copy out all his old entries with this pen. He smiled as he reached the end, then frowned suddenly, eyes wide.

The last few words of the entry read: "Thief! Thief! You disgusting scum of a human being! Don't think we don't know."

Lionel could not believe what he was seeing. "Of course I didn't write that," he said aloud, closing the diary hastily. "No such thoughts ever came into my head. I must have . . . I don't know what." He told himself to bring home some Wite-Out from the office tomorrow, expunge the offending passage, and forget about it.

The following evening, after finishing his entry, he reread it carefully, found nothing out of the ordinary. When he rose in the morning, after a fitful sleep, he checked it again, found it still just as he had written it. He smiled. The offending passage was still whited out. Sipping his coffee, knotting his tie, he whistled absently, then, on impulse, picked up the diary once more before heading out the door. The first thing he noticed was that the offending passage was now slightly readable beneath the Wite-Out, and growing more distinct before his eyes. He looked at the end of the most recent entry.

"Don't think we won't act. Don't think we're not watching. Thieving loser. You always were exactly that. Why do you think I chose—"

The passage ended in midsentence. Lionel inhaled involuntarily, as if sucker punched in the pit of his stomach. He threw down the diary and rushed out of his apartment. When he arrived at his office, he shrugged out of his jacket to find, to his dismay, that he had affixed the pen to his shirt pocket. He tore it free, opened his desk drawer, and slung it inside, then slammed the drawer shut. No sooner had he finished his first cup of coffee and was reviewing the office duty roster than Diane appeared in his doorway with a sheaf of papers.

"The report for the Klineman account has been

proofed and needs your final approval," she announced, setting the bundle of paper in the IN basket on his desk. "Trent would very much like it to go out by lunchtime today." She left the office before he could respond.

Lionel moved slowly through his workload that morning, avoiding telephone calls from clients and buzzes from employees who had questions for him. He got on to the Klineman account report, but paid relatively little attention to the dizzying array of charts and graphs, the long-winded descriptions and interpretations of said figures, the unctuous cover letter thanking them for their business. He stacked the report neatly before him, tore off a sheet from his personal memo pad (which consisted of alternate blue and yellow sheets), and stuck it to the top page. He pulled a pen from the holder on his desk and set its tip to the memo pad sheet, but found he could not write. Not that he failed to find words, but the writing instrument in his hand refused to obey. Or, perhaps more accurately, his right hand refused to work with it. The pen felt like a rough, dirty twig, something he had just pulled off a tree, and attempting to write with it would not only result in unintelligible print, but in injury to his hand. He tossed it aside and grabbed another, but it felt, if anything, more repulsive. Slowly, mechanically, he pulled open the central drawer of his desk, and there, amid the Post-It packs, the paper clips, erasers, the Wite-Out rolls, was the pen. Its gold embossing against the black background was truly stunning. Its surface looked not like some highly refined synthetic material, but something warm and alluring. Something pulsing with life.

He reached in and collected it with the ends of his fingers, felt its warmth, its sweet weight and balance, and he sighed. He wrote effortlessly, in his unmistakable handwriting, instructing Diane to make a few brief changes in the cover letter and then return it for him to sign. He set down the pen and took up his phone, buzzed her. "You can pick up the Klineman account report now," he informed her. He placed the report in the OUT basket on his desk. Diane appeared then, smiling, took up the report.

Lionel sat back, glanced at his watch. He twirled the pen gently, eyes widening. He had no idea he was still holding it. His telephone buzzed. "Ah, I have a question for you," Diane's voice droned. "Can I come into your office?"

"Okay."

She was holding the report and frowning. She set it down before him, pointed to the memo pad sheet. "Is there anything else I need to do before mailing this off, or is this some kind of a joke?"

Lionel looked up at her, eyes squinting, then focused on where she was pointing. "What—" he began, then looked more closely at the memo pad sheet.

"Thief only? You'll hardly get off so easily. Let's talk sick jealousy, resentment, resulting in ... what? Suicide? Everyone ruled that out from the start. Accidental death? Yes, that was the final interpretation, wasn't it? But we know, and you know, differently. Shall I ... or rather you, write the word? I advise you to, otherwise I will. Write it, now."

Lionel swallowed hard, closed his eyes for a few seconds. Then he managed to force a painful smile. "Of course, what do you think? Just trying to save you from another day of hellish boredom around here. Actually, all I need to do is sign the cover letter. . . ."

Shortly after Diane left his office, he realized he had not, as he planned, removed the memo pad sheet from the top of the report. He went out to her desk, but she was not there. Her PENDING REPORTS basket was empty, meaning she had mailed out the report. As no one was immediately about, he scoured her wastepaper basket for the sheet, but could not find it.

"Lose something?"

Lionel whirled around, saw Trent standing outside his office, grinning crookedly.

"Um, no, just checking on the Klineman account report."

"In Diane's wastebasket?"

"Trent, I'm having a very stressful day," Lionel groaned. "I don't need—" He blew out air, stomped back into his office. Throwing himself back down in his office chair, he absently groped at his shirt pocket. The pen was there; had Trent seen it as well? He realized then that he had signed the cover letter with it. The thought caused him to shiver— would his name indeed show up on that line, or would it be some other weird accusation? *How could I be so out of control?* he asked himself, slouching in his chair, eyes closed. *Intend to write something, and write something completely different. What, am I becoming a split personality or something? I'll simply have to proof everything very carefully as soon as I've finished writing it.* Absently he removed the pen from his shirt pocket and began to twirl it slowly, feeling its firm warmth on his fingers. He held the pen close to his face, looked at it intently, brought it a bit closer, not so much to his eyes as to his mouth, stopped when the pen was nearly resting against his lips. He noticed that a Post-It pad lay on his desk, and he set the tip of the pen to it, writing: "Remember, proof everything before letting it leave your desk!" He underlined "Remember" and "everything" twice, with deep, bold strokes, then dutifully read back what he had written, sighed with relief.

Ten minutes later he left his office for a meeting

with some staffers regarding a recently acquired account, which did not end until almost two, leaving him ravenous. On the way back to his office he stopped off at Diane's desk.

"Call out to Fortunato's for a club sandwich and a side of potato salad for me, would you? Is there fresh coffee?"

"Good as done, and yes, there is," Diane responded, then chuckled softly. Lionel paused for an instant, about to ask her the meaning of her action, but set his lips together and headed into his office. He sat down at his desk, found that he was once again holding the pen, twirling it gently with the fingers of his right hand. He saw the Post-It pad, noticed that the top sheet was blank. *Did I tear off that message to myself?* he wondered, glancing around for it. Peering more closely at the pad, he could make out impressed letters on the top sheet. He set the tip of the pen to it and began coloring the sheet until the letters became legible.

"New Year's Eve, was it not? What did you hear Trent say about his car? The battery—"

It ended there. Lionel lowered his head into one of his hands. Slowly he lowered the other hand into his wastebasket, even though he knew he would not final the original Post-It sheet there. He then reached into his printer tray and extracted a sheet of paper, wrote across the top: "Who are you and what do you want with me?" Then he laid it on the desk, determined to watch it for the rest of the afternoon.

He had Diane hold his calls, and he begged out of two more meetings with staffers. Still holding the pen, he watched the sheet of paper. He took to closing his eyes and trying to time one minute, then two, then four and five. He would open his eyes and look at the sheet. Once he actually left his office and went into the men's room. Throughout the afternoon, the words he had written remained on the sheet. As he was driving home, he realized his mistake, was determined to rectify it the next day.

Sure enough, when he reached his office the next morning (having avoided writing in his diary the evening before), the words "Who are you and what do you want with me?" were still on the sheet. He crumpled up the paper and tossed it, then slid the pen from his shirt pocket and wrote the same words on his personal memo pad. Shortly thereafter he had a long conference call with a client on the East Coast; all the while he watched the memo pad, waiting for the change. After the call he commenced the ritual he had begun the previous afternoon. By noontime he was confident enough to go out to lunch, see what might happen in such a protracted absence. When he returned, he found the memo pad where he'd left it, only the top sheet was blank. He studied the sheet, found no writing impressions in it. He stormed out of his office and to Diane's desk.

"Who was in my office while I was at lunch?" he demanded, unable to conceal his rage.

Diane looked genuinely surprised, then confused. She shook her head slowly. "No one. I've been here the whole time, Lionel."

"Someone was in there, Diane. Who was it? Something was removed from my desk."

Diane frowned deeply. "The only person who could have entered your office without passing my desk would be Trent, and—"

"Well, what the hell does he think he's doing? Who does he—"

"—and he's been gone since—"

"—think he is, the disrespectful—"

"—ten o'clock. He's at a meeting with our clients from Helton-Moyer."

"—the . . . Are you certain of that?"

"Absolutely. I was at my desk the whole time you were at lunch. I promise you no one entered your office." Diane's faced creased with concern. "What was taken from your desk?" she asked cautiously, in a low voice.

Lionel ground his teeth, blew out air. "Nothing. It's . . . nothing. Do you have anything for me that's pressing?"

Back in his office, Lionel leafed through a feasibility study he had overseen for one of the firm's most reliable and long-term clients. Despite his agitated state, he managed to concentrate far more effectively than he would have imagined, jotting down notes on his personal memo pad as he read. "All in all," he wrote by way of conclusion, "report well organized and provides info client wants. Could be a little stronger on explaining the residuals that have cropped up the last two quarters, but doubtful it would change the predictive aspects of the recommendations in any significant way." Without realizing it, he then brought the pen to his lips and lightly ran the tip of his tongue over its gold embossing. He drew back, startled at the degree of pleasure it accorded him. A small amount of space was left at the bottom of the sheet. He then added, "Have production proof once more, put into final format and prepare to transmit."

He then left his office and wandered through the building to congratulate the staffers who were responsible for putting together the report. On his way back he stopped off at the men's room, then poured himself a paper cup of water from the cooler. He reentered his office and read the final memo sheet.

"All in all, report well organized and provides info client wants. Could be a little stronger on explaining the evidence against you on New Year's Eve, but doubtful you'll get away with this once all the facts come to light. Have production proof once more, which you failed to do, and prepare to transmit."

He tore the pen out of his pocket and flung it across the room. He gasped as soon as it left his hand, wishing desperately that he could pull it back. It thudded dully against the wall next to his door, dropped helplessly to the floor. He was certain he had broken it. As he got up from his desk to retrieve it, the word that came into his mind was not "broken" but "killed."

He collected it, found it to be no worse for wear, sat down. He ripped off the top sheet of his memo pad, began writing nonsense on the next page until he filled it. "There, you son of a bitch, whoever or whatever you are, make something out of that," he said aloud.

"Is seeing believing?" suddenly appeared at the top of the sheet, replacing the initial line of drivel. Lionel watched, utterly transfixed, as the nonsense letters he had written were transformed before his eyes: "A simple matter of a tiny piece of cardboard. You heard Trent talking about it at the party. The problem with the cable connection at one pole of his car battery. How it was loose. How it would lose its contact with the pole without warning, and all power in the car would be lost. How he used the piece of cardboard to keep the cable secure against the pole."

Give the pen back. Get rid of it.

The words echoed in his head, although he had no idea whence they came. Certainly the voice was not his. He punched the PAGE key on his telephone cradle.

"Yes?" Diane's voice crackled through.

"Is . . . Trent back yet?"

"No, still with the people from Helton-Moyer. Anything I can help you with? You can reach him on his cell phone if it's really—"

"No, forget it. Thanks."

He decided to slip into Trent's office then and return the pen. The only problem was that Diane would see him, might get suspicious of him snooping around Trent's office. Then he snapped his fingers, remembering Diane had gone in with him on the pen-stealing ruse. He sighed, exited his office. He faced her, holding up the pen.

"I've decided to stop the nonsense and return this to Trent," he announced to her. "I think it's gone on long enough."

Diane grinned. "Sounds like a good idea. God knows the man's been even moodier since we pulled that." Lionel turned and strode to Trent's door, pulled on it.

"It's locked," he said over his shoulder. "Do you—"

"No, I don't. Trent's the only one who has a key to his office."

Lionel groaned. "Well, if you want to just leave it

here," Diane offered. "I'll see that he gets it when he returns."

"No. Then he'll start asking questions, like how did you get your hands on it, and so on. It needs to be slipped back in there so he doesn't know who took it or what happened to it or anything like that. You sure you don't have a master?"

Diane shook her head ineffectually. "Anyway, why have you decided to do this now? Why all of a sudden?"

Lionel grimaced. "No . . . reason. Forget it. I'll wait till he's back."

"Is there anything you want done regarding the feasibility report? It's on the fast track now."

He shook his head. "It's good. It's very close. I'll have it to you shortly."

It was only then that he realized that when he had given Diane the feasibility report, he had also given her the notes he had jotted down.

Lionel left the office fifteen minutes later, not bothering to tell anyone that he was not returning for the day. He went to a bar and drank six scotch-and-waters, in rapid succession, then drove home. Once home, he took up his diary and reread his recent entries. They remained tainted, taunting him with their accusations. He reached into his shirt pocket, found the pen there, began to draw thick lines across the offending passages.

The next morning he called in sick to work, but,

fretting over the careless placement of his feasibility report notes, showed up after lunch. He immediately took up his personal memo pad, pulled out the pen, and wrote out a set of instructions.

1. Do not use this memo pad for any further correspondences, notes, or anything else.

2. To ensure this, take the pad to the production room and feed it to the shredder.

3. Type all future memos, notes, etc.

He looked at the last instruction, the pen firm and warm between his fingers, and somehow it struck him as a betrayal. *How could I do this to you?* he thought, bringing the pen close to his lips. His telephone buzzed.

"Lionel?" Trent's voice. "We have a very important meeting with Ronald Klineman in less than a half hour. Are you planning to attend?"

"Of course I'll be there. What do you think, Trent?"

"I'm only asking because you missed our strategy session for this meeting this morning."

Lionel sighed, sat back. He collected his memo pad and looked at the top sheet.

1. Who slipped out of the party, yanked up the hood of Trent's BMW, found the piece of cardboard and removed it?

2. All in the hopes that the car would die on one of those hairpin turns you knew Trent would have to negotiate on his way home.

3. Plus, you knew that he had been drinking heavily at the party, much at your insistence.

Lionel pounded the memo pad with his fist. Then he snatched it, tore off the top sheet, crinkled it up and threw it across his office. "End of the line for you," he muttered, bolting out of his office and toward the production room. He reached the paper shredder only to see an OUT OF ORDER sign taped to the front of it. He stormed back toward his office, confronting Diane.

"What the hell's with the shredder?" he asked, livid.

Diane frowned, then grinned with amusement. "Are you being serious? What planet have you been on? It's been out of whack for almost two months. It's obsolete and we can't get the parts for it, and we don't have the budget at the moment to invest in a new one."

When he got back to his office, he saw that the wadded-up memo pad sheet was gone.

He tossed down the memo pad violently on his desk. Pen in hand, he attacked the top sheet. "Fine, you son of a bitch, whoever or whatever you are. Here it is. I'll even keep it in second person, just the way you want it. Do your damnedest."

He began writing furiously. As he did, his hand began to sweat, and the pen emitted a sweet, sensuous odor that caused him to write faster, more passionately. He felt his heart racing, and heat swelling in his loins.

"Remember how you tried to console Shayla during the party, tried to convince her to leave Trent for you? You told her to follow you home, knowing that she had arrived separately from Trent, as you and Trent were working late. You were drinking heavily, and thought she was. In fact, she had had nothing to drink. You never figured that Shayla had a key to Trent's car, and when he kept insisting he would drive himself home, she wound up taking his car instead of hers, because it was a manual transmission, and she did not want Trent to try driving it in his condition."

He tore the sheet off, crumpled it and threw it toward his door, which was half open. Then he continued on the second sheet.

"Nor did you know that Trent did not have a key to her car, as it had been a Christmas present he had given her only a week before." The pen began skipping, the letters incomplete. Startled, Lionel shook the pen, set it back to the paper. "In that way Shayla made it impossible for Trent to drive. She was trying to save his life, while you were trying to end it. And there she was, barely a half hour after midnight, wrapped around a telephone pole. On one of those hairpin turns three blocks from their house. Accidental death. Thief. Murderer." The last words were almost impressions only on the paper.

He ripped off the second sheet and treated it as he had the first. "There," he said loudly. Then he rose from his desk, kicked both paper balls into the space outside his office. He paused when he saw Diane looking at him. He stabbed a finger in her direction. "Go on! Pick them up! Do your worst!" He slammed his office door, sat down, put his face in his hands. Then he reached, as if by instinct, to his shirt pocket, and wrapped his fingers around the pen. It pulsed in his hand, as if trying to become part of him. He held it briefly in both hands, rolling it gently between his palms. *I'm not going to let you go. I don't care what happens now. Just stay with me. I'll never betray you. Not again. Just stay.*

The door of his office was flung open. He was not surprised in the least by that or by who stood in the doorway.

"You dirty rotten bastard." Trent's voice boiled with venom. His hands were encased in gloves, and in them he held a variety of small sheets of paper—some blue, some yellow and bearing the distinct imprint of Lionel's personal memo pad. "You thought you'd get away with it, didn't you? You—"

"If you've nothing more productive to say, then

don't let my office door hit your butt on your way out," Lionel replied mildly, masking his anxiety.

"—almost did, too. Had you not been a thieving son of a bitch to boot."

"Spare me the name-calling, Trent, please." Lionel tried to sound tired. "Leave my office now, okay?"

"Oh, I will. I will. And you will, too, not long afterward." Trent tapped the sheets against an open palm. "It's all here."

Lionel guffawed, but it knew he sounded hollow. "Oh? And just what might that be?"

"And, you clever fool, in your own handwriting. On your personal memo notes. Covered, as is *my* pen, with your prints. An admission of guilt as pure as if we'd all been there to observe it. Step by step, as if we were all there witnessing it."

"Get out of my office, Trent, and stop acting like such a chump. And as for those papers, you can shove them right up—"

"And now that it's finished with you, I'll be taking my pen back now. I don't want it to get lost in all the commotion that's about to—" Trent was interrupted by the sound of a rapidly moving bodies just outside the door. He popped his head in that direction, then turned back to Lionel with a cruel, conspiratorial smile. "Did I say it was about come down? I'd better grab my pen immediately." He strode to Lionel's desk and held out his hand. Although Lionel had absolutely no intention of yielding to his demands, he felt suddenly powerless, surrendering the pen without the least resistance. Trent then held it up, sighed dramatically. "Beautiful, isn't she? And the way she feels in your hand! Like you could never hold another pen, am I wrong?" Trent pressed the pen gently to his lips. "She won't write anymore. Never again." He looked hard at Lionel. "But then, she doesn't need to." He kissed the pen again, murmured, "We did it, my darling. At last you can finally rest." He placed it with loving care in his shirt pocket and patted the pocket. He turned and walked to the doorway of Lionel's office. Lionel glimpsed Diane somewhere behind Trent, smilingly knowingly.

"I believe the man you're looking for, officers"— Trent called out, motioning toward the interior of Lionel's office—"the man who killed my wife while intending to kill me, and who has been kind enough to provide us with a detailed confession, is right here."

Trent removed the pen from his pocket, kissed it again, and strode out of Lionel's sight.

UNBLINKING

Ramsey Campbell

Dignam wasn't sure if the essays he was marking
defeated him or the gaze of his neighbour did.
Now that the postwoman had delivered to both
sides of the road, the man was regarding him
across it with what looked unreasonably like accusation. With its unyielding stare and its fixed resentful grimace, Dignam could almost have taken
the face for a mask somebody had hung inside the
window opposite. It felt as hostile as all the essays
he'd graded so far—as their insistence that mental
illness could be a gift. He wandered downstairs to
see that the post was even less rewarding than he'd
assumed: a credit card had sent him the same invitation twice. He was about to bin the duplicate
unopened when he realised it was addressed to his
neighbour.

His name was Brady, then. How likely was he to
welcome the item? Dignam was tempted to throw

it away, but it didn't belong to him. He let himself out onto the short path piebald with March frost and fringed with icy spikes of grass. The glazed road was crunchy with frozen winged seeds from Brady's sprawling sycamore. As Dignam stepped between the crumbling stone gateposts under the tree, the man thumped on his window. "Wait there," he shouted and backed into dimness.

Dignam ambled down a path so overgrown it was indistinguishable from the abandoned garden to the front door, which was as scaly as the rest of the exterior. Beside it thick off-white curtains hung inert as paint against the entire interior of a bay window spotted with many rains. He'd started to think Brady had been distracted from claiming his mail when rapid footsteps clumped downstairs and the door was wrenched open with a vicious creak. "I said I was coming," Brady declared, having barely lowered his loose voice.

What had kept him? Not combing his spectacularly uneven greyish hair, nor getting dressed, since he was almost certainly wearing only a dressing-gown stained with egg and toothpaste. This close, his whitish wrinkled puffed-up face more than ever resembled a mask through which his glittering bloodshot eyes peered suspiciously at Dignam. "This is yours," Dignam said. "She delivered it to me by mistake."

"What is it?"

"Just an invitation to take out a credit card, as though there isn't already enough plastic in the world."

"And how would you know how many I've got of those?"

"I've no idea. I meant generally, of course. Me, I've got all I can cope with."

Brady thrust out a hand that involved a smell of stale cloth and turned over the envelope to scrutinise the blank expanse of orange paper before examining the front afresh. OPEN AT ONCE! THIS COULD CHANGE YOUR LIFE! red letters in blue outlines exhorted beneath his address. "Steamed it open, did you?" he enquired.

"Most decidedly not. Why should you—"

"There's where," Brady scoffed, poking a chewed cracked fingernail under the flap. "And you gave yourself away knowing what's inside."

"That's because I received the identical mailing."

"Identical, was it? Had my name on too?"

"Except for that and of course the address. I really must assure you—"

"I'll bet you must." Brady ripped open the envelope and squinted at the picture of a credit card, then stuffed the wad of paper into a dangling pocket. "Teacher, that right?"

"Actually I'm—"

"Don't tell me. A university teacher."

"A lecturer, yes. How did you know?"

"If you don't want everyone knowing, you shouldn't let them see you marking papers and thinking what you're thinking about the girls that wrote them."

"They aren't only girls. Plenty of men as well."

Brady looked worse than vindicated. "I think I'll ask you to excuse me," Dignam said, feeling close to trapped by the man's view of him.

He was almost at the pavement when a stout middle-aged woman tramped by. "Watch out for that one, Mrs Vernon," Brady shouted. "Reads other people's letters. He'll be in our houses next."

The woman frowned at Dignam and increased her speed. "Mr Brady," he called for her to over-hear, "if you spread that sort of tale I'll be forced to take action."

"Got my name now, have you? I'll be seeing about yours. Get off my property right now with your threats or it'll be me that brings the police."

"I haven't time to argue," Dignam said before he crossed the road to escape the shadow of the tree, a gloom that felt too much like Brady's notion of him. As the man's door shut with a victorious slam, Dignam saw the woman peering back at him while she hurried past the variously bushy gardens to the shop on the corner of the main road. An impulse to head off any rumours sent him after her.

Apart from the counter, the small shop was crammed with shelves laden with groceries.

"Here's a newcomer," said the shopkeeper, a woman shorter by a head than Mrs Vernon but compensatively broader.

"Sorry," Dignam felt bound to respond, having passed the shop on his way to work for years. "Just a paper today."

As he made for the counter Mrs Vernon moved aside a little too far for politeness. He rested a hand on the nearest newspaper. "Excuse me, Mrs Vernon, we haven't been introduced . . ."

Her sharp face drew into itself as her lips pressed themselves almost colourless before demanding "Where did you get my name?"

"I heard it just now, if you recall."

"Listening outside, were you? I don't like that, Mrs Timms."

As the shopkeeper opened her pudgy hands in front of her to accept this, Dignam protested "When our friend shouted after you, I meant, of course."

. "If you're talking about Mr Brady," Mrs Vernon said, "you didn't sound very friendly."

"Neighbour, then. Would you say he can be a little odd?"

"I wouldn't, and I'm sure you wouldn't either, Mrs Timms."

"I expect you'd rather not speak ill of a customer. He's certainly got an odd idea of me. All I did was take him some post I'd received by mistake."

"Who are you to say he's not right upstairs?" Mrs Vernon apparently saw reason to object. "You're not a doctor."

"I am of psychology, actually. I lecture on it at the university."

"That's no doctor, that's a teacher. How many nutters have you met?"

"Not a great number. If you put it like that," Dignam said in some rebuke, "none."

"Takes one to know one or think someone else is, more like."

Perhaps a cloud had masked the sun, but the growing darkness felt as if his brain was shrinking out of reach of light. "All I wanted to establish was that Mr Brady was mistaken to say I'd tampered with his letter."

"Sounds like everyone's mistaken except you."

"So you won't be going near his house," Mrs Timms advised.

What else had the women been saying about him? As he turned away with as much dignity as he could gather, there seemed to be far too much clutter between him and the door, and in his brain too. "Aren't you buying?" Mrs Timms said.

"I don't think I've laid claim to anything, have I?" He indicated the counter with one upturned hand, only to discover that print from the newspaper he'd leaned on had transferred itself to his palm. MADAM was the solitary word above a report about a brothel, and the latter portion was reversed like an illiterate tattoo on his skin. He slapped a pound coin on the counter hard enough for the shopkeeper to recoil with a timidity he thought melodramatic. "Here's your money. Keep your wares," he said and marched out of the shop.

The clang of the bell above the door spiked the back of his skull. After the dimness the sunlight felt strident too. He closed his eyes to let the flattened sharp-edged world regain some perspective until he realised he must appear to be loitering to over-hear what the women said about him. They were silent, having seen him eavesdropping. He nar-rowed his eyes and stumbled along the road that seemed at best only vaguely imagined. As he widened them to demonstrate how harshly it was present, he wondered if during the entire con-frontation Brady could really not have blinked once.

He wasn't doing so now. When Dignam resumed his seat at the desk he was met by a glare as un-yielding as the sun that squinted through the branches of the sycamore. "Hope they sting," he muttered, blinking fast, and snatched the next essay off the heap. He recognised Hannah's gener-ously flowing script, and was greeting it with a se-cret smile until his gaze snagged on the phrase he least hoped to encounter.

She thought schizophrenics had privileged perceptions too, did she? If she was so enamoured of his colleague's ideas, perhaps she should go to bed with Roger Douglas instead of with him. The unworthiness of the idea made Dignam nervous of betraying it to the watcher over the road, an absurd fear but nonetheless one reason why he lowered his head. *Many schizophrenics display insights far beyond the average . . . While it is dangerous to regard mental states as contagious, they can sometimes be shared in part by an observer . . . It requires unusual strength of mind to live with unmedicated schizophrenia . . .* Did Hannah mean to experience it or to be connected with a sufferer? Dignam had taken some satisfaction in inking his query alongside the text when he saw that the next sentence made it clear she'd meant suffering oneself. Too late, he thought, and glanced up to see why the light was flickering.

Brady had retreated from view, but a silent white explosion glared out of the depths of the room—the flash of a bulb. He was photographing Dignam, who heaved his window open as Mrs Vernon passed the house, her coat flapping in a wind. "Watch out for your friend with the camera," he called when she peered nervously towards the rattle of the sash. "Lord knows what he'll do with us now he's taken us."

She didn't look at Brady, despite the finger Dignam stretched forth. She fled onwards as though he'd made an improper approach. While the slam of his window was aimed at Brady, it only spurred her faster. He ducked to Hannah's essay in several kinds of rage. When the light flickered again he felt not merely spied upon but found out. "She's a mature student," he muttered. "She can choose for herself."

Did he imagine Brady could hear? He crouched to give the man a shot or several of his scalp, only to bring himself too close to the page to read it no matter how hard he stared. Why was he wasting time? He had plenty of essays to mark in his office on the campus, and it was wholly irrational of him not to want to encounter Roger Douglas. He shoved himself away from the desk and twisted to sit with his back to the window as a preamble to quitting the house.

The route to the university led past the corner shop. Any other was absurdly devious. He might have had a word with the proprietor, but she was talking to a bulky man who frowned through the window at Dignam. Did that mean they were discussing him? "Off to work, Mrs Timms," he called, which made her blink.

Five minutes' stroll, but now two minutes' striding, took him along the seasick pavement of the potholed main road to the traffic lights. On his right a hill was piled with concrete tenements whose balconies always reminded him of battlements, though he suspected that he would have felt most beleaguered by living too close to his neighbours; doing so as a student had often brought him within screaming distance of a breakdown. To his left the cross street grew immediately more civilised as it met the campus, and he promised himself that his mind would. There was really no need to look behind him as he crossed the road. It was having a respite from traffic, and certainly nobody was following him.

He hadn't expected the campus to be so busy on a Saturday. Most of the students were bound for the library, though a few small groups were heading for the pub that faced it. Also on that course was a solitary woman in a dark grey suit, whom he would have taken for a lecturer except for her beacon of red hair. Even tied back so severely, it was unmistakably Hannah's. She was too distant for him to hail without drawing more attention than he wanted. As she stepped delicately into the pub, he told himself that he deserved a drink.

The moment he crossed the threshold, dimness and uproar fell on him. Although the room was at least twice the size of Mrs Timms' shop, the crowd made it feel even smaller. Blinking let him locate Hannah at the bar. He'd taken a pace towards her when he saw she was talking to Roger Douglas.

Surely they resembled a couple only because they were younger than Dignam, but he would have dodged out of the pub if the other lecturer hadn't caught sight of him. Douglas raised his long lean tanned face, pointing his satyr's beard at him. "Look how psychology brings us all together," he remarked to Hannah.

Hannah turned to recognise Dignam. A smile widened her eyes and then her deceptively prim lips. "Oh, Dr Dignam. I didn't see you were here."

"He wasn't, were you, Terry? He was just behind you."

"Hardly just," Dignam said, having lifted a hand to acknowledge them both.

"So long as we are to our students, hey?"

"I can't imagine why you'd think I wouldn't be. May I buy you whatever you're having, Miss Martin? Just an orange, right you are. I shouldn't think that pint will take you long, Roger. Let me come to the rescue."

Dignam felt expansive and in control once he'd succeeded in coaxing the barmaid over. As she levered out his pint he noticed the book on the bar in front of Douglas: *Visions of Schizophrenia.* "Do you always carry your own book with you? I suppose you feel you need to advertise yourself."

"That's our student's copy that she liked enough to buy."

Dignam was swallowing a rusty mouthful of beer to keep down several retorts, by no means solely aimed at Douglas, when his colleague said

"Didn't you have a book in mind once yourself? Will Hannah have a chance to read that too before she leaves us?"

"I'd want to base it on observation. Perhaps I'm less anxious to make a name."

"There's plenty of observation in my book. You should try not just skimming it sometime."

"Observation of yourself when you were taking drugs, you mean."

"Exactly, when I was trying every psychotropic I could lay my hands on, and let me tell you they didn't always look like my hands. No point in being anything but honest, would you agree, Hannah? Nothing good comes of repression."

Dignam was able to hope Douglas had made her uncomfortable until she said "I admired how you didn't hold back."

"Perhaps I shouldn't, then." Dignam saw her face try not to stiffen, though he had no intention of exposing their relationship. "I believe I may have hit upon the subject of my book," he said.

"Do we get to hear?" Douglas urged.

"I've come into contact with a sufferer."

"If you'll accept a word of advice, don't think of them that way. Look on them as an opportunity to share perceptions you might never have otherwise."

"Privileged perceptions, you mean," Dignam said and couldn't resist staring at Hannah.

"They're the ones. Treat yourself to some while you've the chance. They were what you wanted to consult me about, weren't they, Hannah? Forgive me if I don't call you Miss Martin. I like to think of my students as friends."

"I'm sure Miss Martin should be in no doubt as to my regard for her." Shouting this over the hubbub of the bar made Dignam feel walled in by his language. He drained his remaining third of a pint as an excuse to say, "I'll see you at my Monday lecture then, Miss Martin."

"If not before, who knows?" Douglas used a finger and thumb to wipe froth from his moustache, a gesture that reminded Dignam of a villain in a melodrama. "Off to continue your observations, Terry?"

"I imagine that should be the case."

Either Dignam left the pub too energetically or his vision had inured itself to the dimness, because he was confronted by an all-embracing glare. Pressing his eyes shut, even with fingers as well as lids, only trapped it. "Are you okay?" someone asked, and he had to insist that he was. Once he was able to distinguish that nobody was spying on him, or at least no longer, he ran across the campus to his office.

There were essays on his desk, but nothing to contain them. While he searched for a carrier, footsteps advanced and hesitated and executed some further movement in the corridor. Their owner must have been inspecting pictures on the walls, not deliberately staying out of sight or threatening to appear, but the noises made it harder for Dignam to be sure how empty the room was. His rummaging sent dust like the remnants of chalked words into the lethargically inclined sunlight. The essays weren't so urgent that they couldn't wait, and he was suddenly anxious to be home. No doubt this was how it felt to have an idea for a book, an idea that was eager to reach the page.

Words were scrambling over one another in his head as he emerged into the deserted corridor. In under five minutes he was running past the corner shop. He rammed the key into his lock and sprinted upstairs, to be confronted by the man across the road. The unblinking eyes seemed to tug the expressionless face to meet him, unless his own movement brought it closer. He was resisting the temptation to raise a hand in an ironic greeting when he saw that his palm was still imprinted with a word.

Had Hannah and his rival seen it? He licked the other hand and rubbed the pair together as he sat at the desk, until he began to see himself as Brady must see him, washing himself like an animal or worse. He grabbed a pad out of the desk drawer and seized the nearest pen, the red. *A spies on B because he believes A to be spying on him. A's paranoia*

narrows the focus of his mind to B or A. Paranoia is a
form of focusing that excludes insight and any sense of
everything that lies outside the focus. As a substitute for
this lack, the paranoid mind derives delusions from the
subject on which it is focused.

Was this an opening paragraph? It felt more like
notes for several or even for a number of chapters.
Hannah's unfaithful ideas seemed to be interfering
with the clarity he'd thought he was bringing
home, and he reached to turn the scattered pages
blank side up. Then his smeared hand faltered.
Hadn't he tidied them before leaving the house?
Had he failed to notice that he'd left the window
raised almost an inch?

His head jerked up, not quite in time to be able
to confirm he'd glimpsed a mocking grin across the
road. Could someone really have entered the house
and opened the window to provide an explanation
for any disturbance? The mere thought appeared to
send Brady into hiding. When the man thrust his
head out of the front door, Dignam wondered if he
might be on his way to protest his innocence. Instead Brady stalked along the road, the plastic jackets of three library books glinting dully under his
arm. Why should Dignam still feel watched? He
frowned at Brady's house and then couldn't stop. A
face was peering at him from the gloomy depths of
the upstairs room.

He had to lean close enough to the window to

coat it with his breath before he understood that he was glimpsing a photograph on the wall. Indeed, there were several, yet he increasingly felt as if he was staring into a mirror. He sat and waited for the sun to crawl far enough to light upon the faces that weren't really watching him. "You're touched all right," he said, though Brady wasn't there to be told. All the faces were so enlarged that they resembled indistinct ghosts, but they weren't quite blurred enough for Dignam not to recognise at least a dozen versions of his own face.

Brady must have developed them while the subject was out of the house. He hadn't shot them all that morning, however. How long had he been spying unobserved? The question troubled Dignam even more than the pictures did. He craned out of the window to no satisfactory effect, then went for a closer look. Before he reached the end of his path the faces had sunk out of view. As he resolved to work while he kept watch for Brady, he saw what the tree had prevented him from noticing. A bunch of keys was dangling from Brady's front door.

Had he left them as a temptation? It seemed more important that it would take him at least an hour to walk to the nearest library and back. Dignam crossed the road and walked once backwards around the sycamore while pretending not to ascertain that he wasn't being watched from any of the houses, and then he strode to Brady's door. The keys were hanging from a mortise lock. He turned that key, then with a deft twist of the rusty Yale admitted himself to the house. In another second the lumbering door shut behind him.

He wished he hadn't been so swift. Before he was embraced by darkness he'd glimpsed a hall papered with newsprint and a millipede fleeing over a ragged tufted brown carpet to huddle, legs and antennae twitching, at the foot of stairs bare except for discoloured splotches. The house smelled of rot and old paper, and was thick with the lack of clarity he thought only ignorance could bring. He was groping to ease the door ajar when his eyes began to take hold of the dimness. He locked the mortise and advanced along the hall.

His first pace felt as if it was sinking into turf or earth. The sound of his next told him why and perhaps explained the underlying rotten odour. He was treading on sycamore seeds that a wind or Brady must have brought into the house. The noise and the sensation put him in mind of trampling insects, one reason why he hurried to the first internal door. Though the pallid plastic doorknob felt sticky as a second-hand lollipop, he turned it back and forth. The door was locked.

He didn't need to open doors to see. Enough illumination seeped through the grubby fanlight above the front door. Any insects in the hall were either lying low among the scattered seeds or dead.

At least half a dozen sycamore shoots were growing on or between the uncovered floorboards, but
Dignam's attention fastened on the walls. Hardly
an inch of them was visible for the newspapers
tacked to them and overrun with red ink. A marker
pen, if not several, had been used to ring words and
link them with lines, some the length of the hall.

"And" was one of the emphasised words; in fact,
quite a few. And, and, and, and, and, and, and
. . . They felt like threats of a never-ending process.
No sense was to be gained from the newspaper
photographs either. A man's pointing finger was
linked to a woman's hand several yards away,
while another wavering line lassoed both a war
memorial and the chimney of a mansion. Dignam
was trying to imagine a connection when he remembered why he was there: for a closer examina-
tion of the pictures of him and then for whatever
course of action suggested itself.

A single contact with the banister was enough.
The wood was as sticky as the doorknob. He followed his vague jerking shadow to the upper
storey, where the dimness felt like the stale smell
rendered visible. Only the hollow clatter of his
footsteps made it clear that the floor was uncar-
peted. He wasn't surprised the front bedroom was
locked, but finding that none of the keys fitted
threw him.

He crouched to peer through the keyhole. Be-

yond a dishevelled bed he was just able to identify
his own window pinched microscopic, a sight that
made his brain feel shrunken. He lurched to his feet
and backed across the landing to take a run at the
door. Just in time he realised Brady would suspect
him. As he shook himself intelligent he elbowed the
bathroom door, which swung wide.

A toilet roll squatted on the toilet lid, and the
cardboard tubes from perhaps a hundred used rolls
were heaped on the cistern. Three seedlings and a
sycamore as tall as his waist were rooted in earth
several inches deep in the cracked white metal
bath. Another stunted infant tree stood in a sink full
of earth. He hardly knew why he darted forward to
close his fists around all the leaves and crush them
to sticky pulp. As he turned away he saw his
guiltily gleeful face in the smeary speckled mirror.
He started as though he'd caught sight of an in-
truder. His movement was enough to dislodge a
cardboard tube from the top of the pile. Immediately, like lemmings that had found a leader, the
rest toppled off the cistern.

He felt as if something had gripped his mouth
with claws to manipulate it into one or more of several competing expressions. He couldn't judge
from the mirror whether he was grinning or gri-
macing, unless he was about to be overtaken by
quite another look. He stooped to pick up a tube in
each hand, then balanced another pair on top of

them on the cistern, and a third. He was restoring two more to the pile when the whole array sprawled across the tattered linoleum.

How long had he been in the house? Since he hadn't checked when he'd entered, his watch was useless. He abandoned his asinine task and charged downstairs, then up again to shut the bathroom door. The dimness clung to his mind as he raced down a second time and fumbled the key into the mortise lock. He almost slammed the door behind him, closing it stealthily instead. He thrust the key into the lock and twisted it so hard he bruised his fingers. In no more time than it took him to remember to breathe he was hastening across the road in a flurry of sycamore seeds. He was almost at his gate when Brady turned the corner by the shop.

Could he have seen? All of Dignam was desperate to hide—all except his mind. It kept him leaning nonchalantly on a gatepost while he sorted through remarks. "You read a lot, I see." "Fond of words, Mr Brady?" "I hope you didn't write in those books like you—" His fear that he might utter one or more of these spurred him to blurt "Back from the library, then?"

He thought the unrelenting stare was meant to convict him of fatuousness until Brady demanded "Who told you I was there?"

Too late Dignam realised the man was empty-handed. "I saw you taking your books."

"Better taking them than medicine." Brady smirked without moderating his stare. "Keeping an eye on me, are you? You'll need both and a friend's as well."

"Simply being neighbourly," Dignam said and was suddenly afraid that his face was betraying his escapade, a notion that threatened to distort his lips. "It does no harm to look out for others."

"I'll be looking out for you, that's for sure. Any more observations or am I dismissed?"

Surely he couldn't have been eavesdropping in the dimness of the pub. "Please don't allow me to detain you," Dignam said.

"Don't kid yourself you can stop me."

Dignam thought he'd said the opposite. He was sending a silent gasp of relief after the man's back when he remembered that Brady was about to find the keys. Before Dignam could let him do so by himself, Brady spun around. "Made me forget these, did you?" he yelled past the tree.

"I rather think you did it unaided."

Dignam only spoke, but Brady heard him. "And how did you know?" he shouted louder still.

"You told me."

The silence gave him time to understand that Brady hadn't quite before the man bellowed "What's your next trick going to be? Breaking in to see what you can lecture about? Poison me while you're at it, why don't you."

"Don't talk rot," Dignam shouted for any neighbours to hear and strode to his door. He heard Brady's keys rattle as he took out his own. It seemed crucial that he should be at his window by the time Brady went upstairs. He sprinted for his desk as the door slammed like a lid. A seed crunched underfoot as he reached the stairs. His hand must be sticky, not the banister. He sat panting in his not entirely stable chair and tidied the pages of Hannah's essay, then forgot them as he leaned across them. The room that faced him was empty of faces. The sun showed him a blank wall.

He was staring at the wall as if this might force the images to develop from it when Brady entered the empty room with a kitchen chair. He planted it close to the window and sat forward on it, folding his arms, fastening his gaze like twin cameras on his neighbour. Of course he was pretending that he hadn't dashed up to the room before Dignam had reached his. He had needed only to throw the photographs out of sight on the floor. Dignam stood and stretched, but couldn't see them. He felt as if Brady's gaze was weighing him back into the chair to deal with Hannah's thoughts.

Here was the Roger Douglas concept that enraged him most of all: that insanity was somehow magical. She had found more similarities—the ritu-

alistic use of objects, the ambition to alter reality by
the power of the mind, the way witches had once
been regarded and the mentally ill often were now,
a resemblance leading to Dignam's suggestion that
before long the insane would be viewed as sooth-
sayers or visionaries. If people were sufficiently irrational to depend on astrology, he often said, why
not go to the extreme? She clearly hadn't appreciated his irony. Her conclusion felt like a belated attempt to placate him, and overall the essay seemed
designed to mediate between him and Douglas. He
was squeezing the red pen so viciously it creaked
between his fingers when the phone rang on the
corner of his desk.

As he lifted the receiver his gaze couldn't avoid
Brady's. He had to rid himself of a grotesque fancy
that the man had somehow made the phone go off.
"Terry Dignam," he said.

"Terry? Terry," she repeated as if testing her en-
titlement to use the name. "It's Hannah."

"I gathered that."

"I just wanted to ask if you meant what you
said."

"I generally do. It's a peculiarity of mine. Something in particular?"

"I thought you might be saying it so Roger
didn't realise, well, you know. Aren't you coming
to me for dinner tomorrow?"

"I don't think that's going to be possible," Dignam said, holding Brady's gaze.

"Oh."

The syllable was laden with so much disappointment and self-doubt and accusation that he felt compelled to say "I suppose you could do it here if you liked."

"Only if you want me to."

"I thought I'd made it clear I shouldn't have suggested it otherwise."

"You'll need to tell me where to find you."

"I was about to," he said, and did. He hung up the receiver before informing Brady "You've got what you asked for. There'll be someone else to keep an eye on you."

With an effort he lowered his gaze to the essay. 50%, he scribbled in the margin. *Some of your ideas will bear developing—decide which.* He looked up in something like triumph to confront an empty room, and was irrational enough to feel relieved until he grasped where Brady might be. The thought seemed to lodge like an infection in his bladder. He waddled wide-legged to the bathroom and drained himself, then returned to his desk. Brady was awaiting him.

His face was an unreadable mask. Even his eyes failed to react to his subject, who felt as if their scrutiny was puppeting him across the room to sit at his desk like a miscreant under the gaze of a teacher. Brady couldn't know that Dignam had been in his house. If Dignam hadn't, the man would believe that he had, but what did that mean? It made Dignam feel embedded in Brady's view of him. He hunched over the next essay, only for a reference to privileged perceptions to swell into his vision as though it had been freshly penned. He shoved the pages aside to concentrate to his own work, his notes, his book. *The subject sits at a window*, he scrawled, which didn't help him deal with the glare he sensed on top of his brain or in it—didn't reduce his awareness of it or give it meaning. He raised his head and met it. If it came to a contest, sanity must win.

He strove to put everything he knew about himself into his eyes. He continued when they began to sting, because it would seem feeble of him to be first to blink. The first time he was forced to, he pinched his thighs between his nails. His leg was aching in too many places to count by the time he observed that night was falling. When he glanced down at the page he couldn't read his own words.

How long did he propose to sit at the window? He was holding Brady still, but that wasn't necessary; the man would never be able to steal into the house. Dignam took the cramp in his guts for hunger. "Time for some of us to eat," he muttered. "Just make sure it's not poisoned."

He was unhappy to find that he couldn't eat

much. Half the omelette he made to use up milk he scraped into the bin. He still had several bottles too many from trying to moderate his coffee intake and woo sleep. He finished one and bore another into the front room in case it would soothe the cramp in his innards while he allowed himself some television. There was nothing on the many channels to engage his mind: simplistic quizzes, violence whose lack of apparent effect struck him as close to psychotic, comedy shows accompanied by laughter so inappropriate it seemed crazed. While he gazed at the screen, was Brady gazing at the house? The possibility made his mind feel cramped. As soon as watching had tired him enough he stumbled up to bed.

He didn't recall closing his study door, but he resisted the temptation to peer around it to see if his neighbour was spying, which demonstrated how sane he was, as if he needed proof. Once he was in bed he set about forgetting his tormentor. He shouldn't have given the man a thought; by the time he ceased to feel his eyes he couldn't tell how much of the dark consisted of Brady's fancies about him. Certainly it helped Brady come into the room.

At first he only stared at Dignam and leaned close to show that his eyes were lidless, and then he began to shake his huge wild head. Dignam assumed this expressed disapproval until seeds and insects rained on him. He wasn't sure which dropped into his helplessly gaping mouth as Brady towered over him. The man's head was pressed against the ceiling now; some of the twigs sprouting from his cranium bent with a thin creak and snapped off. He reached up with arms longer than the room was wide and plucked a handful of shoots off the cracked scaly expanse of his forehead. He clamped Dignam's eyes open with two fingers of the other hand before planting the shoots between his victim's lips. With a flabby cry that made him feel less in control of his mouth than ever, Dignam jerked awake. Brady was above him, a looming shape more solid than the dark.

Dignam's gasp felt like taking back his cry. It seemed to suck the contents of his mouth deeper into him. He recoiled against the bars above the pillow, and the metal clashed against the wall as he flung out a hand for the light cord. For a moment his fingers felt entangled by twigs, and then he succeeded in tugging the light on.

He was alone in the room. There were no seeds or insects on or around the bed. Nevertheless he felt poisoned by the dream, which he sensed hovering like the man's oppressive presence, waiting to resume its shape. What stale taste was lingering in Dignam's mouth? When he floundered to the bathroom, gargling seemed to emphasise the taste. He threw his study door open to see if Brady was watching in triumph.

A streetlamp cast a net of shadow from the tree over the house opposite—too much shadow for Dignam to be anything like certain if the window was deserted. Poking his head forth didn't resolve the question. His eyes stung, and a taste like indigestion filled his mouth. He slammed the window and hurried downstairs, wiping his hand on his pyjamas between clutches at the sticky banister.

Two could play at the game Brady had wished on him. He drank half a bottle of milk and eased the metal cap off another, then found the seed that someone had tracked into the hall. He rubbed it between his hands, staining his palms, and crumbled the fragments with his nails into a powder he could sprinkle in the milk. He restored the cap and shook the bottle until it looked full of nothing but innocent milk. Having pulled on a jacket and trousers over his pyjamas, he hid the bottle inside his jacket as he left the house.

What did he intend to do? If Brady was watching, only to remind him he was also being watched. Dignam was beneath the sycamore, whose shadow felt as though innumerable seeds were poised to fall on him, before he could be sure Brady's window was unmanned. He strode as quickly as silence permitted to the man's front door. "Milk-o," he said under his breath. "Special Sunday delivery for Brady." He set the bottle on the step with a clunk far more muted than his heartbeat and allowed his uncontrollable grin to lead him back across the road.

He couldn't sleep now. He had to watch. He almost slammed the front door in his eagerness to dash upstairs and resume his post at the desk. He hadn't missed anything; the bottle was still on the doorstep. Its glimmer put him in mind of a headstone too shrunken by distance to move him. What had he done? Nothing fatal, certainly—nothing as poisonous as Brady's effect on him. Perhaps Brady would see that it was best to call a truce once he understood worse could befall him.

Soon Dignam's eyes felt charred by the dark and by watching. More than once the bottle reared up like a pallid larva or executed a jig from willingness to be discovered. "Gargoyle," he called, "gargoyle," but that failed to summon his adversary. In time the streetlamp grew redundant and eventually, without his noticing, dead. At some point he realised he was visible, and snatched an essay off the heap, not that he could make sense of the words just now. They seemed to underline his view of the house opposite, to suggest only that mattered. Once Brady opened the front door, he was all that did.

He didn't see the milk at first. He advanced to the gate and frowned up and down the street. As he turned back to the house Dignam saw him stiffen. He marched to grab the bottle and tear off the cap before swinging around to display how he was emptying the milk over the wild lawn strewn with seeds. In a few seconds he was at the window, holding up the bottle as evidence.

Evidence of what? He hadn't drunk from it, and he'd thrown away the contents. It would be monstrously unfair of him to accuse a neighbour of poisoning him. If he planned to sit there like a dairy advertisement, that was no reason for Dignam to indulge him. Dignam marked the essays almost faster than he could breathe—*confused thinking, too much identification with your subject, too closely observed for objectivity, too narrowly focused*—and swept the heap aside to work on his book. The solitary sentence on the topmost page brought him back to Brady, who hadn't moved or blinked.

How long was Dignam going to let himself be held there? Usually on Sundays he bought a paper to read in the pub on the campus, but suppose Brady took some crazed revenge while his neighbour was away? For once Dignam would have to patronise the corner shop.

He hadn't reached his gate when Brady emerged, flourishing the bottle. "Didn't kill me yet," he shouted. "Have another go."

"Take it as a warning," Dignam responded barely aloud. As he hurried to the shop he glanced back at every other step to ensure Brady wasn't sneaking towards his house. Had the man mouthed something or gestured to make three youths who were loitering outside the shop snigger at Dignam? A furious glance that screwed an ache into Dignam's neck found Brady turning away to speak to a girl in her teens or younger. As she followed Brady up the path Dignam wondered "Is someone up to no good with that child?"

"Dirty bugger," one youth snarled. The others muttered viciously as Dignam dodged into the shop.

Mrs Vernon and the shopkeeper were waiting for him. "Had a bad night, did you?" Mrs Vernon said.

He felt as if Brady's obsession with him had turned into a plague. "What makes you say that?" he demanded.

"Anybody would, the way you're dressed."

He looked down at himself as a preamble to sarcasm and saw the pyjama cuffs protruding from his trousers, the pyjama collar sprawling forth from his jacket. As he gaped in search of words, Mrs Timms enquired "What were you saying outside?"

"Your friend Mr Brady has just taken a young girl inside his house."

"That'll be his granddaughter. She visits him on Sundays."

Dignam retreated to the door and surveyed the deserted streets. "Where did those boys go? Have you any idea where they live?"

"Which were those?" said Mrs Timms, and her

customer added less gently "We thought you were talking to yourself."

Why were they trying to confuse him? If it was what Brady wanted, let him take the consequences. Dignam bought a newspaper and ran home. Suppose Brady had arranged the diversion to distract him? As soon as he'd secured the door he hunted for telltale seeds and did his best to ascertain whether the banister or any of the doorknobs was stickier than it ought to be.

The news in the paper seemed to belong to a world that had become detached from him. At the end of every sentence, and before long of every phrase, his eyes twitched up to focus on the house across the road. The afternoon, though not the paper, was half finished by the time Brady let the girl out. Dignam sprinted to his gate as Brady sent her on her way with not too much of a hug or a kiss. "Excuse me," Dignam called. "You may want to watch out for some young boys round here."

"Hurry home, Jane." Once she had picked up speed the man said "Maybe that's your kind of thing. It won't do for me."

"I didn't mean it like that."

"Then how do you know what I mean?"

"I'm trying to warn you in case you're in danger," Dignam's unwieldy mouth managed to pronounce. "Some people can get queer notions in their heads."

"You'd be the last person I'd need to tell me, Mr Dignam."

"Where did you get my name?"

"I know everything worth knowing about you, believe me."

If his stare was meant to convey this, Dignam was equal to it. His eyes had only begun to sting when Brady turned his back. "It's *Doctor*, so there's something you don't know for a start," Dignam said, but he'd blinked. As Brady shut his door Dignam slammed his and ran to his desk.

Sorting paper kept him busy: the news, the essays, the seed of his book. Soon he was beyond telling which was which. Was he watching out for Brady or hoping the youths would teach him manners? Perhaps they were waiting for the dark that sprouted branches against Brady's house. When a solitary figure disentangled itself from the shadows, he thought it was Brady bound for revenge. Once his peeled eyes recognised Hannah he strove to remember why she was there. Of course, she was anxious to learn what he thought of her essay and her.

Perhaps she would assume he was out, since the room was unlit. She met his eyes, however, as she ventured up the path, a plastic bag swinging from each hand. Now he remembered she had undertaken to provide dinner. The prospect kept him at his desk until she'd rung the doorbell twice, at which point he raced down to enquire "Would you mind telling me where you just got those?"

She looked puzzled and a little hurt. "I didn't just get them anywhere. I brought them from home."

"I'm going to watch you prepare the meal, am I?"

"It's made. All we need is a microwave. I know you've got one."

"Which of my neighbours have you been talking to?"

"None of them. I've never even seen one."

"Well, now you have," he said, jabbing all his fingers at the face among the flattened branches.

She gave it rather too perfunctory a look. "Can I come in now, do you think? It's chilly out here."

He was about to say he was too busy for dinner when he wondered if she might report back to Roger Douglas. If his rival heard that Dignam had been behaving oddly, what might he be capable of saying to their colleagues? "Come in by all means," Dignam said loud enough to be heard across the road. "I've nothing to hide."

Once he'd slammed the door behind her Hannah didn't move towards the kitchen until he led the way. He clawed at the light switch and twisted a chair backwards to sit on while he observed her putting the first carton in the microwave. This done, she was so ill at ease that nobody could blame him for enquiring "What's wrong?"

"Have you only just got up?"

"I've been too busy to get dressed. Do you want me to change?"

"You needn't. I've seen worse." Apparently this was a timid joke, perhaps intended to nerve her to say "Busy marking, would that have been?"

"Marking and working on the book I'm not supposed to be up to writing."

"I've never said that and I wouldn't. I know you have it in you." This was plainly the start of the process of asking "Did you finish your marking?"

"Shilly-shally, Hannah, shilly-shally."

"I'm not sure I . . ."

"That's your problem. Try believing in yourself enough to say what you mean. Have I marked your essay? Yes."

"Am I allowed to hear what you thought?"

"It seems to me you're in two minds. Decide which one you're sticking to."

"Can't I take the best from each?"

"They aren't compatible. By the time I'd finished trying to make sense of your essay my head was splitting in half. You're meant to be writing about madness, not driving people mad."

He thought he might have said too much until some of it silenced her. The hush emphasised how little he was eating. Weren't there seeds in the vegetable curry she served as the first course? He did his best to pick forkfuls nowhere near them, which left most of the contents of his plate untouched. "I'm saving myself," he said and felt the choice of words tug at his lips.

At least the silence let him hear any noises in the street. Before he'd finished hacking spicy chicken off its bones and sifting the rice with his fork, he had dashed into the front room twice. The second time Hannah followed, letting him retreat to the kitchen ahead of her and dump most of his plateful in the bin. Did she suspect? He could think of no other reason for her to replenish his plate. "I know you're worried about work," she said, "but it won't help to starve yourself, will it? Anyway, I don't know anyone who thinks you're past it except you."

How many lies were packed into that? "Don't delude yourself you know what I think," he said, and more slyly "I can enjoy your dinner by watching you eat."

She laid her utensils to rest among the bones. "I made it for you."

Suppose she'd eaten precisely enough not to poison herself? He consigned the remains to the bin and stacked the plates in the sink with a clatter that felt as if sections of his skull were grating together. It suddenly seemed crucial that Hannah shouldn't think he was behaving unusually in any way, lest she tell someone at the university. "I hope that doesn't mean you're leaving," he made himself say.

"Not if you don't want me to."

"You know what I want," he said and unzipped his trousers to demonstrate there was no misunderstanding.

Did she stiffen so that she wouldn't recoil? "Not down here, Terry," she protested.

"Indeed not. Up is best."

As he ensured that she preceded him upstairs, his extension raised itself from flopping against his trousers to sway in her direction. From the landing he glimpsed Brady at the window. If he discharged his task with Hannah in the office chair he could keep an eye out for the youths, but she had already switched on the light in the bedroom. When she sat on the edge of the bed he pushed her as flat as the tousled quilt permitted and eased her skirt up.

Her black briefs were slippery silk, which he felt squeaking beneath his nails until they caught in the filigreed edge. He pulled the briefs down far enough that he could insert himself in Hannah as he clambered onto her. At first he wasn't sure if her moans denoted pleasure or discomfort or simply determination to improve her grades, and then he wondered if they were meant to deafen him to sounds outside the house. He was reaching to lean a hand on her mouth and if necessary her nose as well when he heard shouts and a smash of glass across the road.

Dragging himself out of Hannah was more of a release than he was prepared for. Spurts of solidified dimness preceded him into the study. The sensations this entailed were far more remote than the sight of Brady at the window. The man hadn't moved, and there was no sign of the youths. Dignam wiped himself on a sheet of paper, which he flung into the bin as he resumed his seat. He was peering in search of broken glass when Hannah arrived behind him. "Terry," she pleaded, "what are you trying to do?"

He wasn't so easily distracted; he wouldn't even blink. "Are you asking me to believe you don't know?"

"I can't stay if you're going to behave like this."

"Then that solves a good few problems. I'll see you tomorrow in class."

Why was she loitering? She was about to ask for her essay, of course. "Tomorrow," he repeated so loud that it widened his eyes. He didn't let them shrink until he saw her on the stretch of pavement he was able to keep in view without losing sight of Brady. Once she lost shape and vanished from the rim of his vision he felt as if there had never been anyone except himself in the house.

Whatever the sound of breaking glass had signified, it appeared not to have affected Brady. He was staring at Dignam as if his entire being was concentrated in his eyes, but Dignam was equal to him. He wouldn't move or blink until his subject did. If Brady refused to heed his warning, he would bring whatever happened on himself. The gang weren't likely to kill him, after all. He hadn't made Dignam act out Brady's view of him. He never had.

In time Dignam's eyes drooped, and his head. He stretched his eyes wide until they felt on the edge of sprouting from their holes. He roused himself by pinching his thighs and eventually his penis with his nails. He wanted to think his opponent was having to resort to worse, but there wasn't a hint of movement over the road. How could the man sit so inert and never blink? A stealthy dawn had separated the topmost branches from the sky before Dignam was certain something was wrong.

He began to gesture wildly at the figure across the road. He tried to find the grin that had overtaken his face in the other house, and rocked his head from side to side and popped his eyes. When this had no effect he held up the hand that had borrowed a word from the newspaper in the corner shop and stabbed a finger at it. Next he climbed on the desk, trampling the papers, to wave his penis at his tormentor. None of this earned him a reaction. Brady wasn't just still, he was lifeless. Something—

surely only his mental condition—must have frightened him to death.

In a moment that felt like stepping over the brink of a nightmare Dignam remembered everything he'd done: the milk, the youths. He leapt off the desk, jarring his ankles, and floundered out of the room. He ought to have checked that Hannah hadn't left the front door unlocked for anyone to sneak in, but it was fastened now. He closed it behind him as gently as his shivering fingers could manage and limped down the path.

Could he still be performing Brady's fantasies about him? What if the man had used the photographs to manipulate him? Just as witches had to let their victims know they were supposed to be under a spell, so Brady had ensured he saw the photographs. Or perhaps the seeds crunching underfoot were the key to it all; perhaps they spread Brady's influence. Dignam was so busy sorting out the truth that he was well across the road before twinges in his penis alerted him that it was exposed to the night air. He was stowing it away when with an outraged shout Brady sprang to his feet and vanished from the window.

What kind of a trick did he think he'd been playing? Dignam folded his arms and challenged the front door. He heard a disarrayed clatter of footsteps at the top of the stairs, and then the noises tumbled over one another. They were brought to an end by a weighty thud in the hall, followed by utter silence.

A nervous grin distorted his mouth as he limped on tiptoe to the door and hauled up the rusty flap of the letterbox. He knelt among the seeds and ducked to the metal slot, and had to lever his eyes wide with fingers and thumbs before he could believe what he was seeing. Brady was upside down, his body on the stairs, his head at an excessive angle in the hall. His accusing glare looked strengthened by its inversion, and seemed to require no effort at all.

Dignam met it as if he might still outstare it, and then he shut the flap and staggered to his feet and fled along the path. How long would Brady take to be discovered? Dignam wanted to be present so that whoever found the corpse would see him at his window and know he couldn't have been responsible. He leaned his elbows on the desk and gripped his head with both hands to keep his eyes trained on the house opposite. The deserted window appeared to be pretending Brady wasn't still obsessed with him. Suppose the man never closed his eyes again, or it no longer mattered if he did, since Dignam's last sight of them was embedded in his mind? The sun was helping parch his own eyes when he realised how he was putting himself at risk. He might be suspected if he behaved unusually in any way—if he didn't go to work.

He grabbed the trampled mass of papers from his desk and stuffed them into a carrier bag he found in the kitchen. At his gate he glanced at Brady's house while pretending to collect seeds, but could see no faces, neither Brady's nor his own. "Just off to work, Mrs Timms," he called into the shop. The stained carrier blundered against him as he limped to the crossroads, where the traffic lights drilled colours into his skull with a piercing buzz. Layers of grey matter piled up on the hill, but he succeeded in leaving their ossification behind as he made his swaying way across the campus. Although it was scattered with students, none of them was heading for his lecture. He was about to demand an explanation when he realised he was late.

This was no reason for Roger Douglas to have taken the podium, and why was Hannah on the front row? She gazed up at Douglas as he said "My experience—"

"My course isn't about yours, Dr Drugless." Dignam limped to the podium amid a rustling he mistook for general excitement until he traced it to the carrier bag. "Sorry, that's the last thing I should call you, isn't it? Thanks for filling in for me. You can stop now."

Douglas grasped himself by the beard or held up

a mask. "Are you sure you're—you'll forgive me, but are you up to this?"

"I could ask what you think you're up to. I believe Miss Martin thinks I'm still competent to teach, don't you, Miss Martin? And I'm sure you speak for all your fellow students."

They were certainly all gazing at him in the same way. It couldn't be pity; it must be sympathy—they were on his side. "Thank you, Roger," he said, indicating the auditorium with a hand like a blurred sign.

Douglas stepped down reluctantly but lingered at the back of the room. If he'd decided he could learn from his colleague, perhaps there was hope for him. Dignam emptied the carrier onto the lectern, only to find that the pages were stuck together by vegetable matter. He mustn't let the sight claw at his guts; once the stuff dried he would be able to separate the essays. "So we've been talking about experience, have we?" he said, fixing his gaze on the heaps of faces. "Let's talk about mine, then. My experience . . ."

How could he tell them about Brady? Even mentioning the man would betray he'd watched him. The thought made everything feel turned upside down like the eyes he could see on the stairs. "My experience," he said he didn't know how many times while eyes stared at him. Most of them weren't Brady's, unless they all were. When had Douglas sneaked out of the room? No doubt he was bringing someone else to observe the lecture. Dignam had to demonstrate that he still had plenty to offer, but how? "My experience," he said, and his gaze lit upon his own handwriting. At once he knew both what his opening sentence should be and how he could regain control of the lecture. "A man sits in a room," he said in triumph.

It appeared to mean less to his students than to him. He lowered himself into a chair on the podium and, having tugged his sleeves over his pyjama cuffs, leaned forward to compose the precarious stacks of heads with his gaze. "I'm not going to tell you my experience, I'm going to let you observe it for yourselves," he said. "Observe what distinguishes me from a man with a mental problem. Don't look away until you have."

Some of them must have seen almost at once. Others, not only Hannah, apparently found it harder. He wouldn't relax until everyone had finished the assignment. When refusing to blink began to take away his sight, his innards shrank into him, but soon his inability to see whether he was being watched felt more like peace. He heard people leave the auditorium, and others come in, and voices murmuring. He had to be grateful that they were so anxious not to disturb him. When the voices converged on him and hands helped him up, he was content to be led to rest now that he'd carried out the task he was paid for. A solitary thought was enough for him. He need see nothing that he didn't want to see so long as he never blinked.

THE DIRTY PEOPLE

David B. Silva

They came in the middle of the night.

The Dirty People.

Their silhouettes pasted against the drawn shade of the attic window of the neighboring Victorian.

I noticed their arrival by chance. Both by chance and by purpose, to be perfectly truthful. The hour was near midnight. I was on my way downstairs for a can of Pepsi, hoping the rush of caffeine would keep me writing another hour or two. As I passed by a window, I noticed the light in the attic window across the way. The Victorian, which had been built the same year as my own, had been vacant for months. The owner, a gentleman by the name of Harvey Shoemaker, had passed away after a coma brought on by hypoglycemia. His sister had placed the house on the market the very next day, asking an obscene amount, even for these supposedly prosperous times. It was by the chance of a glance that I noticed the light, though I must confess I had been experiencing an odd pull toward the house throughout most of the day.

Along with my can of Pepsi, I brought a pair of binoculars back upstairs with me to my office. I turned the light off as I entered. The can of Pepsi went on top of the filing cabinet, next to the door. I hadn't been thirsty in the first place, and now that I was wide awake with curiosity I had lost what little interest I'd had in the drink.

I sat at the desk, to the right of the computer, where the desktop was less cluttered. There was a pair of casement windows at the back of the desk, covered with blinds so I wouldn't be distracted when I wrote. I turned off the last remaining light source in the room, the computer screen, then raised the blinds to allow myself to peer out without being noticed.

Silhouettes.

How many of them, I could not tell. Four. Perhaps five. Milling about in the attic, somewhat aimlessly, as if they were lost, as if they were familiarizing themselves with a strange environment.

The FOR SALE sign was gone from the front yard, where it had been sunk in a patch of sand and ice plant for months, the metal already beginning to corrode from the salty spray of the ocean. It had become an eyesore, and I freely admit I was pleased to see it gone.

But who were these people? These silhouettes against the shade of the attic window?

I could not write for wondering, and fell asleep near three o'clock in the morning, the Pepsi still sitting on the filing cabinet, unopened, the blinds covering the casement windows behind my desk still raised so I might watch the activities of my new neighbors without them watching me.

I dreamed of a dark place with gradient shadows of black and gray, where the inhabitants blended almost seamlessly into their surroundings, where night was forever. It was a place I had visited often in my recent dreams.

This is the writer's life, I have always argued. To live in quiet solitude. Away from the distractions of a pop culture that bombards us with the images and morals of a *Jerry Springer* or a *Survivor* or a *Big Brother*. These voyeuristic excursions into the lives of our modern gladiators. Who will survive? Who will be the savage? Who will be meek and compassionate and therefore suffer the consequences of their humanity? It is a mistake for a writer to play witness to such events, for fear he may begin to believe what he sees is reality.

It is not reality.

Reality resides in the writer's soul. It feeds his

thoughts, his dreams, his perceptions. It is his wisdom, his truth, and it belongs to him and him alone.

These are the reasons I live the life I live. Outside the circles that seem to consume the lives of the masses. It is a writer's responsibility to elevate, to introduce new thought, to shed light on the shadows that cast darkness over truth. It is no light task. I take it seriously.

It is for these reasons I had always confined myself to the surroundings of my house as much as humanly possible.

It is for these reasons I tended to sleep late into the day and work late into the night.

The following day, after a night of difficult dreams, I came back to the world a little after two in the afternoon. Every window in my Victorian was covered with blinds. I had done this to keep the sun out. Yet there were thin slits of light defying my efforts throughout the house. The morning fog had burned off. The sun was out in full force.

I pulled back the blinds in my bedroom and spent a long time staring at the attic window of the neighboring Victorian.

No silhouettes by daylight.

No activity.

No voices.

Apparently, they slept later than myself.

I did not know these new neighbors, but already

I did not like them. They were intruders. They had moved into my comfort zone and I did not care for it. Not at all. Because there would eventually be activity. There would be noise. And other distractions. A man cannot do his work with distractions.

Still, a writer writes.

I did my best to maintain my usual routine. I showered and ate a breakfast of toast and eggs—the mind needs protein to function at its peak. After breakfast, I did a light workout on the treadmill—the mind also needs oxygen—then spent several hours reading *The Holographic Universe*, by Michael Talbot, followed by a few chapters of *Beach Music*, which had been on my reading pile for several years.

The sun had begun to dip below the horizon of the ocean by now.

Normally, I would sequester myself in my office for the remainder of the evening and well into the night, working on whatever was my current project, which in this instance was a massive novel spanning multiple generations of the family Cain. It was a project I had been working on for nearly two years now. There was still no end in sight. It did not help that on this day, in the late hour, I found myself once again peering out through a small opening in the blinds at the movement of my new neighbors.

They were back, it appeared.

I could see silhouettes once again stirring behind the shade of the attic window.

It was difficult, having something so little to work with as a shadow against a light, to distinguish either the number of inhabitants occupying the neighboring house or the distinct characteristics of said inhabitants. However, I began to keep notes on my observations.

I believed there were four altogether. Three men and a woman. Perhaps a mother, a father, and two sons? Perhaps an arrangement less respectable.

The men cast similar shadows of long hair, down over their shoulders, with beards which appeared equally as long. They were tall, neither thin nor fat, and dressed in a manner which I found impossible to determine by silhouette alone. The woman, who I came to refer to as The Matriarch, because she always seemed to be in the middle of things and at times I had the distinct impression she was in control, was rather slight in stature. It was for this reason and for the full, distinctive outline of breasts that I determined she was female.

What they were doing in the attic at night, I was unable to discern.

Yet I watched just the same.

Mesmerized.

I should have been writing, I admit. A writer writes, as the old cliché goes, and as I have already stated. But I found myself both fascinated by and distrustful of the activity next door. Who were these intruders? What so fascinated them in that old Victorian attic? And why had I yet to see them under the glare of daylight? Out in the yard? Unpacking? Arranging? Making the house theirs?

I dreamed again that night. A dream of faraway places where gradients of gray and black shadowed the landscape, where the inhabitants blended chameleonlike into their surroundings, where night cast a never-ending shadow over the terrain. It was a busy land, overgrown with weedlike tendrils, mushroomlike plants, dark green grass, everything growing close to the ground.

I woke out of the dream shortly after six in the morning, left with an overwhelming sense of disorientation. It felt as if I had awoken in a foreign land. The feeling remained with me for nearly an hour, until I was finally able to fall back to sleep again.

It was a few minutes past one when I climbed out of bed. I abandoned my normal routine, for reasons I cannot fully understand, and found myself in my office, once again staring out through the window at my new neighbors.

There was no activity in the attic—I had expected none—and no activity anywhere else in the house so far as I could tell. However, in my efforts to thoroughly observe the Victorian, I discovered something I was not expecting. The house was showing signs of neglect.

It was most notable beneath the windows, where dark patches of a greenish black mold had developed overnight, leaving an appearance similar to mascara running from the corners of a crying woman's eyes. Around the footing of the foundation, weeds had sprung up. Paint had begun to peel in sporadic patches across the siding. Some sort of spiderwebbed growth covered several of the windows.

What was happening over there?

I spent two, maybe three hours observing the old Victorian with no sign of activity in the house. Late sleepers, perhaps. Night people. Not the kind of people who belonged in a house like that, in a neighborhood like this.

I finally showered. It was too late for breakfast, so I fixed myself a tuna fish sandwich, then spent half an hour on the treadmill. It should have been longer, at least an hour, but I didn't feel up to it. Not today. Not with the new neighbors doing heaven only knows what next door.

After my stint on the treadmill, I ended up taking a short nap. I had been unusually tired lately. Run down a bit, though I didn't feel as if I were coming down with anything. I did come out of the nap with a rather peculiar sense of loss, however. I couldn't remember if I had dreamed, which was probably for the best considering the nature of my recent dreams, but I also had trouble remembering things that should have come effortlessly to mind.

The title of my current book.

What time the postman usually delivered the mail.

The name of the grocery story in town, where I usually did my shopping.

The date of my birth.

Little things. Numerous little things that should have come to mind without the slightest need of encouragement. And yet they would not present themselves in any manner whatsoever. I found myself digging through the yellow pages until I was able to finally put a name to the grocery store . . . Sunshine Market. It wasn't until I rifled through the papers on my desk that I was able to determine the title of my book . . . *The Cain Chronicles*.

Every lost memory had been recoverable, at least for the time being.

However, that failed to address the underlying enigma: where had these memories gone in the first place? Why were they suddenly out of my natural grasp?

The late afternoon and early evening hours troubled me with the worry that perhaps something was wrong with me. A dementia, perhaps? A stroke? Some sort of neurological damage that had occurred without my full comprehension?

I had no desire to write.

Three days in a row now I had not written.

A writer writes.

Since the arrival of my new neighbors.

For the better part of the evening, I involved myself in word games and crossword puzzles, in Trivial Pursuit and a card game called Concentration, which I believed my mother had taught me as a child, though I could no longer be certain of that fact. Anything to test the functioning of my memory, the extent of my knowledge.

There was, without question, a loss. An unexplainable loss.

By midnight, I found myself watching the house next door again.

A light show had started in the attic. Yellow, blue, red. Flashing on and off like some sort of Frankensteinian reanimation scene. The sky was clear, the stars bright, or I would have expected bright flashes of lightning to come down from overhead.

There was something else, too.

It took me a moment to identify what it was . . . a humming sound like you might hear from an electric shaver, only lower than that. Much lower. So much so I could feel its vibration humming inside my body. As if it were coming *from* me instead of *to* me.

Tonight the silhouettes were not at the window, though I had little doubt my new neighbors were up there somewhere, milling around in the attic like animals trying to get acquainted with new surroundings. Perhaps it was the lights that masked their presence? Perhaps it was the vibration humming through my veins?

Sleep caught up to me sometime around three. I napped at my desk until after four, then dragged myself off to bed.

The lights were still flashing next door.

My dreams returned me to the familiar landscapes of the past several nights.

I don't recall what time I awoke the next day. Later than usual. Only a couple of hours before sunset. The sun had already begun to turn a soft orange after its white-hot midday glare. It wouldn't be long before it would dip below the horizon of the ocean, and night would slip quietly in to take its place.

I abandoned my usual treadmill routine, skipped my shower and shave as well. It had occurred to me how much of my day was consumed by these activities, and how they were primarily activities of appearance. They had always been my way of trying to fit in, and suddenly they seemed foreign to me.

The Victorian next door had continued to deteriorate in both appearance and condition. Paint had peeled away from huge patches of the siding, exposing the raw wood beneath. Black mold had spread across the building in broad, ugly swathes. Windows had been broken. Weeds had sprouted up along the foundation walls like gopher holes in a garden. The framing around the windows had pulled away from the siding and a number of boards were dangling by little more than a nail or two. And . . .

And . . . the shade was absent from the attic window.

I had moved my desk away from the wall by now, and set up a chair so I could be more comfortable in my responsibilities as an observer. But I nearly fell out of my seat upon the discovery of the uncovered attic window. Finally, I could gather a complete and accurate portrait of my new neighbors. Unfortunately, it was also true that they could now observe my presence as well.

That was a thought that disturbed me horrendously.

For a good part of the evening, I fought my own curiosity and kept my distance from the window. I filled my time returning to the word puzzles and brain teasers I had dragged out the day before. During the night, I had again lost vast regions of my memory.

My mother's name.

Where I had been born.

My age.

Nearly all my childhood memories.

I was, I began to believe, deteriorating much the same as the old Victorian next door.

Late in the dark of the night, I found myself drawn back to my neighbors again. I moved the chair to the window, raised the blinds several inches, and took out my binoculars.

Lights were flashing, as they had the previous night. Only brighter tonight, because of the missing shade.

I found the attic window, expecting a performance not dissimilar from the night before, but instead was shocked to the point of fear when the form of a man stepped into sight. He appeared to focus his attention directly upon me, though I could not be certain of this because he did not appear to have eyes. Nor did he appear to have a mouth or a nose. There was a thick mat of hair covering his face, something like you might see on one of those old wolfman sideshow exhibits at a traveling carnival. However, as I have stated, he did not appear to have any of the other features one would expect to find on a human face.

He stood in the window, looking down at me, until I began to feel that low humming vibration stir inside my body again. Not a sound as such, but a . . . *communication*. He was *communicating* with me.

I dropped the binoculars, and retreated back into the darkest corner of the room.

Not only was he communicating with me, but I believed I knew what he was saying: *Time for your return*.

I was unable to find the courage to return to the window again that night. I spent my time pacing the main floor of the house, not unlike a rat in a maze, I suppose. What did he mean, *Time for your return*? Who was he? *What* was he? My return to *where*? The questions nagged at me like an open wound, unanswerable, until I eventually succumbed to a state of exhaustion that led to sleep.

I dreamed again of a dark place, of shadows, of weeds growing close to the ground. Unlike my other dreams of the past few nights, this one had familiar inhabitants: my neighbors.

When I awoke again, it was still dark outside and I felt exhausted. I lay in bed, a strange numbness settling over me like a shroud. My name forgotten. My surroundings unfamiliar. Still drawn, however, to the activity next door.

Once I was able to gain a sense of my bearings, I climbed out of bed and stumbled, rather unceremoniously, into the bathroom, where I was faced with the unimaginable. During my hours of slumber, my appearance had transformed dramatically. Quite similar, if not identical to my new neighbor of the last few nights, my face was now overgrown with hair. My hands trembling, I parted the mass and discovered not only that my mouth and nose were missing, but that my eyes were missing as well.

Then how can you see?

I did not know.

Nor did I know how I could smell, yet the strong, salty fragrance of the ocean was unmistakable.

Finally, when I could not stand before my reflection a moment longer, I turned away, my legs weak and struggling to carry me. I stumbled out of the bathroom back into the bedroom, and made my way to the window, where I tore down the horizontal blinds. The room filled with a palatable darkness that engulfed me, and made me part of its own.

Time for your return.

And I understood. At long last, I understood.

I came to think of them as The Dirty People, though I fully realize this was unfair. They had come from another place, that same dark, shadow-gradient landscape that had inhabited my dreams those few but painful nights.

They had come for me.

I had always known I didn't fit here. I was the

outsider. I was the restless child in the quiet, easy-going surroundings of a small town. I was an accident, an evolutionary mutation, an anomaly. *The choice is yours.* All that matters is that I did not belong here.

But I did not belong *there*, either.

I told them as much, The Dirty People.

They understood.

When I woke the next morning, my world as I had known it was in place again. I knew those things that I should know: my mother's name, my date of birth, what time the postman delivered. I had eyes that could see, a nose that could smell, a mouth that could taste. My hair was considerably shorter.

The Victorian next door was its old self again. The windows restored, the weeds gone, the FOR SALE sign back standing in a patch of sand and ice plant out front.

Yet nothing would ever be the same again.

Certainly not me.

I spent the day opening the blinds and windows throughout the house. Then, as the first signs of evening began to show themselves, I took a long walk on the beach.

It was the first time I had ever walked the beach.

I liked it.

It made me feel alive.

GLYPHOTECH

Mark Samuels

Franklyn Crisk did not mind the job or even his colleagues in the office too much. Certainly, both bored him. No, it was the noise and the heat that were becoming intolerable. Outside the Mare Publishing House building, on the crossroads, some men in boiler suits were working on the road. Though the noise they made was more like fingernails clawing across a blackboard than the juddering of a pneumatic drill, which is what one would expect to hear. It was the middle of summer but the office workers were forced to close all the windows in order to stifle the sound. Since the company did not regard the comfort of its employees as its concern, there was no air-conditioning and the temperature inside the cramped offices was unbearable. The clean shirt he'd donned this morning was soaked with sweat and his head throbbed painfully.

He wondered how he'd wound up being employed by this company, housed in a whitewashed four-storey structure on the corner of Fytton Square. It was obvious to him now that he had spent too long overseas. Twenty years in Kyoto, Japan, had rendered him almost unemployable back in his home country. He had, without being particularly aware of it, picked up the Japanese obsession with ritual and social custom to the degree that even his speech patterns betrayed a clipped formality that set him apart.

This job at Mare was the only vacancy that had been offered to him, despite several other positions he'd fruitlessly applied for and for which he felt he was more qualified. His work was drudgery: inputting book royalties into a computer system, printing them out and then mailing the statements to authors. It meant eight hours staring at a dim monitor screen. The computers utilized by the firm for these tasks were almost obsolete. Their lack of modernity meant that there was no spare memory capacity for any other programs that might serve as a welcome distraction. There was no access to the Internet or even email to connect him with the world outside.

And now this ceaseless noise and heat! The worst of it was that the laborers always worked behind a tall screen that they'd erected and no one could see just what it was they were up to. The junction looked like a patchwork quilt, with different shades of gray indicating the age of the tarmac that had been overlaid there.

The men were only glimpsed when they emerged from behind their screens, walking to or from their dirty green van. Strangely, one never seemed to see them carrying shovels or pickaxes. Invariably clad in their nondescript black boiler-suits, despite the heat, the operatives were not of the type that one would willingly approach directly in order to ask their business. They had none of the raucous bonhomie common to laborers, but were silent, unsmiling individuals with pale white faces, mouths like slashes and eyes like huge inkblots. Their abnormally long hands and fingernails were caked with dirt and one of Crisk's office colleagues joked that perhaps they dug with their bare hands.

The name on the side of the vehicle read GLYPHOTECH RECONSTRUCTION CO. But when one of the Mare staff dialed the telephone number that was also blazoned across the side of the van, he said he obtained a connection that rang without ever being answered. After a few days, however, the screens were taken away and merciful quiet reigned again. Strangely enough this happened to coincide with the onset of thunderstorms after the intense heat. A double relief, since as well as the ir-ritating noise being gone, the temperature dropped.

* * *

"Sir," said Crisk in that clipped Japanese manner that he could not shake off, "please be good enough to explain. You say that I should go. But why you have not made clear. Respectfully I ask, of course."

"I am just," James O'Hara responded, wincing at Crisk's strangled English, "making a suggestion that may improve your quality of life. I've been watching you for a while and it seems to me that you're down in the dumps a lot of the time. What Glyphotech can provide is a focus in your life; a way of realizing possibilities that you yourself might not have thought of."

Crisk stared at O'Hara for a brief moment, considering what response he should give. His superior merely stood there smiling with his hands folded behind his back. Crisk remembered the name "Glyphotech"; it had been written on the side of the van of the workers who'd been digging up the crossroads weeks before. But he could not fathom just what they had to do with this other venture. As if picking up on his thoughts, O'Hara interjected.

"Yes, yes," he said, "Glyphotech is a diverse company. As well as undertaking the reconstruction of buildings and roads, their course of psychological transformation is one of the aspects of their enterprise. I really would recommend that you take the course, Crisk. Bear in mind that several of your colleagues have already signed up and not to do so might appear, well . . ."

He had to say no more in order to convince Crisk. Here was his office superior telling him that it was best to conform. The idea of falling out of favor was not pleasant to Crisk. He needed the job, even though he was bored by it. He had a duty, after all, to Mare Publishing House.

"Sir," he replied, stifling the slight bow he wanted to make by force of habit, "of course, I agree. Further discussion not necessary. Let me know time and meeting place. Gladly I will take part."

When Crisk got back to his desk after the meeting with O'Hara, he discreetly asked his colleagues whether they too had been asked to attend the course run by Glyphotech. All had been requested to do so—some, they said, with the clear implication that not to accept O'Hara's suggestion would be severely frowned upon. From what Crisk could gather, most of his coworkers viewed it as some kind of motivational seminar that would improve efficiency in the workplace and raise staff morale.

Later that same day one of the office juniors came around the various departments to hand out flyers. The heading bore the Glyphotech Reconstruction Co. logo, with the same design that Crisk had seen blazoned across the side of the workmen's van. In bold letters, underneath the logo, were the words: *"Do not underestimate the effect our process can have on YOUR life!"*

In smaller characters beneath this was the following short text: "Do you feel drained, hopeless or adrift? At the mercy of what life throws at you instead of in control of events? We guarantee to provide empowerment and a sense of purpose you might never think you could achieve! Using our proven mental technology you will overcome all obstacles without fear, you will enjoy a renewed sense of purpose and success in both your private life and in your workplace environment. Attend our introductory seminar in the spirit of openness and friendship. Your life is too urgent to waste! Join us!"

The flyer provided details of where and when the seminar was to be held: at the Grantham Hall Hotel, only a few minutes walk from the Mare Publishing House offices. When Crisk saw the hours involved, however, his spirits sank. It was a two-day affair, lasting from ten a.m. until ten p.m. and repeated the next day. Moreover, it was to take place this coming weekend.

There were stifled groans around the office as each individual got to this part of the text and realized they'd been duped into giving up not company time but their own personal time, and on an ostensibly voluntary basis.

In the days leading up to the weekend a dull sense of resentment permeated the offices of Mare Publishing House. Though nothing was actually said aloud. This was undoubtedly due to the fact that the only one of those duped who had been brave enough to confront O'Hara about the deception was instantly dismissed from his job. The person, David Hogg, found his desk cleared within five minutes of his speaking to O'Hara. He was forcibly escorted off the premises by security guards moments before his personal belongings were flung out onto the street after him.

Crisk had been standing beside the doorway from which Hogg was ejected. The company had a strict no-smoking policy and Crisk would, at a quarter past every hour, enjoy a crafty cigarette at that spot. After helping the bewildered ex-employee collect the various odds and ends not connected with work now strewn around him, they had a brief conversation.

"I am sorry . . ." said Crisk, "but if it is okay for me to ask, why did Mare Publishing so harshly treat you?"

Hogg groaned.

"I know all about those Glyphotech seminars," he finally replied. "I told O'Hara there was no way I'd go along with it. I'd warn the others to stay away. We had a hell of a row and he told me to get out. I could tell you things about Glyphotech that . . ."

Crisk trembled inwardly at Hogg's audacity. To upset O'Hara was to challenge Mare Publishing itself. He looked around him, horrified at the prospect of being seen even talking with the ex-employee. To give up one weekend in order to curry favor was something Crisk was more than prepared to do. Backing away from Hogg as if the man were contaminated, Crisk made his apologies, mumbled a word or two of consolation and scurried back inside the building. Crisk knew that O'Hara would find it easy to justify Hogg's immediate dismissal, for he had only very recently been hired by the company and was often drunk at his workstation.

When Crisk was back and seated at his desk, he again looked over the Glyphotech flyer that had been handed out to everyone. Surely it was a wild overreaction to make so much of a fuss over nothing more than a motivational seminar.

At ten a.m. sharp on Saturday (O'Hara had warned everybody that being late for the seminar would not be looked upon kindly) Crisk was seated amongst about a hundred other people in a ballroom within the Grantham Hall Hotel. There were the usual murmurings and muted conversations one would expect in a crowd of that size. As he looked around he spotted a number of his colleagues and nodded at them in recognition. Seated right at the front, he noticed, was O'Hara.

At the end of the room was a stage with a raised dais and behind it a screen on which slides could be projected.

Someone at the front of the room made a signal to a person at the back and the heavy panelled doors opened to admit a figure. The man, immaculately dressed in an expensively tailored suit, walked confidently down the aisle between the rows of seats toward the dais. His bearing was impressive; he seemed to exude an aura of unshakeable confidence. And yet, at least to Crisk, there was also something of the arrogant mixed in with it.

The man mounted the dais and smiled dazzlingly. He was in his mid-forties and his well-groomed black hair was swept back high over his forehead.

"Welcome to all you strangers, soon to be friends!" he said in a voice that rang out across the hall with clarity and purpose. Here was a man well used to public speaking.

"I want," he continued, "to congratulate each and everyone of you for deciding to come along to the seminar. You've made a decision that I know none of you will ever have cause to regret. Let me introduce myself. I'm Hastane Ebbon. Now I know"—again he flashed that dazzling smile, looking around the room with a mock-comical expression —"that some of you may be wondering just what you've signed up for. I want to say one thing right now. You're free to leave. Really. But if you do you're going to miss out on the rest of your life. Over the next few days, you'll experience a personal revolution."

Someone in a row toward the back tittered. Crisk looked over his shoulder and saw that it was a very overweight woman in her early thirties, wearing glasses and dressed all in black.

"Hey, that lady out there is only expressing what a lot of you are thinking. I mean, come on, these things are simply a moneymaking exercise, right? Wrong, my friends. If you take what we offer, I mean, if you're really *open* to it, believe me, things will never be the same for you again."

He paused.

"ANYONE WANT TO LEAVE?"

Ebbon was staring and smiling at the overweight lady. She lowered her head, and looked a little sheepish.

"NO?"

There was a ripple of tension in the ballroom. At that moment, thought Crisk, it would have taken someone with a degree of self-assurance equal to Ebbon's to have stood up and walked out. And no one did so.

Crisk was suddenly very uncomfortable. This wasn't like any motivational seminar he'd been to before. And he'd been forced to attend a number while employed by agencies over in Japan. This was something quite different. For perhaps the first time, he began to wonder whether his sense of company loyalty was not misplaced.

Ebbon grinned.

"Well this is unusual, let me tell you. You're obviously a lot more intelligent than the last crowd of seminar attendees we had. But then they came from the south of the city. . . ."

A number of people in the audience laughed and the tension dissipated.

What Crisk realized after a couple of hours was that a significant number of persons attending the seminar had actually done the course previously. They were there to guide the newcomers and instruct them in the correct protocols that Glyphotech wished them to follow. For example, asking questions without permission was just not done. Daydreaming was not allowed. And in what few breaks there were, for meals or coffee, newcomers were encouraged only to mingle with those who were there for their guidance. Talk centered around discussions and explanations of Glyphotech's "technology" and a series of terms such as "eureka moments" and "routines" were frequently employed. The first referred to, apparently, a juncture in one's life where the possibility of happiness was within grasp. The second referred to an individual's habits; the displacement activities he would use to justify avoiding doing something he knew he had to do.

There were many more such terms, but Crisk lost interest in hearing about them. It seemed to him that this was simply some junk mixture of psychology and counseling, with elements of Zen Buddhism tagged on to give it an ethereal sheen.

What came next turned his stomach. Back in the ballroom, persons were encouraged to come up to the microphone and expose their weaknesses, traumas and failings before the rest of the attendees. By the time the tenth had gone up (she seemed to be well versed in this form of communal confession) Crisk actually suspected that many welcomed the opportunity to bare their souls in public. He wondered whether they had not become addicted to the experience. For what it brought in its wake, after the tears and sobbing, was a round of thunderous clapping from the audience. The first one or two confessions had been greeted with hesitant applause, but once things really got going tears dribbled down the cheeks of most participants. Such was the wave of warmth and mass acceptance generated it was with great difficulty that Crisk restrained himself from joining in with the process and advancing up to the dais himself.

He could not help noticing throughout this part of the seminar that O'Hara kept glancing back at him from the front of the hall. Crisk was the only one of the Mare Publishing employees who had not yet succumbed to the hysterical atmosphere in the room.

Ebbon returned to make periodic appearances on the stage, one of which was to explain the concept of "monologues" Glyphotech had developed.

"Monologues," Ebbon said cheerfully, his teeth flashing with that fake smile, "are the way we come to interpret what's happening to us, and of dealing with things that make us uncomfortable. Now let's take an example. Say your boss shouts at you because you're late for work. What's your reaction? You're angry, you're annoyed, YOU MAKE EXCUSES TO YOURSELF! And then you convince yourself he's a bad person, just because he's made you upset. You're using your monologue to avoid dealing with the real issue. Now here's the deal: don't get upset. He's not the problem. YOU'RE THE PROBLEM. Yes, get that and get it good. You see what I mean now? A monologue is when someone is talking to himself and not listening to someone else because he's angry or afraid. Aren't some of you doing that right now——EVEN WHEN I'M TALKING?"

Crisk squirmed uncomfortably in his seat. All the people around him were now nodding enthusiastically as if lightbulbs had been turned on inside their minds. They were hanging on Ebbon's every word. A horrible kind of blind faith and exultation spread palpably throughout the ballroom.

After Ebbon stopped speaking he invited people to share their own examples of "monologues" with the rest of the group. There was almost a stampede to the dais, and a queue had to be formed.

One after the other people poured out their stories of how they'd neglected their mothers, their children, even their work, because they'd shifted the blame unreasonably instead of taking responsibility themselves. Yet what was worrying, at least to Crisk, was that he felt that some of these people had, by any reasonable and objective standard, been right in feeling resentment. One person told how he came to detest his dying mother who had been bedridden for four years. He'd cleaned up after her, fed her and the only thanks he'd got was to be told that she hated him and wanted to see her daughter who could not bear to see her in that state. Why shouldn't this person have had the right to resent such ingratitude? It was clear that he loved his mother, but to deny him access to a quite natural response, where was the logic in that? Another person told of being raped and was encouraged to forgive her attacker, to declare that she bore some complicity in his attack. And this plainly was not the case except through a deranged reading of the facts.

Rather than the light that had illuminated all those other minds in the hall, a cool and comforting darkness, like shade in the summer sun, entered Crisk's own mind.

I don't want my pain blanked out, he thought to himself; I need to keep my pain. It is a part of who I am, every bit as integral as the joy I've felt. It is not a mental cancer.

And, to his own astonishment, and that of all the others in the ballroom, he calmly rose to his feet, ignored the cold glare of O'Hara and walked out.

"Please excuse," he muttered in his strange English to anyone who might listen, "but this is no more than simple brainwashing exercise."

Outside the ballroom, in the corridor, a man whom Crisk didn't recognize accosted him. He was flanked by two boilersuited operatives, the kind Crisk had seen emerging from the Glyphotech van that had been parked outside Mare Publishing.

"Are you leaving?" the man said, in a tone that was firm yet offered the prospect of reconciliation. "I'd advise you not to. The very fact that you desire to quit now is the strongest indication of how much you are in need of our assistance."

He didn't acknowledge the presence of the two menacing figures on either side of him though their unspoken participation in this blatant attempt at coercion was clear.

Crisk saw that the workers of Glyphotech looked even weirder close up than from a distance. For some bizarre reason the sleeves of their black boilersuits were too long and flopped over at the ends, totally concealing their hands. Their deathly white faces were absolutely expressionless, so much so that their features, the slashlike mouths and inkblot eyes, looked uncannily as if they'd been worked into soft white putty rather than flesh.

"I made stupid mistake," said Crisk, "absolutely the blame is mine. Further explanation not necessary. Now I will go."

The other man just stood there silently, as if weighing his options. Crisk became uneasy. His eyes flickered to the name badge the man wore (no one was permitted to remove them while the seminar was in progress) and to the indistinct faces of the Glyphotech operatives. He addressed the man personally.

"Mr.Collins, I will have you let me pass," said Crisk, his voice admirably level and betraying no sense of the fear gnawing at his innards. "Have told friends that if I do not call them at five p.m. they are to come here and collect me. If necessary, with police. Reason being, warned by colleague against attendance at Glyphotech reconstruction seminar. Such precaution unfortunate but necessary, I felt."

"Not in the least necessary, I assure you, Mr. Crisk. We are not in the business of press-ganging people into our circle of friends. If you feel that you must leave, then do so. You are free to make whatever choice you wish." Collins replied. There was an edge in his voice though, and the last few words were almost a hiss.

Crisk brushed past the three men, through the lobby and out of the Grantham Hall Hotel. He was already beginning to dread the reception he would receive from O'Hara when he turned up for work on Monday morning if, that is, he still had a job at Mare Publishing.

But on Monday morning it was as if his conduct were forgotten. O'Hara greeted him with a pleasant smile (though Crisk admitted to himself that the sight of O'Hara grinning was horrible in its own way) and Crisk began his computer inputting as usual. He did detect a new furtiveness in his colleagues, however, but it was hardly sinister—more like they felt somewhat sorry for him. He could not help noticing that they now employed Glyphotech terminology in a lot of their talk, and went about their duties much more assiduously than before.

It was only after he got home to his flat that same evening that he was made aware there were, after all, certain consequences resulting from his having failed to complete the seminar. The phone rang at seven thirty p.m., just as he was preparing some sushi for dinner.

"Hello, Mr. Crisk, it's John Collins here, from Glyphotech. I hope you don't mind me calling but I wanted to go over the conversation we had when last we met, at the seminar, you remember."

Inwardly, Crisk groaned. He felt the urge to slam down the telephone but his sense of gentility prevented him from doing so.

"To speak the truth nothing more to say," Crisk responded. "Now busy preparing food. Cannot talk, even prefer not to—"

"This won't take long, I assure you," Collins said, cutting in. "I just wanted to let you know that there's another course beginning at the end of this week and that we'd be happy to welcome you along. Forget what happened before, and make a fresh start. Many of our best friends took their time coming around to total acceptance of the benefits Glyphotech can provide."

"Sorry, but I have no interest." Crisk said sharply.

"Please reconsider. No need to be hasty. Think about it. I'll call you back tomorrow or whenever is convenient. You see it's not possible for you to phone us, it's against protocol."

"Do not call again. How did you obtain my number at home? Intrusion of privacy; will advise telephone company of this outrage—"

"Let me be frank with you, Mr. Crisk. We checked. We know that what you said about your friends coming to take you from the seminar was just a monologue you'd created. You see we have lists of your calls; the phone company understood it was for your own good. Their managers and employees found a recent Glyphotech seminar of great use in reconstructing their—"

Crisk hung up. Then he dialed the operator's number.

"Hello, operator?" He said. "I am Franklyn Crisk, calling from phone 456 67304. I wish to report unwelcome intrusion of privacy by Glyphotech Recon—"

"Of course, sir," a dull voice cut in. "I'll transfer you to the appropriate department."

But the number he was transferred to just rang and rang without ever being answered. And when he spoke to the operator for a second time he was transferred nearly immediately to the unanswered line again, without even being given the opportunity to utter a complete sentence. After the seventh attempt he gave up.

A scant two days later Crisk realized that what he had at first taken for amused condescension on the part of O'Hara and his colleagues was the primary stage of tactical psychological warfare. Crisk suspected that he had initially been given the benefit of the doubt. Their belief in the validity of Glyphotech's reconstruction seminar made them think that he would eventually come to embrace its tenets, despite his faltering start and refusal to cooperate. But as the days passed and he was still clearly as antagonistic to the idea as he had been when he'd walked out of the seminar in front of everyone, their attitude changed slightly. Although never outwardly hostile, it became obtrusive. Scarcely an hour would pass without some employee making a remark about how Glyphotech's technology had improved their lives beyond recognition, how much happier they were in their work, or how much they were looking forward to socializing with their fellow seminar attendees. These comments were made deliberately within Crisk's earshot, presumably with the intention of making him feel left out, peculiar or downright freakish in not having realized Glyphotech's benefits.

John Collins or some other Glyphotech devotee still telephoned him at his flat, sometimes three or four times an evening, but Crisk would cut the conversation short by slamming down the receiver the moment he realized who was calling. That they had resorted to using a rota of individuals so that he was off guard when he answered almost drove him to distraction. And Crisk's attempts to contact the phone company and have the matter dealt with proved as futile as before. He was beginning to believe it really was just another branch of the Glyphotech phenomenon.

Although these developments were unnerving enough in themselves, they were not as unnerving as the fact that Crisk discovered he was being watched. A Glyphotech Reconstruction Company van had parked itself on the street directly opposite the building in which his flat was situated. In the evenings, when Crisk glanced out of his window, it was always there, a dirty green vehicle with white-faced operatives clearly visible through the wind-shield, who peered up at him with eyes like dark smudges.

Another week passed. Crisk had given Mare Publishing no excuse to terminate his employment, since he ensured that his work and timekeeping were beyond reproach. O'Hara and his colleagues became increasingly resentful of his intransigence and their former cheerfulness seemed somehow brittle, as if his own presence was a factor in their discomfort. Whether this was the case or not, he was sure they would never dare admit to it. He began to suspect that the persons who had com-pleted the seminar and who claimed to have gotten the most from it harbored a real sense of dread at letting Glyphotech down by admitting any tiny doubt as to the success of their psychological re-construction. All of them were now paying considerable amounts of money in order to attend advanced courses. Mare Publishing gave interest-free loans to those who could not afford to pay so that their continued participation was ensured.

The effect the stress had upon Crisk was that he suffered episodes of insomnia. Still, he felt some comfort, at least, from the fact that the Glyphotech phone callers had finally ceased their campaign to persuade him to change his mind. However, when at work, and when walking home to his flat from the office, he thought he detected unusually intense and hate-filled stares from passersby. Moreover, he could not rid himself of the persistent notion that he saw alarming physiognomic alterations in large numbers of the people whom he encountered. Those who stared at him for too long seemed to be developing black smudged eyes that were sinking back into their sockets, while their hands, digits and fingernails were of a horribly abnormal length.

An open-top lorry carrying scaffolding equipment had recently joined the van parked outside Crisk's flat. The lorry also bore the Glyphotech logo on both its sides. Crisk had noticed that the company had recently added scaffolding to its ever growing list of enterprises. It made some vague sense, seeing as they had, he'd read in a newspaper, secured contracts to refurbish a large number of buildings throughout the city. The latticed scaffolding structures and plastic-sheeted fronts with their logo were becoming evident almost everywhere one looked.

Although Crisk hoped that this new activity might, at least, divert some of their energies away from their bogus psychological reprogramming of the populace, he tried as much as possible to avoid passing buildings fronted by the Glyphotech scaffolding. From behind the sheets of opaque white plastic attached to the poles and clamps, he clearly heard the sound of scratching, as if dozens of long fingernails were clawing over and over again at glass, brick and concrete.

In order to calm his nerves after his fractious working day, Crisk would often pass a couple of hours drinking at a bar in a back street close to the Mare Publishing offices. None of the other employees spent time at this bar anymore, teetotalism being Glyphotech protocol. It was a quiet, dark place, and good for reflection.

As he sat there sipping a pint of beer, a man whose head was wrapped in bandages entered. Crisk tried not to stare but couldn't help pity the fellow. He must have been involved in quite a nasty accident. Instead of going up to the counter, however, the stranger made straight for Crisk and slumped in the seat directly opposite him.

"How are you, Crisk?" he said in a voice that,

though croaky, Crisk recognized as belonging to the former Mare employee David Hogg.

"I have troubles," Crisk replied, "but none to compare to your own, I think. You have met with an accident, I suppose. It is very unfortunate, especially coming after your dismissal."

Hogg's eyes, staring out through holes in the bandages, were watery. Beneath the wrappings there seemed to be neither a nose nor cheeks, only deep hollows. He spoke again:

"I thought that those at Mare who didn't succumb to the Glyphotech brainwashing might come in here now and again for a drink. The converts hate the stuff of course. But I admit that I didn't think you personally would reject the seminar, seeing as you were such a loyal company man."

Crisk wasn't certain whether Hogg was complimenting or denigrating him—perhaps a mixture of both.

"Glyphotech repulsive organization," Crisk said. "Attack free thought, harass ones who speak against it. Any honorable man who understands duty would do as I did."

"Could you buy me a drink, Crisk? I'm sorry to ask. But I have no money, and I need one rather badly. In return I'll give you some advice. It's a small price to pay in exchange, believe me."

"Advice? Explain please."

"After the drink. Please," Hogg responded.

Crisk returned to the table with another beer for himself and a double Scotch and soda for Hogg. He guzzled the amber fluid rapidly through the mouth-slit in his wrappings, spilling a few drops onto the bandage around his chin.

"How far into the seminar did you get?" Hogg asked, putting the half-empty glass down.

"First day, about five hours. Left when—"

"I did the whole day," Hogg cut in, "and most of the next. They nearly got me. That was back before I joined Mare. I left my previous job because I saw what the Glyphotech seminar did to the company. But Glyphotech wouldn't let me reject what it was offering. They kept phoning me at home, and my then colleagues ostracized me for not enrolling, since they themselves had all done so. By now, you must be experiencing something similar."

Crisk nodded. He felt a deep sense of shame at having badly misjudged Hogg.

"They no longer ring me." Crisk responded.

Hogg seemed to be agitated rather than soothed by the news.

"You realize they don't actually have a working center of operations, don't you?" Hogg continued. "I mean, they say they do. But it's just an empty old office somewhere with a desk and a telephone and no one around to answer it. The calls they harass you with don't come from there. I don't even know if that swine Ebbon has ever been to the office. It's against protocol to ask about the place."

The bandaged man reached for the remains of his Scotch and soda and downed it with a single gulp.

"Another, how about?" Crisk asked him.

"Get the bottle," Hogg replied, coughing a little as the alcohol made his throat tighten.

The two men drank heavily.

"You know," Hogg said, his voice slightly slurred by the booze, "what happens on day two? They tell you about the core of their mental technology. The bastards repeat their propaganda over and over again, until it begins to make sense, until, as they say, you reach the understanding. It's called the suicide resolution. Funny isn't it, in a grim way? The suicide resolution. When you accept that final piece of the jigsaw, you belong to them, utterly and totally. I didn't. What they tell attendees is that the suicide resolution is the secret of extracting the maximum joy from life, living each day like your last: because soon it really will be. And everyone, by then, is so brainwashed they believe it."

"Too fantastic: ask people to kill themselves?" Crisk responded. "Such things cannot be, except in trashy horror tales of the worst type. Why not inform the police?"

"You don't understand, they *run* everything." Hogg spluttered, "Anyway, you didn't get as far into it as I did. By day two you'll swallow all they say. Brainwashing only works when the victims refuse to accept they've been brainwashed. The suicide resolution is bad enough, but it's what comes after that's even worse. Things don't end there; suicide's just the beginning. The technology somehow works on parts of the brain we don't normally use. It ensures you come back afterwards so that they can carry on with the reconstruction process, carry on with it even after you're dead. Glyphotech never lets go. Never, ever."

Crisk suspected Hogg had gone mad. He was pointing to the bandages in which his head was swathed.

"I'm telling you they nearly had me, Crisk! Leave while you still can. Don't hang around like I did. Those ghouls managed to get to my face before I—"

Crisk stumbled to his feet. He didn't care whether Hogg was telling the truth or not; he could take no more, and left the bar without looking back.

"Get out of the city, Crisk," Hogg cried behind him. "When they stop calling you it means they'll take more drastic measures."

The next day Crisk left Mare Publishing for good. What Hogg had told him the previous night made a horrible kind of sense, even if he could not accept every word of it as literal truth.

He had, however, noted the same physiognomic mutations occurring in his office colleagues that he'd observed in the people on the streets. Perhaps it was some disease, but he was baffled at the fact no one had commented upon its having been allowed to spread unchecked.

He would quit his job without giving notice, go home, pack some of his belongings in a couple of suitcases and leave the city by the first available train out. Unless he took this decisive action he felt he might well trip over the edge of reason and go completely insane, as Hogg had done. He told no one of his plans and walked out of the Mare Publishing offices at six p.m. as usual.

Only O'Hara saw him depart and, to Crisk's horror, his boss raised a hand with abnormally long digits and nails and gave him an ironic farewell wave. There was a horrible knowing smile beneath his smudgy eyes.

It was a ten-minute walk, at a leisurely pace, from the office to Crisk's flat. But he covered the distance in half that time, breaking into a trot as often as he could and only slowing to a normal pace when breathless. Already he was going over in his mind what he would take with him: the bare essentials, cash he'd saved for an emergency, some clothing, toiletries and perhaps one or two treasured items he'd brought back from Kyoto; his tea set and sake bowls. Yes, they had "wabi" and could not be left behind.

Crisk tried to avoid looking at the people he passed in the street and at the buildings. He knew the way almost by instinct in any case. When, however, he finally reached his flat he saw, with a jolt of panic, that Glyphotech scaffolding covered the front of the building all the way to the top. On the other side of the street the truck with the poles was no longer there, though the other vehicle, the dirty green van, remained. However, there didn't seem to be any Glyphotech operatives inside.

Had he not needed the cash he'd put away in the drawer of his bureau for the train fare, he would have abandoned any notion of going up to his flat, deeming the risk too great. Instead, he stood out on the street and then cautiously moved toward the sheets and poles, straining his ears to detect noise from within the structure. He waited for several minutes, but heard nothing. Perhaps, if he were quick, he might get in and out without being noticed. Crisk always bolted his windows from the inside and was confident that any break-in would have aroused too much attention, so he doubted that intruders were lying in wait for him within the flat itself.

He let himself in through the front door, passed along the hallway and ascended the stairs. The light bulbs had blown on the second floor, so he had to pass through a pool of darkness before reaching the third where his own flat was situated. Unlocking it quietly, he opened the door halfway, reached in and turned on the light switch just to the right of the entrance. Then he entered.

Everything was as he'd left it that morning and he saw, with relief, that the windows were still bolted and closed. The scaffold platform and its opaque plastic sheeting closed off the usual view. But there was no one out there. He left the door slightly ajar behind him for a quick exit should it prove necessary.

After removing the cash from his bureau and transferring it to his wallet, he took two suitcases from underneath his bed and began packing them as swiftly as he was able. The tea set and sake bowls were the most troublesome, as they were quite delicate and required careful wrapping in layers of newspaper.

Then he heard loud scuffling noises. Several people seemed to be frantically climbing the ladders that led from one platform of the scaffolding to the next. They were headed in his direction; there could be no doubt about it. Crisk spun around to the door, his only escape route, and saw a horribly long hand snaking around the edge, as if someone were about to push it open and enter his flat. He dashed across the room in and tried to jam the door shut, trapping the hand. It was attenuated and spiderlike, and the fingers twitched convulsively as Crisk put all his weight into his shoulder, ultimately succeeding in forcing the door shut. As it closed tight, the digits on the hand squashed and broke off as if made from damp putty.

Directly behind him Crisk heard the sound of fingernails scratching on the windowpane. He turned and saw half a dozen deathly white faces leering through the glass. The things were all clawing idiotically at the surface.

Crisk picked up the telephone and frantically dialed the operator. He was transferred to another line at once, without saying a word, and heard the familiar ringing tone begin. Perhaps if he could get through to Glyphotech, he hoped, if he could persuade them he'd changed his mind, there might still be a chance.

"Answer it," he mumbled to himself, "answer it, answer it. . . ."

Just before the window shattered and the things crawled over the sill toward him, raking their hellish fingernails across everything they touched, Crisk thought of the dusty and empty office, long disused, where an unattended telephone rang and rang.

Dedicated to QSC

Spider Dream

Michael Reaves

The black widow spider scrabbled up his naked arm, moving incredibly fast, its eight legs leaving pinpricks tattooed on his puckered flesh. In another moment it would disappear up his shirt sleeve. He sucked in a terrified, whistling lungful of air and swatted at the horror, fingers flicking the bulbous body—a big one, his mind jabbered, got to be the size of my thumb, at least—away. It sailed out in a long arc, trails of silk threading the air behind it. He glimpsed the distinctive scarlet hourglass, vivid against its shiny black underside—and then, suddenly, he had no idea how, it was just there again, on his bare leg this time, flickering toward the inviting darkness between the loose material of his shorts and his inner thigh.

He screamed this time, batting at it, trying to knock it away again, but somehow he couldn't hit it, it was moving so damned fast, and it disappeared beneath the baggy cotton, heading toward his groin and he screamed again and then he—

Then he woke up.

He sat up in bed, drenched in sweat, heart thundering in his chest, trying to shake the remnants of the dream. The curtained darkness pressed in on him, and he turned on the bedside light, then turned to sit on the edge of the mattress. The clock's readout told him it was four a.m. He rested his face in his hands.

Jesus Christ.

A spider dream—he hadn't had one in years. He'd forgotten how bad they could be, how unerringly vivid. Always about black widows; they'd been everywhere in the small desert town where he'd grown up, and as a child he had been absolutely terrified of them. His mother had told him that their poison was ten times more deadly than a rattlesnake's, and that one bite could bring instant death. While he knew today that such a reaction was very much the exception rather than the rule, still the fear had remained. The dreams only came to him when he was under a huge amount of stress, and God knew his life was stressful at this point, what with the divorce and custody fights and the pay cut and all. His therapist had told him that the spider represented all his fears, from childhood on, wrapped up in one tiny black symbol of death. Not a symbol, he thought. The real thing.

Was there now or had there ever been on Earth a creature that projected such pure, unadulterated malignancy than the female black widow spider? If there was, he didn't want to know about it. With its black satin skin and that scarlet hourglass on its underbelly—as potent a reminder of patient, grim death as the Reaper's scythe—the black widow represented the epitome of designer fear. Even other arachnids that were equally as venomous, like the brown recluse, couldn't come close to generating the kind of terror it inspired. He'd rather deal with a tarantula as big as his hand any day.

He rubbed the back of his neck. When he was awake, when the California sun was high in the sky, its light and heat baking away the fears of the night, then he could tell himself that he wasn't particularly afraid of spiders, although they weren't his favorite life forms by any stretch of the imagination. He avoided them, but didn't go into a fit of hyperventilation when he saw one. After all, spiders were a fact of life in the desert. He was a grown man now, not a child.

He grimaced ruefully. Yes, a grown man, and should he ever be in danger of forgetting that, the divorce and all its attendant psychodrama were there to remind him. There was an obvious parallel to be drawn between his anxiety dreams and his unfortunate reality. . . . Somewhere in the afterlife Freud was no doubt chuckling. He knew he would get no more sleep tonight. He decided to get up, make a cup of coffee; maybe he could get some work in before the day's grinding pace began. . . .

He looked at the rumpled sheets and blankets, remembering how, as a child, he would sit in the center of the bed and scrunch himself into the tightest possible ball and wait out the night, sure that at any minute one of the ebony horrors would come up from behind the headboard and be upon him before he could even move. A frisson of dread shook him then; he whipped about, staring behind him—

And the spider was there, coming at him, seeming to almost float over the white sheet, and Jesus Christ, it was bigger this time, the size of a golf ball, those eight jointed legs each three inches long at least. How could it be bigger? But even as his brain screamed the question, the thing was on him again, heading up his bare arm toward his shoulder and neck, and he leaped from the bed, bleating pure panic and hitting frantically at it—

And he woke up.

Holy fucking shit.

He was standing next to the bed. He could smell the reek of his fear, combined with the sharp tang of urine. He had wet himself.

At this point he didn't even care that he was standing in a warm puddle of his own piss. He moved slowly around the bedroom, turning on all the lights, trying to come to grips with what had just happened.

A dream within a dream.

To the best of his recollection, such a thing had never happened to him before. He'd heard of them, of course—"recursive dreams," his therapist had called them. Dreams—and nightmares—nesting two, sometimes even three deep, one inside the other. He looked about the room and the inevitable question arose: How did he know that he was awake now?

It didn't feel like a dream. Dreams—his dreams, anyway—were usually shifting, surreal fragments that seemed perfectly logical at the time, like chocolate cows melting slowly over his third grade teacher's face. He pinched his arm, feeling a bit foolish doing so, and was relieved at the comforting pain that resulted. He put a hand against the wall.

It was reassuringly solid.

No, it wasn't a dream now. It couldn't be.

It was, he told himself, definitely time for a cup of coffee.

He slipped on his robe, remembering a time when he was nine years old. His father's way of relaxing after work was to do wood turning and light carpentry, building cabinets, whatnot shelves and suchlike. The family car, a '56 Ford Fairlane, had been banished from the garage, which had been converted into a workroom for the old man's pride and joy: a Shopsmith Mark V. His father would work late into the night sometimes, yellow light spilling from the garage door, along with the screech of the table saw ripping through lumber.

One night he had run from the front door toward the garage on some now-forgotten errand. Just as he entered, a spider had dropped from above on a single strand and swung right into his face. In his memory it seemed as big as a cat; it landed on his cheek, and he had swatted it away, screaming in fear. He clearly remembered the look of disgust on his father's face at his reaction.

He shuddered convulsively and stepped into the dark hallway, groping for the wall switch—

And the spider was there, dropping down from the ceiling on a silk strand like a climber rappelling down a cliff. It had grown again—still a black widow, but now the size of a large tarantula. A shriek ripped from his throat and he jerked back with enough force to overbalance; he fell on his back, his head cracking painfully on the hardwood floor.

The spider dropped toward his face.

He barely managed to jerk his head aside, lurching to his feet, clawing at the doorjamb for purchase. He tried to scream again but his throat was too constricted with fear.

The spider sprang at him. He turned to run, felt

the impact as the thing hit his back, felt it clinging to the terry cloth robe as it ran up toward his neck—

And he woke up.

He barely managed to reach the bathroom before vomiting. Acidic bile scorched painfully up his throat and through his nose. Most of his stomach's contents missed the bowl and splattered the white tiles. He choked, gasped, and managed to stand. His bare feet slipped on the slimy floor, and he barely saved himself from falling again by grabbing the sink.

He looked in the mirror. A pale, gaunt thing looked back at him from out of shadowed eye pits.

Was he awake now? Or would these nesting nightmares just go on and on, until . . . what?

He splashed water on his face, rinsed the sour taste from his mouth. God, please, let it be over. Let me be awake now. He looked at himself again in the mirror—

And the spider was there, clinging to the wall, its body now swollen to the size of a large man's fist, its eight eyes glittering in the glare of the ceiling lamp. Against the white wall it looked like a bizarre Rorschach blot. Then it started to move, running along the vertical surface, heading straight toward him; in a moment it would jump and—

He lunged toward the door, knowing that there was no chance of him avoiding it in the bathroom's confines. He sprawled on the bedroom floor, kicking the door shut. He thought he had trapped it in there, but suddenly it came out from under the bed and shot toward him. He backed up quickly, vaguely aware that he was making a sort of whinnying whimper, because the damned thing had grown again, this time to the size of an eggplant, its legs a foot long at least. He realized he'd backed into the open closet, and that he was trapped, there was no place left to run. His hand, groping frantically for something, anything, to use as a weapon, closed on a pole standing with the rest of his ski equipment behind the shirt rack. The spider leaped at him again, and he grabbed the pole, pulled, thrust it forward with the little strength he had left—and felt the shock of impact vibrate up his arm as the giant black horror impaled itself on the sharp point.

His grip was suddenly nerveless; his muscles turned to water and he dropped the pole. He pulled himself to his feet, and staggered forward, not daring to congratulate himself, to celebrate victory, just yet.

He looked at the bed. It was over—he'd killed the spider. Maybe he'd gained some great and subtle victory over his inner demons, but he didn't feel any better or worse—just tired, drained.

This had to be a dream. Even if it was the most realistic dream he'd ever had, still it had to be a dream. Black widows don't grow that big in real life.

So why didn't he wake up?

He turned slowly and looked behind him.

The spider still sprawled on the floor; the ski pole still transfixed it. The eight legs curled up and inward, almost like a supplicating hand.

One of the legs twitched.

Then another.

He screamed again—it ripped like fire up his raw throat—and ran for the bedroom door, yanked it open and ran into the hall.

The kitchen light was on at the far end—a beacon, a signal beckoning him to safety. He ran toward it, down the long hallway, but the hallway began to stretch, to elongate, and he seemed to be running slower and slower. The light was only a pinpoint now, very far away, and as he ran the floor beneath him began to slant downward, the angle growing steeper with every stride he took. And then he wasn't running anymore; he was falling, falling down a lightless shaft, and he had time to think, it's still a dream—only a dream, and then suddenly his fall stopped. He was entangled in filmy strands that looked like old decayed lace. They were strung every which way, in random patterns, and the more he moved, the deeper enmeshed in their sticky lines he became.

He knew where he was.

He stopped struggling. He hung still, exhausted, his mind hanging motionless as well, emptied of all except the fear. Then he felt the web strands that imprisoned him begin to twitch and shift once more, and a vast shadow passed over him. He looked up, and—

The spider was there.

BEHIND THE MASQUE

Jeffrey Thomas

"I found myself within a strange city . . ."
—Edgar Allan Poe, "Eleonora"

In the same story, Mr. Poe also said that "the question is not yet settled, whether madness is or is not the loftiest intelligence—whether much that is glorious—whether all that is profound—does not spring from disease of thought." Now, I am not saying that I think Diego Kaji was a profound man in any way. Though he was a man of great wealth, I do not think he was responsible for producing anything glorious, unless one would consider his large house perched atop the Turquoise Tower to be glorious (many consider it an aberration). But there is no doubt that he was a man of great intelligence and creativity, a man with distinct esthetic tastes, however unconventional—a man with a personal vision, however diseased that vision might seem when perceived through the eyes of others who are not Diego Kaji.

Nothing more about Diego Kaji would ever be learned from his own lips. Only by observing his environment, his possessions, could we the living hope to understand him now. Diego Kaji had committed suicide by hanging himself from the chandelier that overhung the foyer of his mansion atop the Turquoise Tower in Beaumonde Square, one of the most affluent sections of the city of Paxton.

Paxton is a colony city on the planet we Earthers call Oasis. We call Paxton (the "town of peace") Punktown, because this is a more fitting appellation. Crime and violence run rampant in the streets of Punktown. The perpetrators are human and nonhuman, mutant and automaton alike. Their crimes are often as shockingly alien as their physical bodies: Who could imagine that a race of beings from one world might want to run up to you in the street and paint a yellow stripe down your nose? While this might merely exasperate and inconvenience you or me, it would be the greatest of malicious thrills to this race, akin to rape. Not so terrible in our eyes, you might well say. But you would doubtless be more alarmed to have a member of another race, from another world, leap upon you from an alley mouth so as to clip off one or both of your thumbs, because these resemble closely their jointed phalluses, and are used to concoct aphrodisiacs in unlicenced apothecaries. Yes, it can get very unpleasant—downright dangerous—down on the street level of Punktown. It should be no surprise that a man of wealth would want raise himself high above these floodwaters, to sequester himself safely atop a plastic turquoise edifice protected by armed security teams. Though no security team had, in the end, protected Diego Kaji from violence by his own two hands.

His crime upon himself was not so alien, so unfathomable, I suppose. Kaji was on the board of directors of a company that produced cloned laborers. These clones were cast from a master set of six males; convicts sentenced to death had signed over rights for their likenesses to be produced for these purposes. Because it was illegal, you see, to produce clones of living people at that time. The moral and ethical questions of cloning slosh back and forth endlessly like amniotic solution in a lab tech's beaker. For some years, this cloning operation made its owners quite wealthy. But lately there had been scandals, not the least of which was the murder of Ephraim Mayda, an important union figure, at the hands of an escaped clone. It developed that this seemingly vengeful clone was actually the pawn of larger forces. There had come investigations; the media had made much of the controversies. And so it was that Diego

Kaji—my employer—stood upon the railing of his balcony and stepped off into empty space with a cord around his neck, causing the great glistening chandelier to sway and scintillate like a crystallized jellyfish, its glittering tentacles tinkling slower and slower as the circles Kaji traced grew smaller and smaller. He was dangling utterly still when Lan, one of the servants, spotted him in the morning. Her screams summoned others. I myself saw him before he was brought down. . . .

I can't say I liked Diego Kaji. I respected him, because I was paid to do so. I did appreciate it when he inquired about my wife's welfare after she was mugged and beaten by a group of youths; he even gave me paid time off, sent a basket of rare fruits and a veritable rain forest of endangered blossoms to our apartment. But truthfully, I felt better when I did not encounter him face-to-face in my movements about his mansion. I was thankful that he spent most of his time at his office within the cloning operation. But he had an office in his home, as well, and one time he called me into this room to share a glass of brandy with him. I accepted his invitation, though I respectfully declined the cigar he offered. He seemed slightly drunk, and maybe a little bored. Perhaps even lonely. He was between wives. His girlfriends changed so frequently that I could scarcely remember what names to address them by. At any rate, this night he was chatty, and the chat went pleasantly enough until he patted my knee, and the patting became a rubbing, up and down my thigh. Taken by surprise (though, having seen some of the parties at the house, I shouldn't have been; no, not at all), I stood abruptly and excused myself. I was afraid that he would dismiss me from his service for rebuffing him, but the next day when we chanced upon each other in one of the hallways, he simply smiled at me and said hello as cheerfully as if I had dreamed the whole incident.

I was not close to him, not a butler or bodyguard or chauffeur—though he had those. I was the head of maintenance at the mansion. I made sure that every machine, and every living body in my team, was performing its task properly. The cleaning crew answered to me. It was my responsibility, too, if a fountain of wine stopping spurting. If holographic nude male dancers with arrows jutting out of them like Saint Sebastian started dancing in slow motion or speeded-up motion or vanished like elusive ghosts altogether. I did mention that Diego Kaji was a man with unique tastes? Jaded tastes. There was enough to do to keep me and my people and my several automatons busy every day. The house he had built upon the flat roof of the Turquoise Tower was very large. It was a synthesis of every style that appealed to him, a Frankenstein's monster of grafted parts that somehow all came together in an unlikely whole. Towers and gables and gargoyles. There was an adjacent chapel with a steeple and it had stained glass windows that portrayed beautiful naked women with batlike devil wings. Various wives and girlfriends had posed for these demonic likenesses. Many an orgy had taken place upon the chapel's floor, with Diego Kaji presiding over the events at the altar.

I had never participated in these revelries, had done my best to be out of the house when they occurred, though I was always on call. My wife and I had once received a formal invitation to one of these events, ostensibly a Halloween costume party. On the card, it was called a "masque." Somehow my wife and I were able to decline, and thankfully my employer had never invited me to attend one of his special events—as a guest—again. It was disturbing enough to have to replace a circuit chip in a pleasure robot while lovely teenage girls looked on and giggled. Unsettling enough when I was called upon to lower a man tightly bound in a cocoon of black leather when the chain he dangled from would not deliver him back to the floor.

Maybe I'm a prude in my old age, but I'm not so sure that even in my youth, unmarried, I would have fit in with the revelers at Diego Kaji's "masques."

After Kaji's suicide there was a lot of activity of a less pleasurable variety about the big house.

Lawyers removed computers, while business partners fretted in the background. Ex-wives squabbled over ownership of this painting or that sculpture; a two-thousand-year-old Kodju vase was dropped and shattered during one particularly ugly confrontation of this type. And I was given duties. Very solemn duties. They were considered an extension of the cleaning I had always overseen during my employment . . . which I knew was soon to end.

"Good man, Rod," one of my boss's former business partners muttered, patting me on the back for no apparent reason, as I met him coming out of Mr. Kaji's home office. This was the cocooned man I had helped get down that time.

I erased the memories of pleasure robots. I removed and burned holograph chips of underage nude mutant girls cavorting. It gave me satisfaction to see some of these things destroyed at last, though another part of me was disgusted at myself for aiding in their disappearance. For cleansing Diego Kaji's memory.

"Ah . . . did you get rid of that enema robot yet?" one former guest of the house whispered to me outside the huge, bi-level library. He was obviously a little embarrassed to ask.

"Yes, sir," I assured him.

"Oh," he said, and I realized he was disappointed, had wanted to take it with him. He nodded at the threshold to the library. "Those books of erotic art prints from Ram?"

"I think Mr. Blemish took those," I reported.

"Bastard," the man mumbled, whisking away, maybe hoping to locate Mr. Blemish elsewhere within the mansion.

I had things to do, at that moment, in the library. I entered it. I touched a code on the keypad by the door frame. I heard the big double doors of violet Ramon wood clunk into place, firmly locked. Then I turned to face the high-ceilinged room.

My boss had been a voracious reader. He loved books as artifacts, as objects, preferred to read from actual volumes rather than off a monitor. This room held quite the collection even now, however much its contents had already been pilfered and censored. I approached a locked cabinet set into a section of wall that was not filled with built-in bookcases. This showcase held some of Mr. Kaji's most prized, most priceless volumes. One of the items displayed behind glass was an original copy of *The Pioneer* magazine, in which was printed the story "The Tell-Tale Heart," by Edgar Allan Poe—Diego Kaji's very favorite author. But it was from the displayed copy of *The Stylus*, a literary journal edited by Poe, that Kaji's people had managed to isolate and extract the correct DNA. Oil from a thumb, a bit of rubbed-off cell, still clinging to the brittle paper even after all these many, many years. . . .

I was one of the very few people in the mansion atop the Turquoise Tower who knew about the switch hidden under the lower edge of the glass showcase's frame—and the foremost of those few was already dead. I flipped this switch, and with barely a whisper, the section of wall in which the cabinet was set swung inward. I passed through the narrow portal, and pushed the hidden door back into place.

The corridor was too cramped, too chilly, and quite unnecessarily murky. Into its walls, cells were recessed. One cell had only bars to contain its occupant, but it had no occupant now. Mr. Kaji had sold his clone of motion picture actress Jayne Mansfield to a friend. I didn't know much about her other than that she and her little dog had been killed in an automobile accident in the twentieth century. Mr. Kaji had acquired her "death car" and it was still displayed in his adjacent garage, a miniature museum of motor vehicles. It was from this that he'd had her blood, and thus her DNA, extracted. I remembered seeing her at some of the masques. Even when she was attired—in some glittery sheath from which her ample curves seemed ready to burst—her eyes flailed the walls, the ceiling, the groping people around her in a vacant, drugged panic. She had less than the mind of a little dog, now.

I was relieved that I would not have to destroy her, scrub her like a lichen off the face of Diego Kaji's tombstone. Despite all that I had done for him over the years, I had never had to kill a woman—even a cloned woman—before. . . .

The next cell had a clear wall, like that glass showcase containing several of Poe's works, and from within a man seated on the closed lid of a toilet gazed out at me warily. He had a glittering, shimmering cape around his shoulders against the chill, but otherwise he was naked. A white jumpsuit lay crumpled, soiled, upon the floor. The crusted tray of his most recent meal rested atop his bolted-down table. The man made a little grunting sound; hardly the beautiful music that had achieved his fame. His hair drooped in greasy black spikes across his forehead, though the blue-black color was dyed; the servants saw to this when they drugged him and washed and shaved him. Some clones were placid, but this one tended to fight, become violent, thrash around madly like a martial artist fighting off an army of assailants. I'd heard he'd been gleefully tortured one night after breaking the nose of one of Mr. Kaji's female guests.

"Hello, my man," I said to him soothingly. Sadly. I had listened to the man's music; one could hardly miss it, as Kaji had often played it loudly. But the sadness I felt was not for the destruction of a great talent. That talent had died many generations ago. No, the regret I felt was more like that which one would feel bringing a sick pet to the vet to be put down. Not even that regret, really, because this had been Mr. Kaji's pet, not mine.

I activated a separate clear panel set seamlessly into the larger cell wall, and it slid aside. The man grunted again, looked ready to rise from the toilet, perhaps expecting one of the treats he liked, such as a doughnut. Instead, I raised the handgun I had brought with me—a Scimitar .55, metallic gold with a dusting of red sparkly flakes—and pushed its barrel through the opening and pointed it at the man on the toilet and like the angel of death I squeezed the trigger. The gun emitted only the slightest *poof*. The man emitted only a soft third grunt before he toppled off the toilet and began melting.

Only when he began dissolving—the blue, glowing plasma spreading rapidly and consuming his cells—did the clone begin to kick and thrash in a mindless attempt at survival, but it was much too late. I slid the opened panel shut to avoid smelling the fumes as the plasma did its work. The thrashing became a subdued writhing as the man lost shape under the corrosive blanket, his limbs shortening, and then there was no more movement but that of the plasma itself. It being a blue plasma, it only consumed organic matter, and so all that was left when it was finished was the man's shiny cape, barely stained and empty on the floor of the cell.

The next few cells were empty (for which I was again grateful) except for hanging chains or props and decorations related to their former famous occupants. Maybe Diego Kaji had foreseen his own end longer ago than anyone had suspected, and had thus let his most trusted friends take some of his clones. His most tight-lipped friends. I knew that other angels of death would be visiting some of his *less* trustworthy friends, but fortunately that was not on my own list of chores. After the last of my work was done in this mansion, this Graceland atop the Turquoise Tower, I would take my savings and move my wife to another city—another colony on another world, perhaps—and change my name and pray that no other servant of the late Diego Kaji ever deemed me a threat to the sanctity of his memory.

I came to the only other remaining clone. The second of the two men that for whatever reason had been idols of Diego Kaji. Perhaps he had thrilled to this man's stories of madness. Been deliciously chilled, or even titillated by their brooding atmosphere. I had, at my employer's prompting, read a number of his stories and poems and I could understand Mr. Kaji's enthusiasm more than I could his affinity for the music of his other idol.

Maybe Diego Kaji was a frustrated author, a would-be singer, and all his own accomplishments were merely what he had made do with.

The other cells I had passed had once been closed off by invisible fields of force—nearly invisible, at least, in that they gave off a pale violet tint so that one would know they were activated. But this cell had no bars, no glass wall, no magnetic field. I came to a wall of brick, as if some of the other servants had already set to work sealing off all traces of this jail. This zoo cage. The front of the cell was entirely bricked up except for one small area at the level of my eyes. This was open, and I could smell an unclean odor wafting out even before I brought my face close to it warily.

No arm shot out to rake at my eyes. No spittle came flying at me. In the murk beyond, lit only by the holographic flame of a mock candle fixed to the wooden tabletop, I saw a man dressed in a torn and shabby black suit, seated before the candle. Its wavering glow gleamed off his bulbous forehead, made black pools of his mournful, deep-set eyes. Though his hair was in disarray and he was due for a shave, his small mustache still looked neat. The head lifted slightly. Silently. From within their pools of darkness those eyes contemplated me, almost as if there were actually a sharp mind behind the waxen mask of fame. The living Halloween mask that this entity had worn to the masques, to the delight of Diego Kaji's guests.

You can clone flesh and bone, but you cannot clone talent, or memories. We knew who this man was. But he did not know. This man was as lost as he had been when for five days he had disappeared, perhaps in a drunken stupor, on the streets of Baltimore, Maryland, in AD 1849.

One of Mr. Kaji's guests, a movie producer, had once asked him if he might borrow this clone, so that it might help script a film for him. Imagine the selling hook in such a project! But my boss had only chuckled and wagged his head. Even if he had been willing to make known to the public the unlicensed cloning of this man, the creature was simply not capable of writing so much as his own renowned name.

"Hello, my man," I said to him softly, the Scimitar .55 hanging down by my leg. There was enough room for me to point it through the gap in the wall of mortared brick . . . but I did not raise it yet.

It was not illegal, technically, to clone a dead man. But any cloning for personal—rather than industrial—use was against the law. Though clones did not possess the rights of us "birthers," there were still too many sticky areas of legal ground. There were groups that cried out in protest at the mistreatment of clones, at *any* use of clones. One could not legally clone himself in the pursuit of immortality, and surely Mr. Kaji hadn't, or else why even kill himself in the first place?

Unless that had been a sham to throw off the authorities. Perhaps the *hanged man* was the clone. Perhaps Diego Kaji—the Diego Kaji with a mind and with memories—was already in another city, another colony on another world.

Yes, I thought. Though I had not been a friend to the man, a close associate, not even a butler or bodyguard or chauffeur, I felt I knew him well enough that this was a real possibility. It rang true to me. I knew the man not so much by his words to me, but through his tastes—his environment, his possessions. His possessions such as this clone. This human being.

Regarding the man in the tomb, as he regarded me, I thought again of the works of his that I had read and been so impressed by.

Squeezing and unsqueezing the handle of the gun resting against my thigh, I said aloud, as if to remind an amnesiac of these words, as if teaching them to a child for the first time: "He had come like a thief in the night. And one by one dropped the revelers in the blood-bedewed halls of their revel. . . ."

I paused, as if to gauge whether these words moved the cell's occupant in any way. He appeared not to have even heard them, however. He seemed deaf, no matter how intense his stare upon me. I felt suddenly uneasy, as if he were the one observing a prisoner, as if I were the one behind this brick wall gazing out at freedom. As if he were taking mental notes so as to pen a story about me at some later date. As if it were *he* considering *my* ultimate fate.

I could not bring the gun up. If only he had grunted, animal-like, as the other clone had. If only his eyes had been less clear, however shrouded in their darkness. If only I hadn't read his stories. . . .

I swore under my breath, very softly, as I unsealed the door that was hidden skillfully within the wall of brick. I swung it open, and gestured to the man at the table with my free hand . . . still gripping the pistol in the other should he come flying suddenly toward me with his arms extended, his fingers like talons. I remembered the occasion when Mr. Kaji's bodyguard had had to shoot an undrugged clone who had gone berserk at one of his masquerades. This female clone had attacked her master, who was dressed as a kind of robot, I guess, that night . . . a man of tin. The clone had been a person named Judy Garland, cloned just to the age of a young girl in pigtails. Poor child. I had been relieved to hear that she had been returned to the ether, in a sense. . . .

After several long moments, the man rose from his chair. I gestured to him again, and at last he came shambling toward me. Out through the narrow doorway into the dimly lit hall. He allowed me to take him by the elbow, and guide him back through the passageway toward the locked library.

As we walked together, as if to train him, I said, "Lo! Death has reared himself a throne . . . in a strange city lying alone. . . ."

In the vaulted, balconied library, I unlocked that glass cabinet and removed the copies of *The Stylus* and *The Pioneer*, and I stuffed these yellowed, crackling magazines into my companion's jacket. He submitted dumbly like a child having a winter coat pulled on. Then I unlocked the library doors of violet Ramon wood and peeked out into the hall. When I thought it was safe, we emerged. We moved stealthily while we made our way to one of the doors that exited the mansion built atop the Turquoise Tower in Beaumonde Square in the colony city called Punktown.

The man and I descended to street level in an elevator. With my hand still on his arm to guide him, we continued along the avenue. Finally, we came to a little café and went inside for coffee and pastries. It was an upscale café and the man's stink attracted the disgusted eyes of neighboring patrons, but I ignored them as my chewing companion did. After we had eaten, we returned to the street, and I tucked a hundred munits in bills into the man's pocket, though it was mostly a gesture for my own sake. I wasn't convinced he would know what to do with them. I even considered giving him my gun, but that was too unrealistic a gesture, so I kept it in my shoulder holster.

And it was on the street that we parted ways. I clapped him on the back, as a cowboy in an old movie might slap a horse to get it moving away on its own. Stumbling a few steps, the man glanced back at me. And then I watched him as he staggered along, until his famous bobbing head became only one of many anonymous bobbing heads, and I lost sight of him down at the end of the great avenue. Swallowed in the flood that Diego Kaji had sought to rise so high above.

Sometimes I think of the man pushing a crumpled bill across a counter to buy himself a drink at a bar, a bottle at a store. Most often, I think that his body must be lying in its own filth in an alley, its skull bashed in and its pockets turned out. Or perhaps he isn't dead yet, not yet, but lies there starving and sick, muttering unintelligible words—like a young bride dying of tuberculosis as her grieving husband helplessly watches. Muttering garbled words like a dreamer suffering fevered nightmares and talking in his sleep, as if to convey those nightmares to whoever will listen. In his delirium, clutching his magazines against his breast. And I hope they are soaked in spilled wine. Stained with vomit. Caked with congealing blood. Because I know it would agonize Diego Kaji to see those prizes defiled in that way. He, who would think nothing of defiling a clone of Jayne Mansfield, would have cried out in horror just to know that I had removed them from their case. . . .

If Diego Kaji did indeed escape into the world alive, he should have thought to take those publications with him. But perhaps he had been afraid to give his greatest secret away by doing so . . . the secret that he, too, walks the streets still breathing when he should really be a dead man.

In any case, those objects were in the hands of the man to whom they truly belonged. And if those pages crumpled, and those hands decayed, then that was the way things belonged, too.

LAST STOP

John Pelan

Schumann whispered to the man in the overcoat, "Time to go, we're closing up." The overcoat man was always the last of the homeless stragglers in the library. There was no sign of him having heard Schumann, no acknowledgement of his presence, the overcoat man simply rose, and without a word or gesture shuffled toward the elevator. Schumann seethed inwardly; the magazine the overcoat man had been "reading" was an issue of *Time* from some weeks back that hadn't been opened, meaning that the overcoat man had just sat there quietly staring off into space for the better part of six hours. Compounded by the rest of the homeless that considered the public library a multimillion-dollar shelter or entertainment center, it wasn't too bad, merely irritating that *real* scholars like that gentleman with an entire cart of bound volumes of *The New Yorker* couldn't find a place to do their research due to the abundance of human flotsam like the overcoat man.

Schumann shrugged and went to turn off the computers; as usual they were all logged on to porn sites, some of the most disgusting stuff that he could imagine. Were there really that many women who would couple with horses? He shook his head and went to the elevator. The squad of janitors would be here soon; in the morning he'd see that they'd successfully worked the magic of making the somewhat grubby and antiquated structure seem sparkling and new. Of course, by noon the place would be filled with the overcoat man and his ilk, and the miasma of dirt, dust and foulness that seemed to follow them about would take over, and Schumann would sit and suffer in silence until closing time.

The worst of the lot was the overcoat man. He'd never really had a good look at him as the man wore a floppy hat pulled low on his head and kept the collar of his overcoat turned up, no matter what the season. Schumann had read that many schizophrenics behaved that way, either wearing layers of clothing or bundling themselves up as "protection" against whatever bedevilments or risks they imagined. Schumann wasn't unsympathetic to the unfortunates, he just wished that they'd find somewhere else to while away the hours besides the library, and it wouldn't be too much to ask that they bathed once in a while. . . .

The blinking light told him that he'd reached the

first floor. Charlie the security guard was still sitting at his station; he'd be on duty until an hour or so after closing, just in case someone had hidden in a restroom or something. Last year they found a lunatic in a stall in the ladies room licking a copy of M. R. James' *A Pleasing Terror*. Apparently the loon was trying to loosen the glue on the card pocket so as to abscond with the book. Apparently he had no idea that the tiny chip affixed to the jacket would set the alarms off and summon Charlie from his chair. Schumann chuckled at the thought—at least the fellow had actually wanted a book, unlike the dregs that just came to take up space and play on the computers.

"G'night, Charlie."

"'Night, David. You going to catch the game?"

Schumann looked at his watch. It would already be the third inning—the way the Mariners were playing these days it was probably already seven to one or some damn thing. Hardly a worthwhile investment of time or money.

"No, I'll probably just have a beer or two and head home. Tomorrow's another day. See you."

Schumann headed out into the darkening night, overcast in the middle of July. The darkened skies threatened rain. The smart course would be to go straight home and work on his entomological research, but the allure of the bright neon farther down the street was far too strong. Schumann threw caution to the wind and decided a couple of drinks before dinner couldn't possibly hurt.

Christopher's was one of those spacious and overlit establishments with enough potted plants both faux and natural to stock a small jungle and waitresses who had such eerily similar smiles and perfect teeth that he couldn't help but think of *The Stepford Wives*. Looking at the rather extravagant prices on the menu, he decided that he'd better skip dinner and just have something when he got home. He ordered a drink from the overly cheerful waitress and glanced at one of the several TV screens located around the bar. He located the one set not turned to a baseball game and moved to a table closer to the screen. It was just the local news, but that was bound to be more interesting than watching an athletic contest between two dismally bad teams. The newsman was one of those robotic good-looking sorts, obviously reading from a teleprompter. He droned on for several minutes about the horrendous commuter traffic between Seattle and the East Side, a subject that was hardly "news" to anyone living in the area.

Schumann paid a bit more attention as the newsman went on to discuss the finding of yet another mangled corpse in the downtown area. The police were asking for information from anyone who may have seen suspicious characters in the vicinity. Schumann almost laughed at that; more than half the people he saw every day could easily be described as "suspicious characters." The details were few: apparently a man in his late forties had been set upon by an assailant or assailants sometime in the late evening hours. The story again mentioned hideous mutilation. Schumann ordered another drink and turned his attention to two young women playing a game of pool. Both were very attractive blondes in their mid-twenties, the sort that Schumann hoped in vain would someday come into the library and ask him about a book. Unfortunately, that possibility was as remote as the chance that both women would ask to join him at his table. At least the perky waitress was being attentive; he ordered a third drink (or was it his fourth, he found he wasn't sure).

Standing and weaving just slightly, Schumann went to the men's room; when he returned to his table he noted that the efficient waitress had supplied him with another drink. He didn't really want it, but couldn't see any way clear of refusing to pay for it without a confrontation, and she seemed like a very nice girl. Thoughtful of her to make sure he had a fresh drink when he got back. Maybe she was interested. . . . Schumann dismissed the ridiculous notion and turned his attention to his drink. Since he felt obligated to pay for it, he also felt he should drink it. . . . He looked at his drink closely, imagining the swirl of molecules as the Jameson's mixed with the soda. After hesitating a moment he seized the glass and gulped the contents down as he stood up and pulled some bills from his wallet, leaving far too large a tip, and went out into the street.

The mix of misting rain and neon made the street shimmer and Schumann felt vaguely disoriented, as though he was seeing this street for the first time. Of course that was nonsense; the bus stop was right in front of the drugstore. A short ride of about ten minutes and he'd be home and off to bed. Schumann leaned heavily against a lamppost; he was drunk—far drunker than he'd thought. . . . He shook his head, trying to clear it, and was gratified to see the twin headlights of the approaching bus; he needed to get home.

The bus pulled up and Schumann paid his fare, mumbling a greeting to the impassive driver. Glancing down the aisle at his fellow passengers, he decided to take a seat toward the back, well away from the boisterous college students laughing and chatting at the front. Besides the little group of four couples in the front, the only other passengers were a middle-aged man reading a newspaper and a young woman wearing a security guard uniform, obviously on her way to work. Schumann found a seat in the rear of the bus, where someone had thoughtfully left the evening paper, and sat down, opening the paper to the local news.

Damn. He could have sat in front after

all. . . . The students all piled out at the next stop, obviously one more club to pop into before retiring. Schumann felt a twinge of regret that he couldn't sleep through a morning class and be none the worse for it—no, the library demanded he be on time for his duties as babysitter to society's dregs. Schumann tried to focus on the paper, but the type seemed to swim and dance before his eyes. The jolt of the bus stopping caused him to look up—the young lady was getting off and another passenger was boarding.

It couldn't be. . . . But, yes, yes it was. The overcoat man, his daily albatross, was on the bus and *heading toward him*. Schumann quickly held his newspaper up to cover his face and peered around the page. The overcoat man had taken a seat directly behind the other passenger and was leaning forward, no doubt wheedling and pleading for money. The bus jounced along and Schumann closed his eyes for just a moment. . . .

He jerked awake. Damn it! He'd missed his stop and the driver hadn't bothered to check for passengers. He looked out the window. The bus was parked in a completely unfamiliar part of town, the lights off, the driver gone. Schumann staggered to his feet and made his way to the front of the bus. Something tripped him; he flailed out and caught the handrail, turning to see what he'd stumbled over. It was the foot of the man with the newspaper; he must've dozed off as well. The driver should be fired for being this careless about his passengers. Odd that the impact hadn't awakened him. . . . Schumann peered at his fellow passenger and gasped, fighting back the urge to vomit.

Half of the man's face and neck were missing; red muscle and white bone reflected dully in the darkened bus. That he was dead, there was no question. *The overcoat man*? Could he have seen something, been involved somehow? Schumann knew he should call the police, but he was the last person on the bus—they'd detain him for questioning, there would be no explaining this to his superiors. He ran to the front of the bus and forced the door open and went out into the night.

The neighborhood was alien to him and the alcohol was still making everything swim in a surreal haze. Neon signs shouted out LIVE GIRLS, XXX and BEER & WINE, but none of these establishments seemed as though they would provide sanctuary. Stumbling over broken glass and garbage, Schumann hurried toward distant streetlights.

He walked briskly toward what appeared to be an intersection and to his relief saw a taxicab parked just a block away. Hurrying toward the cab, Schumann heard another set of footsteps. He turned and saw the overcoat man a short distance behind, not chasing him exactly, but purposefully matching his stride. Schumann almost broke into a run as he neared the cab. Swinging open the passenger door and leaping in, he gave the cab driver his address and sank back in the seat, almost afraid to look out the window. The overcoat man stood on the street corner impassively watching as the cab drew away.

The ride home was uneventful; Schumann cursed himself for a fool when he saw the outrageous sum on the meter of the cab. Grumbling, he paid the driver and stumbled up the stairs to his apartment where he fell into a nightmare-ridden sleep, the faces of the mangled dead man and the overcoat man chasing him through endless alleys.

The buzzing of the alarm clock brought wakefulness and with it a brutal hangover; Schumann had to gulp down a cup of instant coffee and some aspirin before he could face the prospect of a shower and shave and preparation for work.

Schumann bravely faced the day with a hellish hangover. The madness of the preceding evening seemed a nightmarish hallucination and nothing more; in the hour before opening the library Schumann scanned the local news stations' Web sites for any mention of a body being found on a bus. There were none. Had he imagined it—imagined the mutilated features and the relentless pursuit through the deserted streets to the safety of the taxicab? No, it had been all too terrifyingly real; surely there would be some news later in the day. . . . For now he had to play St. Peter to the shuffling, stinking throng that would fill the library and make it impossible for real scholars to work.

It was nearly the lunch hour before the overcoat man came in. As was usual, he grabbed a magazine seemingly at random and sat staring at the unopened periodical. Schumann's heart raced. Should he call the police? What would he say? That he had been drunk? That he had seen a murder that seemingly hadn't been reported? That was lunacy. Schumann watched the overcoat man. After the events of last night, there was a sense of menace to the way he sat quietly with the unopened magazine before him.

Schumann spent the day in a state of agitated distraction, trying to perform his duties while keeping one eye on the seated figure. Why was he there? What purpose was there in sitting in the library throughout the day? The minutes dragged into hours as the figure remained motionless. As the clock neared eight, Schumann's motley pack of regulars began to file out of the building, the overcoat man among them.

Schumann breathed a sigh of relief and after a quick check of the premises headed for the door himself, barely nodding to Charlie as he bolted out.

There! At the bus stop was a gaggle of the homeless men, the overcoat man standing off to the side of the group. As Schumann watched, he saw the overcoat man produce a bottle of something from within the folds of his coat and gesture to one of the men. The others seemed oblivious to this motion and continued waiting at the stop while the overcoat man and his companion headed off up the street. Schumann followed, keeping his distance and doing his best to ensure that he was not seen by either man. He had his cell phone tonight. If the overcoat man attempted another killing, he'd be ready. . . .

The two men turned onto a decaying side street. The only businesses that had not yet fallen victim to the urban blight were peep shows and a solitary convenience store that did ninety percent of its business in cigarettes and fortified wine. Schumann followed, keeping a safe distance to prevent being observed; the two men seemed to be passing the bottle back and forth between them as they walked. Schumann's heart gave a start as they turned and went into an alley. . . . What should he do? Obviously the overcoat man meant to kill his companion now. . . . Schumann looked up and down the street for a policeman. There was no sign of anyone likely to be of any help at all, let alone an officer he could hail for assistance.

There was a faint sound of glass breaking! He

stole toward the alley and peered around the corner expecting to see a scene of horror as the overcoat man tore at his victim. No, they were nearing the end of the alley and turning back out onto the street. Instead of following, Schumann raced to the corner and waited. In a moment they appeared, still walking together, though there was no sign of the bottle being passed—that must have been the noise he'd heard. The two men crossed the street and started heading toward Schumann on the opposite side of the street. Schumann stood and pretended to examine the contents of a bookstore's display window as the two men reached the corner and crossed, walking by him as though completely oblivious to his identity. They were heading back toward the library. Schumann followed and stopped as he realized that their circuitous route had brought them back to the bus stop, where they stood waiting.

Schumann turned and headed in the opposite direction; there was another bus stop only a block and a half away. He'd take a seat in the back and be waiting when they boarded. He patted the pocket containing his cell phone. Yes, this time he'd be ready. He'd see justice done and a murderer apprehended!

Schumann fidgeted as he waited for the bus. Possibly he should just tell the driver to keep an eye on the overcoat man and disembark. But no, that was no good, the driver would think him a lunatic. He had to see this thing through.

There! The bus was pulling up to the stop; Schumann paid his fare and looked around. Perfect! There was a seat in the back where someone had left the evening paper. Schumann made a beeline for the seat and unfolded the paper, peering around the edge as the bus pulled in to the next stop. Sure enough, the overcoat man and his equally shabby companion got on, sitting next to each other near the front. Schumann glanced around at his fellow passengers. The bus was a bit more crowded than the other night; of course this was an earlier run, so that was to be expected. Schumann felt the tingle of adrenaline-fueled excitement tingle through him as he surreptitiously spied on the two men. They took no heed of him, or anyone else for that matter. The two figures sat, heads bowed, engaged in a mumbling conversation.

One by one the passengers disembarked. Schumann peered at the street signs, trying in vain to orient himself; somewhere along the route of twists and turns the bus had ended up in an unfamiliar part of town. The numbers of the buildings indicated that they were just past the downtown area, but nothing looked even remotely familiar. Schumann reassured himself that he had his cell phone handy.

The overcoat man's hand shot up suddenly and

pulled the cord to signal for the next stop. Schumann debated his best course of action. Should he go one more stop and try to retrace the route and chance losing sight of his quarry? Would he tip his hand by getting off here? As the overcoat man and his companion headed to the front door he made his decision. A split second before the bus pulled out, he shouted, "Wait! This is my stop." The driver was an obliging man; he waited for Schumann to hurry to the front of the bus and smiled and bade him a good evening. Schumann hurried off the bus and looked around.

It was the same general part of town he'd found himself in the night before. Streets dimly lit by cheap neon signs and guttering street lamps. The two men were just a block ahead of him, walking slowly and leisurely, the overcoat man taking his companion's arm and gently steering him down the street. Schumann glanced at the street sign. SHEA STREET. He'd lived here all his life and never heard of Shea Street; 1st Avenue, the street the bus had followed, was of course a main thoroughfare. Well, there were bound to be a few unfamiliar streets in this forsaken and decaying part of town. Schumann followed the two men, senses at alert in case he needed to bolt as he had the previous night.

His worries were unfounded. The overcoat man was oblivious to his presence and his wine-soaked companion would have been unlikely to notice anything short of Schumann leaping at him and yelling "Boo!"

Now Schumann recognized the neighborhood—there was the seedy peep show and the all-night convenience store he'd seen the preceding night. His quarry stopped at the latter and went inside; Schumann stopped and waited for them to emerge. After a couple of minutes they reappeared, the overcoat man's companion triumphantly brandishing a small brown paper bag. Obviously they picked up another bottle of rotgut wine and the overcoat man was letting his victim drink to a state of anesthesia. *Just like some horrible human spider*, thought Schumann, *he's softening him up for the kill*.

They'd now gone at least half a mile down Shea Street and Schumann worried if perhaps he should turn back—six blocks was a long way if he had to run. . . . Wait! They were stopping; the overcoat man was pointing to a brownstone with boarded-up windows, but with a small illuminated sign saying simply ROOMS. Could this be where he lived? Schumann stood quietly, pressing himself against the lamppost, trying to be invisible. He was right! This was where the overcoat man lived! The two men walked slowly across the street and up the short staircase to the front door. The door was apparently unlocked; the two men went through it. Schumann had a brief glimpse of light from inside and then the door closed.

Schumann stole forward. Should he just walk right in? How would he know which apartment the man lived in? Checking to see that the cell phone was close at hand, he walked up the steps, gingerly avoiding the stinking piles of refuse that littered the stairs. The door was still unlocked. Well, he hadn't really expected it would be a security building. . . . Schumann went through the door, the charnel stench hitting him as he stepped into the maw of Hell.

The lobby of the building was a scene from the nightmares of Giger or Bosch. The furniture was covered with layers of black mildew and small gray mushrooms, the floor littered with bones and torn clothes. In the midst of the abattoirial pile crawled white insectoid creatures, swarming to the fresh meat that was laid out before them.

The overcoat man was there with his companion, though it took Schumann a moment to reconcile the ghastly bone-white insectile creature with anything that could ever be mistaken for human. The thing in the overcoat had discarded its hat and opened its coat to reveal two additional limbs, which were hooked and barbed like those of a mantis. The hooked arms were clutching the other man, holding him up in a sitting posture, though he was obviously unconscious. The overcoat man's upper face looked more or less human; though now Schumann could see that his eyes were solid black pools and that there was no nose to speak of. It was the lower face that was the worst. His jaw had opened sideways revealing mandibles that he was using to tear chunks from the unconscious man's face and neck while the small creatures swarmed to the man's legs and torso, tearing through cloth and flesh alike with sharp mandibles and barbed limbs.

Schumann retched and staggered back toward the door, fumbling for his phone. He turned and almost collided with a figure coming up the stairs. He stared for a moment. The hat was subtly different, the filthy overcoat perhaps a slightly different shade of gray . . . *another* one. Schumann elbowed past the figure and ran. Glancing over his shoulder he saw the figure get to its feet and start down the stairs, then suddenly turn and head back up to the place of the hellish feasting.

Schumann ran. He had to get out of this area, call the police, maybe the army. . . . No telling how many of these things were infesting the city. He could call the police when he reached home; he didn't dare dally in this neighborhood. If there were two of them, there might be more lurking about, maybe even other nests.

Schumann raced through the filthy streets, nearly tripping several times over bottles and other debris strewn on the sidewalks. The late afternoon gloaming had turned dark and a light rain was making everything shimmer with the reflection of the neon lights that were just now coming on. He turned and headed toward what he recalled was the street that led to a main arterial, peering over his shoulder to make sure he wasn't being followed. No sign of pursuit; perhaps the things had been so absorbed in their feeding that they hadn't noticed him. Were they of human intelligence? Hard to say. They certainly knew enough to adapt to camouflaging themselves, but that could be some sort of inhuman instinct, not necessarily intelligence.

Schumann slowed to a walk. The next block was filled with brightly lit storefronts—granted they all seemed to be disreputable businesses like peep shows and sex shops, but at least there was the comforting buzz of humanity milling about and not the nameless terrors that inhabited Shea Street. Schumann spotted a row of taxis parked by a newsstand and made his way to the first one in line. Sliding in to the backseat he mumbled his address and closed his eyes, feeling his racing pulse finally starting to slow to normal. Schumann saw the horrible scene from the rooming house as clear as a Polaroid in his mind's eye. He shuddered; tomorrow would bring police, the National Guard, whatever it took—they'd raze the nest of horror to the ground. He'd probably get some mention in the papers. . . . Best of all, he'd never have to worry about seeing the overcoat man again. The police would know what to do.

He started—the driver had apparently made a wrong turn. They weren't heading the correct way, the cab had turned and headed back down Shea Street. Schumann angrily banged on the one-way glass that separated the driver from the backseat.

Schumann yelled, "Hey, what's wrong with you? This is the wrong way! Turn this thing around!" He wasn't used to having to argue with people or raise his voice, but after what he'd been through, he was damned if he was going to let some gypsy cabbie run up the meter on him. Maybe he should have just found a bus stop. . . . A lot of these cabs were run by immigrants who didn't know the city and could get hopelessly lost, or by swindlers who would deliberately feign ignorance so they could run up the fare. Schumann hadn't been born yesterday, he wasn't about to be taken advantage of. The horror he'd experienced faded, to be replaced by righteous indignation over the dishonesty or stupidity of the driver. He rapped on the glass again after glancing at the meter that was blinking redly in front of him: $4.80 in the wrong direction. . . . The hell with that.

"Driver! Stop the cab, you went the wrong way! You need to set the meter back to zero and start over. I'm not paying for you going the wrong way.

Reset the meter or I'll complain to your owner and to the City. You could lose your license, you know!"

The cab slowly pulled over and Schumann felt pleased with himself—a little assertiveness worked wonders with these people. The cab came to a complete stop and he heard the driver open his door and step out. A tingle of apprehension ran through Schumann; hopefully the driver wasn't some sort of loon who would pick a fight with a passenger over so trivial a matter.

A gloved hand pulled open the door to the backseat. Schumann saw the filthy overcoat and looked up into black compound eyes that shone with a pitiless hunger. A crazy thought struck him just before the hooked arms reached for him: Schumann wondered where the overcoat man had learned how to drive.

A Bottle of
Egyptian Night

Jessica Amanda Salmonson

I had long wished to find one of those curiosity shops so common to legend, wherein a romantically minded lady, such as I fancy myself to be, might purchase some homely object that turned out to possess an extraordinary property. I am thinking of such items as that mummified foot purchased by the Parisian Romanticist, Théophile Gautier, and belonging to the Princess Hermonthis who came to him in order to reclaim it, and, not incidentally I believe, to exchange flirtatious sentiments. I should like to have an adventure of that sort.

Thus I am willing to stop at any foolish roadside attraction, dollar-museum, curio or souvenir stand, in worn-out parts of towns and cities, or along old back roads and touristed seacoasts, in the hope of one day being led into more than a commonplace encounter. Perhaps the reality is that I have merely wiled away my life in foolery, awaiting some grim and tortured destiny none of us can ever fathom beforehand. We all need something to keep us from reminding ourselves that our existence is but an interlude to our nonexistence.

Along the jaded years I've chided myself about my hobby-quest, lacking as it does refinement or good taste. I had long before given up any idea that I might actually stumble upon something as magical as Aladdin's lamp. Nonetheless, I found such shops amusing and vulgarly wonderful, preying as they do, naively and innocently, upon forgotten dreams and childlike imagination. Thus I have been known to travel ungodly distances in order to inspect the mere rumor of a ridiculous establishment of "curious" intent.

My odd hobby had become so much a part of my routine that I wouldn't have thought existence quite worthwhile without my periodic journeys north, east, south and west, in search of the sorts of places my intellectual chums would be too embarrassed to enter. (I venture they *are* intrigued, however, for I am often asked to talk about my journeys, and not entirely out of these chums' eagerness to nettle.) I have sometimes imposed on this or that friend to venture with me, and they've not been disappointed, but neither were they true converts who must thereafter seek such silly haunts repeatedly.

I had all but forgotten the romantic origins of my eccentric and tireless interest when, finding myself going gray of hair and far less slender of build, I stumbled upon a quaint little store in my very neighborhood.

I am quite the one to walk about the city. My urban apartment is in a neighborhood which, after a period of decline, has become fashionable. There are many unique and individualistic shops, both new and old, many of artistic intent or leaning. The nicest shops by my standards—those that had been part of the neighborhood for years and even decades—have tended to be crowded out in these upswing years as buildings are refurbished, rents are tripled, and the previous quaintness is replaced bit by bit by glitzier, less practical styles of entrepreneur. The greatest loss was of a century-old dimestore with soda fountain, which even the newest generation had loved sufficiently to circulate petitions against the eviction—to no avail, as the square footage is today replaced by four small gaudy, costly boutiques.

One hears (from my generation) many complaints of "the rich" taking over, though it seems to me these invaders present merely a pretense of wealth, while beneath their artificial posturing and mortgaged lives, there is neurotic fretfulness that amounts to a gloomy fear of tomorrow. Still, the veneer of wealth and youthful success has unquestionably transformed my once-ignored corner of the city. Even so, a few of the old shops remain, particularly those not on the central shopping boulevard.

I am on first-name terms with many of the older proprietors. I can lament with them the loss of charm that seems inevitably to follow a neighborhood's rise from bohemian decay. Knowing the district's past and present as well as I do, having trod many times every alleyway and thoroughfare, you may imagine I was startled to find, on my way to grocery shopping, a curiosity shop entirely new to me. To me! I have visited every such institution in twenty-seven states of the Union and half as many countries during the last twenty-odd years of penny-pinching travel. To find one within blocks of home and never to have known it was there!

Nor did the shop appear to be newly ensconced. The sign, which said CURIOS FOR THE CURIOUS, was a badly faded, homemade affair, nothing to compare with the glistening backlit signs of the main boulevard. Nor could that sign have been moved from some other location, for the nails holding it to the wall were old. Rust stains streaked the wood with bloody tears.

The shop itself had beveled, leaded glass windows, two or three sections replaced by thinner, un-

beveled glass. I noted etched lettering—CUR and
TY—visible on two small panes, interrupted by a re-
placement pane void of letters. The door had been
painted years before and was badly flaked, dark
wood bared beneath curls of dirty pale green.

There was no question but that it was an old
store. How unaccountable that I had never noticed
it! Does one take her own neighborhood so for
granted that certain shops might go unseen for
years? Do our daily trodden paths and routines
stay so narrow that unknown regions await us always, a mere one block left, a scant two blocks
right? I had become so jaded both by my hobby and
my pleasing neighborhood, I had become least sensitive to an interesting shop where it was closest to
home.

Needless to say, I set aside my grocery errand
and went into the store to acquaint myself with its
contents.

It was astonishingly prosaic. Jewelry carved by
craftspeople of the hippie era, and by Eskimos, or
imported from India and Taiwan, reposed in a pal-
try cultural jumble beneath scratched glass, mois-
ture having smeared the ink on price tags. It was
old stock, to be sure, underpriced even for such
junk as it was. The African trade beads were the
real thing. Little Japanese jades were pre-war. There
were carvings of seagulls (these I consider overpriced at any price at all) and soapstone whales of

a variety common to all Northwest souvenir shops and tourist centers. There were cheap toys such as were given out at midcentury carnivals and midways as consolation prizes. There were dusty, broken dolls—a few of which might be valuable if professionally repaired—with tattered dresses and eyes half-closed and sad.

Then there were magic tricks as appeal to boyishly adolescent mentalities (I confess these have always appealed to me) and a great many "gags," such as the nail through the finger, arrow through the head, palm buzzer, whoopee pillow, soap that turns the fingers black, calling cards that read plainly, MY CARD, and similar minor idiocies. There were party favors and decorations that children ought not to see and adults ought not to enjoy, though both do, and an excessively cute plastic doll that peed on my blouse when I picked him up. There were soap-flavored candies, a "sampler" of horse-apples instead of chocolates, exploding cigarettes, and a kaleidoscope that left a sooty ring around the eye of anyone stupid enough to peer into it. (Happily I had a couple of napkins with me with which to rub my eye clean.)

In all, it was a dreadful novelty store, as far as merchandise was concerned. I could not believe the average age of an excited customer would be much more than ten.

The room was decorated with "not for sale" and

"do not touch" artifacts, more interesting than the stock to be sold, though not by large degrees. Stuffed turtles and toads stood on their hind legs holding musical instruments. A monkey-mermaid was suspended from the ceiling by means of tarnished wires, trailing cobwebs. Two-headed creatures floated in dark, half-evaporated alcohol. A three-foot-tall mummy labeled PIGMY was patently a dried-out baby orangutan with its fur shaved off. A faded, stuffed parrot—dusty and pathetic—gazed my way with one pale green eye of glass.

There were arrowheads, fossils, and old bottles, along with foreign coins and paper money, that *were* for sale, and a molted mongoose mounted with a wrinkled cobra in its teeth, dabs of red enamel placed to affect blood.

Some of these objects were protected by glass cases so scratched and dirty that it was difficult to see within. This increased their mystery and charm while hiding their rank deficiencies. Other items were sitting out and had been pinched and rubbed by so many intrigued hands across the years that they were falling to pieces.

I looked at the inevitable shrunken heads and decided they were quite possibly authentic.

As I sauntered about the close confines of numerous claustrophobic aisles, I saw no proprietor, but smelled a horrible unclean pipe.

When I reached out to stroke the fur of a type of

wildcat scheduled for extinction, an old woman popped into view, her face distorted through the glass of an antique druggist's case, a filthy corncob pipe in her yellow teeth, her eyes squinting.

"May I help you?" the apparition demanded.

I tried to spark a real conversation with her right away, for I did enjoy the shop in spite of its extraordinary triviality and uselessness. I didn't let on that I found her establishment wondrously tasteless and singularly devoid of imagination, but conveyed, instead, my sense of glad surprise that such a shop existed, unbeknownst to me, mere blocks from my home.

"Nowadays it is rare," I said, "to find a store such as yours in an urban environment. The modern world has left curiosity behind. Youngsters derive their sense of wonder from violent electronic games or still more violent movies; so what is a whaler's spear to them?" I eyed the spear mounted high on the wall as I said this, and continued. "Their amusements are packaged by Hollywood, and a stuffed mermaid is nothing anymore. It is sad, don't you agree?"

The old woman sucked on her vile pipe until it went out. She stared at me with pretended interest, her narrow eyes half-seeing, her ears likely half-hearing. She nodded vaguely, not helping me with idle chat.

"But I suppose entertainment hasn't deteriorated

so much," I ventured, "for the overpriced sensational paperbacks of today are certainly no peg down from the dime novels of a vanished age." I pointed with my chin at a pile of rare, torn, yellowed Victorian magazines and penny dreadfuls. "Still and all, things have lost a certain innocence. People scoff at innocence today."

The old woman continued to stare. I was growing uncomfortable.

"Well," I said, "it's been nice. I was on my way to do some grocery shopping. Might I buy one of those souvenir spoons from you before I take my leave?"

"You don't want a spoon," she said gruffly. She had sensed the token purchase as an act of pity, I suppose, but her senses were mistaken. The silver spoons on her rack, black with age, were no longer made in quite those designs, and I had a young cousin who collected them.

"I've a relation in Connecticut," I said soothingly, "who has a big set of them. Yours are very nice and inexpensive."

The old gal shuffled between aisles with me in tow. She tapped her dirty pipe on the edge of a counter, then pushed the dottle into a handily situated box on the floor. I could see by the stains on the wooden frame of the glass case that she usually emptied her pipe in that exact place. The box had a great deal of horrible ash in it. It was a wonder she had never burned the place down, the box being only cardboard.

Behind a certain case she dithered with items not generally on display. She came out with a small India ink bottle. She set it on the counter-glass, looked me straight in the face, and declared, "I can tell you're a connoisseur. You don't require a spoon at all. If you've a friend who wants one, I'll let you have it without charge. But *this* will just suit your own requirements." A bony finger unfolded to point at the stoppered bottle of ink. "It is one of a kind, of course," she said. "It will cost a pretty penny, even considering the free spoon I am throwing in. But as you're an enthusiast, and expert in rarity, I'm certain you won't quibble with price. It's ten dollars."

I was about to say, "For a bottle of ink?" Old ink bottles can be had for half the price even from pseudoantique vendors who inflate their prices on the basis of criminality or self-delusion. But she had circumvented complaint by the suggestion that I was above haggling. Quite clever of her. In fact I was never above haggling. Still, one tends to live up to others' expectations. Rather than dicker, I glared at the small bottle as though tentatively interested. Inwardly I was flabbergasted at the old gal's grandiloquent presentation of so patently worthless a trifle. Taking my silence for awe, she continued.

"You've seen to the heart of the mystery at once. A less observant individual would have thought it a bottle of ink, rather than the Egyptian night it happens to contain. But do you know who once owned it?"

"I think not," I said foolishly.

"It was in the possession of Sophia Hawthorne of Salem, in about the year 1840. It has passed through few hands since."

"*The* Sophia Hawthorne?" I inquired, rather boggled.

"None other," she said. "Although, she was not quite a Hawthorne when the bottle came into her possession, though already versed in kabbalah."

"I had no idea she was a kabbalist," I said.

"Well, a general occultist of the time; it was Sophia who got Elizabeth Barrett interested in such matters. Sophia gave the bottle to her husband after they were wed. It was later left behind at the Mosses mansion when they moved to Concord. I spent some while tracking down its history. My granddaddy, less observant than you and I, had mistaken it for a bottle of ink, stuck up in the rear of the antique hall-desk that had been the main object of granddaddy's auction bid. He was long in his grave, and I for many years the proprietress of his old establishment, when I stumbled upon a surviving record suggesting that Emerson possessed this bottle when he was writing his *Nature* studies;

but that record was spurious, assuming as it did that the bottle once contained ink, which is not so. Nathaniel Hawthorne makes a reference to the bottle of Egyptian night in one of his lesser tales, "A Virtuoso's Collection." Though the reference is facetious, we may guess he was less offhand about the object itself, or it would not have been left behind when he and Sophia moved. He was a bit of a neurotic, you know, and probably afraid of it.

"It came down through the Ripley family, until a liquidation auction of minor odds and ends put it into my granddaddy's hands. He displayed it in this very shop as Emerson's inkpot, missing its true merits altogether. When I took over the shop many long years ago, I set about to discover what pieces of my granddaddy's stock were authentic and what were cheap fraud. I can assure you *this* is the very bottle of night belonging to the Peabodys and then the Hawthornes themselves. It has never been offered for sale until this minute."

"Then . . . I shouldn't."

"Nonsense. When I'm dead, what will become of this rat-infested hole of a store? It'll be torn out and a shiny stainless steel and orange plastic restaurant will rise in its place. Whatever of my stock isn't burnt will end up in a thrift shop, charity to the terminally inane. It isn't often that a connoisseur finds her way here in these tragic days. I may not have another chance to place this into appreciative hands."

"Oh, you'll have plenty of chances to drop things in *my* hands," I protested. "Now that I've found your store, I'll come by often." And I rummaged in my bag for a crumpled ten-dollar bill. I wouldn't get so many groceries as a result, but who could help but take pity on the imaginative old lady? She had given me a good ten dollars worth of entertainment in any case, with her wild tale. I took the ink bottle and the free spoon and toddled along my way.

She had been the most curious thing about her cluttered shop and doubtless I was her only paying customer of the day, if not the week. I felt I had done a good turn to buy something from so lonesome an eccentric. I completed my shopping and, before I reached home, had all but forgotten the ink bottle. I found it in the bottom of my purse a few days later, remembered the engaging encounter with the oldster, and placed the bottle on top of the refrigerator where it gathered dust. In the meantime I attempted to visit the shop again, being as I am attracted to odd people and their tales. But the store was never open.

I wondered if the poor soul had died or was in the hospital. I tried upon occasion to see into the dark shop but caught no glimpse either of her or smoke from her pipe. A few weeks later, on my way to the grocery, I saw the old sign was down and the windows were boarded with a large, bright signboard that read, Future Home Of Hasty-Tasty Burger Giant, beneath which was the eerie legend, We're Growing. I shivered and took a different route home from the grocery thereafter.

I hadn't known the name of the proprietress and had no means of looking her up, whether in the phone book or the obituaries. I made an effort to trace her through realtors and read the obituaries for any mention of an owner of a curio shop, but could find out nothing.

All this made me terribly sad. To think an entire life could come and go without notice! Three generations of curio-collecting and selling, swept away as if by evil magic, decades of a family's concern erased by callous businessmen who knew nothing of their newly gained property except what it represented as investment.

It made me feel my own life was thinly rooted in this material world. Who would miss *me* when I passed on? What mattered my small nest, wherein every corner was decorated with useless geegaws, every wall hidden behind shelves of foxed and odorous books? We are dust in the end, as we all well know and hate to ponder.

I could not sleep that night. I was bothered by thoughts of the grave, of the pointless meanderings and accumulations of so few years prefacing death.

Then I recollected the bottle of Egyptian night, that oh-so-foolish purchase, the last remaining speck of some old woman's years on earth. I rose in darkness, padded in my slippers to the kitchen, and flicked on the light. I took the bottle from the top of the refrigerator, dusted it carefully, fondled the cool glass and its cork stopper. I wondered if, after a century and a half, ink remained in it. Doubtless it had nothing but a black crust of dried ink on its inner walls, affording the illusion that it was full.

I pulled the stopper out.

My first thought was that the electricity had gone out all over the city. It was not only pitch-black in the kitchen, but I could see no hint of streetlight through the curtains, nor the faintest outline of the kitchen windows.

No one realizes how *bright* urban life is, even at midnight in a residential neighborhood where streets are lined with trees, until one experiences, for the first time in life, absolute darkness in one's own kitchen.

I felt I would lose my balance in such a void, so I reached to brace myself with one hand against the refrigerator, whence I had taken the ink bottle. I almost dropped the bottle's cork when, to my astonishment, the refrigerator wasn't where I believed. I reached farther, and still could not touch it.

The blackout must have disoriented me. I

reached left, then right, trying to find purchase
against refrigerator or cabinet.

My kitchen is long and unusually narrow, so it is
not possible to stand anywhere in it where absolutely nothing is in arm's reach. I was rooted to
the spot, afraid to move, the absurd notion in my
mind that the floor may have opened up on all
sides and I would fall into an abyss by taking a single step in any direction.

Utter silence, as much as utter darkness, is unknown to city life. Yet I could hear nothing. The fine
hairs of my arms stood and tickled my flesh as
goose bumps raised in chilly anticipation of some
dreadful thing about to happen.

No sound, no sight; but I could *smell* something.
It was a scent alien to my kitchen, though I seemed
to recall something vaguely similar from my travels. Herbs and dryness came to mind, if "dryness"
can describe an odor. My mind played with many a
description: musk incense, rusted emptiness, old-
ness or decaying purity . . . nothing was accurate; it
was indescribable.

Yet this alien odor became my overwhelming reality, for my other senses were dulled or absent,
with nothing to feel, hear, or see. I could not even
feel the bottle in my left hand, the stopper in my
right. For this reason the inexplicable darkness did
not immediately strike me as the product of the ink
pot. I had virtually forgotten the little bottle until I

had exhausted every other unlikely possibility to explain my predicament. When all reasoning proved to me the unreasonableness of what I was experiencing, when it became clear that there was no *possible* explanation, I began to consider the impossible. And I recollected the bottle I had uncapped.

Only by great concentration could I detect that I did indeed grip something in each hand. How difficult it was to put the parts together again! With the senses dulled, the simplest act can become a complicated puzzle. Yet I brought the stopper to the bottle. The alien odor faded into the familiar scents of my kitchen. Sight and sound returned. I stood with gaping mouth and wide eyes, glaring at the innocuous bottle in my grasp.

Rather than relief at my safe return from blackness, I felt as though reality were an intrusion. I had a muted sense of puzzled happiness over the simple fact that Wonder, after a lifetime of searching, had at long last entered into my life.

I had been unable to sleep before my odd adventure, but now I was extremely weary. Sleep is a kind of escape from incomprehensible situations. Dreams help us cope with strange emotions or events. I was not about to fight against the healing or the resolutions sleep can offer. I set the bottle aside and returned to my bed, knowing I would sleep well.

The gentle weariness may not have been a means of escape, however. Rather, for the first time in long years, I felt a peaceful satisfaction, a sure knowledge that there is more to this existence than can ever be reduced to the ordinariness of science. I liked better the idea of living in a mysterious universe wherein the outcome of our individual existences is no longer as logical, as consistent, or as irrevocable as our last breath.

Over breakfast tea I glared at the tiny bottle beside my teacup saucer. How wonderful, yet how strangely disconcerting was that object! It scared me, but how could I ignore my life's ambition: my desire for a remarkable encounter with the unknown?

That day, I pottered around the city, trying to forget the bottle. I investigated dusty corners of used-book stores, my regular haunts, forgetting curiosity shops and bargains found therein, thinking instead of moldering grimoires purchased for a dollar, with recipes for spells to bring knowledge or wealth or power or doom—some volume, perhaps, from the private library of that inveterate collector of occult books, Sophia Hawthorne. Ah! I was too far along in life, too set in my ways, to replace one foolish fancy with another. Mine had never been a quest for the magical book, but for the magical object. Now that my old dream was in the midst of its fulfillment, I could not turn my back upon it to seek grimoires instead.

Late in the afternoon, I returned home to the little bottle of darkness.

No reasoning woman, nor a fanciful one for that matter, puts herself willingly in peril. I had thought through the previous evening's adventure and decided that for all the peculiarity of the event, and from all that I could judge, I had been quite safe, for I returned from that Otherplace without extraordinary effort and in no great harm.

I felt I would be more prepared a second time. Nothing would take me quite so much by surprise. I wouldn't be thrown off guard for lack of sight, sound, touch . . . nor would I risk dizziness in the void, for I first sat myself upon the bench in my breakfast nook.

When the stopper came out, once more I was cast in darkness. I felt as though I were squatting in the air and, furthermore, could not touch the breakfast nook's table, though a moment before, my elbow had rested on it. I tried not to move at all, realizing my lack of touch was more acute than on the previous night. The table *must* still have been there, and the bench as well, or I would certainly have fallen from my crouch.

Again, as before, I could not hear, but this time, neither could I smell. Rather, and unexpectedly, I could only *taste*. One takes the sense of taste so for granted that it is a shock to be confronted with the fact that our usual environment has a specific *flavor*. When that flavor suddenly alters, it is as though a toxic gas were drifting into one's throat! I was gagging at the acuteness of the darkness's flavor, but quickly calmed my emotions, convincing myself that the air I breathed daily was probably more polluted than the strange atmosphere that presently invaded my mouth and lungs. Indeed, it occurred to me that it was *purity* that was most alien, that never before had I experienced the flavor of the world, or of the universe, untainted by careless, destructive human actions.

My nose was absolutely useless so I stuck my tongue out to test the air more carefully. Surely I looked the idiot, but it was not possible to see or be seen, so why care? The air tasted of . . . oh, how can one say? I was about to say "persimmon." The fact is, the senses of smell and taste are so bound into one another that perfectly familiar objects become indistinguishable if tasted without the nose aiding in the recognition.

I worked the puzzle, so to speak, and got the stopper back into the bottle. I found myself in the familiar breakfast nook, no worse for wear. Prepared though I thought I had been, the episode had unnerved me. I was still working my tongue around in my mouth, striving to categorize the lost flavor of *different* air, of wholesome, musky dryness.

I went into the living room with the bottle and, pulling out a volume of short stories entitled *One of Cleopatra's Nights*, put the bottle at the back of the shelf, and replaced the volume. I tried not to think about that bottle for a few days.

It wasn't fear that I was feeling, though perhaps I was more frightened than I realized. I felt fascination rather than revulsion. Even so, I had to let it lie, let the thing that was happening to me settle into a more philosophical, if never a totally reasoning, comprehension.

"Out of sight, out of mind" as the cliché-mongers say, and I pretty much forgot about the bottle for some while. I had a busy couple of weeks, but that hardly explains my not dwelling on the bottle's existence. The truth is, the psychology of the mind is unfathomable, for which reason all psychiatrists are either mystics or quacks. I was not ready to cope with the phenomenon of the bottle, so I simply did not think of it. But a couple of weeks passed and one evening I took down a volume of ghostly tales by Gautier, thinking I would reread "The Mummy's Foot" and reacquaint myself with the delightful Egyptian princess of the tale, but was distracted from my intention when I saw that by removing the book from its place, I had exposed the presence of the little black bottle.

I cozied myself into a tattered, stuffed chair and took a deep breath of readiness. For long moments I cupped the bottle in my hands and stared into my lap. The sudden darkness on unstopping the bottle was hardly a surprise by now, though no less uncanny.

Again there was absolute silence, but neither could I taste or smell the atmosphere on this occasion. My hands and fingers were exceedingly aware of the bottle and stopper they were holding. The chair had been comfortable before, but now felt as unyielding as concrete.

I tucked the stopper underneath the bottle in my left hand so that I would have one hand free to reach outward. Carefully I stood, the press of coldly solid flooring seeming exaggerated through my shoes, as though I walked on a huge slab of stone.

I felt the touch of ghastly tiny insects crawling over my instep, then realized it was gritty earth. An exceedingly light wind delicately touched my face, bringing neither scent nor sound.

My right hand felt along a rough stone wall. I made my way through darkness. I imagined the layout of my apartment and tried to find my way through some place of the imagination with familiar rooms. But it was soon clear to me that I was in a labyrinth and no bend was familiar, no room was one of mine. This realization filled me with an unexpected dread. Again, I had thought I was prepared, yet I hadn't until that moment considered the possibility of getting lost in the bottle's night.

On the previous occasions I had barely moved from a single spot. This time I had wandered where my sense of touch had led me, only to discover that the place was a maze.

My moment of terror was telling me to restore the stopper to the bottle as quickly as possible and hope for the best. But the awesomeness of my situation overwhelmed even my terror. Something had distracted me and I realized this distraction was nothing more tangible than my fingers touching Wonder.

The hand that caressed the wall communicated fantastic imagery to my consciousness. It was not merely a rough surface; the wall was covered with engraved designs. I wanted desperately to set the bottle down and use both hands to solve the patterns. I dared not, for in such pitch night I might not find the bottle again. Someone born blind, and whose tactile sense was well honed, might instantly have understood the wall's carvings, but these things do not come naturally. My brain agonized over the problem, deep in painful concentration.

I thought one design might be a serpent, but again it might have been a gnarled stick or a wavy sword. Another shape my fingers traced suggested a war helmet or an eagle's face.

Still fretting that I may have lost myself far from the sanctuary of my living room, I decided at last to stopper the bottle, thereby discovering I had ventured no distance at all. My comfortable if somewhat lumpy easy chair was so close behind me, I nearly touched it with my calves. Evidently, I could wander all I wanted within the Egyptian night and always return to the original area of prosaic reality.

I was awakened early the next morning. A woman I've known since childhood called to inform me that a mutual friend was in the hospital.

"Her lungs?" I asked, for Virginia had been a pathetically addicted smoker and couldn't give it up even when diagnosed with emphysema.

"Yes," Helen answered. "Her lungs."

Helen picked me up in her Datsun and we drove out to a suburban hospital. The halls stank of chemistry and rubber. I hated to imagine dying in such stench and flavor. Virginia lay in a dismally white room with white curtains, her bed and respirator by a window overlooking whitewashed auxiliary buildings.

Physicians are, ultimately, high priests and mercenaries of death, nothing more. The whiteness of their cathedrals struck me as a shocking contrast to the womblike comfort of my small home in the city. Such whiteness was all the more shocking as my mind tried to withdraw into the protecting memory of my magic inkpot's darkness.

Virginia couldn't speak. She managed a few illucid phrases between gasps behind her respirator mask. It was evident that she was unable to tell Helen and I apart, whether because of medication or deterioration of her mind, I would never know.

She had been the strongest among us, physically and emotionally—six feet in height and a constant jester. In many ways she was the most beautiful and heroic woman I had ever known. As I gazed at her lying there helplessly, it seemed as though there wasn't enough left of her to say good-bye to.

Helen and I left in shared despondency. She took me to a Thai restaurant in the nearby village. We pushed noodles around with chopsticks and eventually ate some of them. We spoke of spirited adventures we had had as a threesome over the years. Our adventures became fewer as we grew older and more staid, yet the accumulation of derring-do was impressive viewed in retrospect. We even managed moments of rowdy laughter that late afternoon, commingled with our glistening tears.

Then Helen fell to gloomy seriousness. Her elbow was on the table and she placed her forehead on her palm. She said, "It's over so soon, isn't it?"

"What, Helen?" I didn't *want* to know what she meant, though of course I knew.

"It just ends. Why do you think that is?"

Helen made herself sit tall, forced herself to buck up and smile.

"That nasty old patriarch, Time," she said, "gets all of us eventually. Yet I always thought the three of us had a few good years left. She was handsome in her day! Weren't they good times?"

Actually, life for each of us had been marked by pain, struggle, and failure. Those times Helen had in mind, when she and I were rivals for a young Virginia's attention, were days of naïve and powerful emotion, especially as regarded that sweet, slim giantess in our closed and closely knit community—the giantess who now lay dying.

Helen and I had known each other since grade school. We grew to be prissy young women, girlishly coy and passive, and each quite certain the *other* was the one who was a bit, well, peculiar, but forgiving it. Then we met Virginia, who wasn't prissy at all, nor coy, nor passive. For a while Helen and I were worst enemies as a result, but we got over jealousies soon enough. The next few years after our awakening were fiercely romantic and discouragingly foolish.

"Once I thought Virginia was immortal," said Helen. "A goddess shouldn't die. Where does everything go?"

I couldn't answer. I wished I couldn't even think about it.

Then she laughed in offhanded impishness and asked, "Why were you and I not lovers?"

"Too much like sisters," I said, a ritual reply after all these years. I was drawn into Helen's memories, the days when Virginia was new to both of us. They were days of frightening conservatism in a world where being lesbian meant you risked not only loss of employment and social standing, but might actually be imprisoned in a mental institution and tortured by physicians. The current generation has no idea what it was like to have someone in one's private sphere suddenly vanish, only to return a year later with dulled senses and a lobotomy, performed on women (especially any who expressed "irrational" outrage when confronted by indignities and monstrous injustices) incarcerated in the Western State Hospital after a diagnosis of incurable sexual deviance.

Our only outlet, the center of our demeaned community, was a dark, spare tavern that called itself a ballroom. The jukebox alternated between big-band hits and early rock and roll. Those of us who were the "femmes" sat in a row of folding chairs up against a wall. Helen and I would sit with our legs crossed, waiting, hoping, watching the "butch" group who wore pants, cut their hair short or slicked it back, and leaned on the bar ogling those of us in chairs.

The butches of the day were riotously funny parodies of teenage boys, but we never laughed about it. We found it sexy for all the demented silliness of role playing. It was a painful, heart-racing reality and at the time we could imagine no other way to express ourselves.

"Remember that old ballroom, Lady Whisker, way back when?" asked Helen, still with her sad, sly smile.

"I was just thinking of it," I confessed.

"It was a terrible place, wasn't it? It's where we first met Virginia. And when I discovered she wore men's Fruit of the Looms, I laughed and laughed! But she was so exciting. We were so young, so unknowing. How things change."

"Some things change for the better," I said.

"Except we get old. We disappear. And new generations start again from square one. Sometimes from farther back than square one."

I pondered the changes the three of us had witnessed. I think it was during the "flower child" era, when bisexuality was the inspirational reality of young women growing up immediately behind Helen and I. Those daring, pretty girls in long country dresses and sandals, storming into Lady Whisker all flutters and giggles! They asked femmes to dance, bold as could be, though as near as we could judge, they were themselves femmes and ought to sit properly and wait to be asked. Stranger still, they asked butches to dance! They walked right up to those tough, handsome girls standing at the bar, totally oblivious of protocol. Some of the butches were offended. Most were titillated. And none of us were the same after those gently rebellious years.

Women like Virginia, who could never quite get over *being* butch, became anachronisms and suffered, whereas Helen and I were probably liberated by those times, and more comfortable with life afterward.

"Memories," said Helen. "What are we but the sum of our memories? A pity it evaporates, with nothing left to show."

"Maybe there's something," I said. "If we'd had this discussion a couple of months ago, I might have nothing to add but my own morose disappointment in the way things seemingly have to be. But lately I think life might not end."

She laughed weakly and shook her head.

"Mark my words. There's more to this universe than meets the eye."

"If there is, is it something that makes the struggle worthwhile? Or is it only another dirty trick, followed by another, and another."

"We can't know that one way or another, before the end. Virginia will know the answer soon."

We talked on and on, passing through variously colored moods of jollity and sadness. Secretly, vague ideas had settled into my thinking during that meal, far too thinly formed to express to Helen clearly. Echoes of that question, "Is it something worthwhile?" resounded in my heart. And I kept answering myself, "I don't know. I don't know." But I felt as though I were on the brink of an answer.

That night, I stood by the bookshelf with the bottle in my hand. I unstopped it. This time, in the darkness, there was no sensation except . . . *sound.*

When Valentino as the Sheik first rode out of the Sahara and across the silent silver screen, what music echoed in the young, enraptured hearts of our grandmothers or great-grandmothers? I believe it was the music I heard in the universe of Egyptian darkness, the eternal music of the spheres the Ancients pondered and mistook for the pounding heart of God.

Suppose, if you will, that whatever foolishness Faith and Religion may become, the root of that Faith is a scent, a flavor, a thing touched, or a sound that is instantly recognizable as an aspect of Otherness and Elsewhere. It is a moment of nirvana that cannot be conveyed to another and cannot even be preserved within the self, for it is a wisdom at once ephemeral and unending.

The efforts of a sincere mystic to communicate such knowledge would sound no less idiotic than the love-pablum packaged for sale at thousand-dollar seminars held by gurus on whirlwind tours of the richer nations. We are unable to tell actuality from fraud where there exists no rational measuring stick. Therefore there can be no teachers and no priests except those which are within ourselves; and if there is nothing in us that can see into the darkness with our own power to dream, then *that* is the only reason we are not immortal.

I lay in my bed late in the night, remembering the sounds of darkness. Reduced to words, it sounds absurd, or it sounds like nothing very important. The sound of bells, cymbals, drums, wind, shifting sand, camels braying, the padding of dancing feet and the tinkle of silver anklets, the songs and laughter of women, the strings of their harps . . . all this and more than this. If recreated on the material plane it would amount to chaotic racket. But I cling to it in my memory as an exquisite peace, a quietude rich with melody.

Yet there was also the roar of wild beasts, the cries of ailing children, of torture, shattered glass, and fire. There was horror in the universe as well as peace, an amalgam of everything we've imagined to be Heaven and Hell, which are one and the same.

The song of the sparrow, and the last sad sigh of its short life, are recorded forever in that darkness, and both are music, and both are beautiful, and both are at once transient and eternal.

I slept the remainder of the night in a state of

restfulness unequalled in all my life before. A weight had been lifted from me. A fear that each of us carries in our hearts had been replaced by the splendid harmony of an eternal Egyptian night.

The answer I imagined myself to have found was *not* evidence that we survive. It was only that, by logic, we cannot know, whereas previously, science and logic had seemed to deny all greater possibilities. I had discovered *something else*. It made hope more than a feeble plea to a blind, unyielding cosmos. If I was Pandora, the bottle was Her box. Or, I had become Aladdin's genie. And if magic were real, if fairyland existed, then anything was possible.

The things we discover in our dreams, the answers we invent that heal emotions, are usually forgotten in the dawn. Yet we are wiser nonetheless, and for the moment, healed. I sat up, dawn peeping between my bedroom curtains. Though I had not slept very many hours, I was thoroughly refreshed.

I knew, from forgotten dreams, if not wholly by deduction, that my mystic bottle was nearly done with me, for I had already experienced scent and taste and touch and sound.

Next time, I should *see* the place of darkness.

Next time, I would be granted vision.

* * *

I wandered the city streets in the early afternoon, seeking especially those corners I have most loved through the years.

Near the Hebrew College, in a woods left more or less wild, there stood for many years, inside a stone niche on a hill's face, a huge table made of three enormous slabs of stone. The largest slab, which previously rested atop two broad legs, had in recent years been broken in half by vandals; it now lay outside the niche in two fragments, adding to the impression of this being an ancient ruin rather than a site of prayer only two or three decades in disuse.

The site was grown over with vines and shadowed by the last old-growth timber in the city. There was an auxiliary parking lot nearby belonging to the college, but even this was so long out of use that roots, scrub maples, and tall grass lifted the concrete and poked upward through the cracks.

From the vantage point provided by this place, it was easy to envision the wilderness reclaiming the whole of the city, once people were deservedly extinct.

No echo of city life reached this solitary place where insects chirruped and birds sang and a small silver lizard eyed me quizzically before darting into a crack at the rear of the rocky niche. I've no idea when the niche was created, by means of mortared stones, or what its varied uses through the years must have been. It has remained virtually unknown as a landmark, and has therefore escaped graffiti and, until relatively recently, evaded vandals as well. It couldn't be older than the college itself, which was built at the beginning of the twentieth century. But in my emotions, it was thousands of years old.

I felt like the ghost of a Druid priestess who, in accordance with ancient customs, stood ready with her dagger, to sacrifice the king supine on the altar.

I was caught between sensations of having passed far back in time to a world primitive and verdant, or eons forward where the horrors of civilization were blessedly devoured by age. I sat upon one of the broken halves of the tabletop, meditating and listening to the birds, and watching for the lizard to peer forth once more, although it never did.

After a while I stood and went along the narrow brick-paved road that led soon to newer, concrete streets. Shortly I was back in a residential neighborhood. I strolled through alleyways admiring the decaying garage doors, weedy patches of neglected lawns, and crumbling back gates. From the main streets the houses all looked well-to-do, but from the alleys there was an illuminating disintegration.

What has fascinated me all my life about the heart of this city is the manner by which one can stroll from a finite little area of wilds, to a district crowded with the large houses for the wealthy, to smaller houses and the horrible low-rises of the poor, and ultimately to the hectic business streets which were themselves mere preludes to down-town office towers. I only rarely went downtown per se, for everything that one requires is here in the neighborhoods of The Hill. The closeness of everything, the variety, the peculiar and unwhole-some *beauty* of the city had kept me here all my adult life, more or less glad of it, or at least happier than I could have been elsewhere.

The drawbacks of the city include its youth ori-entation, making it less *my* home as I grow older, and the increasing dangers of the street; and, the worst thing of all, as one's perspective grows longer, the rapid changes one looks back on with regret; the losses that accumulate yearly. . . .

As though it were not enough to have destroyed wildernesses and replaced them with all manner of architecture and roads, even that artificial environ-ment must be destroyed as a matter of course, blithely replaced by things that are larger and de-creasingly pleasant. The city environment was for-ever changing—not so much due to a dynamic nature as to an imbecilic humanity's losing battle against chaos, a battle that is itself chaotic.

I had arrived at a feeling of living in a phantas-mic world of shifting castles made of sand, all its inhabitants prematurely buried in order to make room for others.

The unbearable failures of our lives are reflected in these ineffectual renewals and replacements of things that were themselves mere echoes of a greater, graver, and unrecoverable past. Refinement is illusion, a prelude to vulgarity, as life merely preludes our oblivion.

Everything I ever loved was here in these city streets, but the underbelly had been revealed to me, and I was stricken with sadness.

I trod the streets for hours, inspecting shops and little parks and odd corners here and there. I hardly marked the time until it had grown dark. I wound my way home again, filled with the sense of having said good-bye to more than one friend who, though breathing and alive, had long ago died away from me. It was only healthy that I let go.

When I returned home, there was a message from Helen on the answering machine. Virginia had died two hours before. I lifted the receiver to call Helen, but could not follow through. I no longer loved the world, and did not regret Virginia's absence from it. Rather, I regretted my own presence, and Helen would not understand such sentiment as anything but rage or melancholy, though it was neither.

*　　*　　*

The curtains and blinds were closed against the night. The lights within the room were turned out. I sat in my overstuffed chair with four things in my lap: the bottle, a flashlight, and my own two hands. My breathing was deep and quivering.

I removed the stopper and was surprised to discover that on this occasion I could smell and hear. I felt that the overstuffed chair had turned to stone beneath me.

But I could not see.

Having thought it out beforehand, I was somewhat prepared for the darkness. This was to be the voyage of sight, but still within a place of blackest night.

I safely tucked the stopper in my palm underneath the bottle. Then I clicked on the flashlight. For long moments, the light revealed nothing to me, for there was only blackness all around. I shined the beam on the arm of my chair and saw that it was indeed carved of granite. If permanence were the thing missing from the world I'd known, and transience the thing that horrified, then it was only rational that here, in this other place, a stuffed chair might be transformed into harshly angled stone.

I stood. With no point of reference, even though my senses were intact, I felt disoriented. Then in my torch's beam I saw a looming stone wall. Upon the wall were bas-reliefs of Egyptian beasts, peoples, deities, and household objects, painted in muted ochre, brown, and gray.

I had been an armchair Egyptologist in my young years, but had forgotten so much that I could make only broad interpretations of the hieroglyphics. The images, and the stories they implied, were so weirdly but imprecisely familiar, I felt as though I were walking in fading portraits of my amateur studies, a place of dream and half-remembrance, and not a place with material existence.

I walked along a corridor that stretched, for all I could judge, into infinity, rapt with the images revealed by my torch.

Here, Hathor-Sekhet the Divine Light waded in the blood of humankind, thrashing her sword of fire until even the eternal pyramids were char and dust. She only stopped her wild onslaught when the hawk-winged solar disc of Ra brewed from the clouds such quantities of beer that for thirty days and nights Egypt lay beneath an ocean. Hathor-Sekhet drank all the seas and became so intoxicated that the last human souls were accidentally spared.

And here, the horned goddess Isis was creating a poisonous serpent from the slaverings of an aging and infirm Ra. The serpent slew the sun god. Isis restored him to life in exchange for godhead. She was thereafter the supreme being.

And here again, the Universe, personified as Nut, her skirts studded with stars, straddled the firmament, giving birth to deity upon deity. One of her daughters, Nephthys, goddess of Death, lamented over the remains of Osiris. Her grief resuscitated him to a semblance of life, while a sexual rite performed by Isis restored his mind.

The dominance of the feminine principle in these hieroglyphics gave me to believe I was in the tomb of an Egyptian queen.

So caught up was I interpreting the endless murals, I had failed to consider the limited life of my torch. At first I didn't notice it was dimming, my eyes having so adjusted to the lessening light. At length the tired batteries could not be overlooked, and I switched it off.

Curiously, I could still see, though only after a strange fashion. Mottled shapes formed and reformed before me, ghostly presences that at first I took to be phosphene or tricks of the brain. I turned on the flashlight anew, thinking to disperse illusion or to clarify actual objects, but the light was too dim to resolve the formless undulations surrounding me.

One drifting shape became more and more material, shining palely, then shining more clearly, until I was able to recognize the form of a young girl limping toward me from the black distance. Her thin arms were encircled by serpent bands and bracelets. Her hair was woven into long thin cords;

and coiled around her hair and forehead was a young cobra with upraised head.

Her full lips, wide nose, and burnished copper coloring revealed her as a Copt, and a singularly beautiful example of her race; indeed, she was all but perfect in her youthful, shocking beauty.

By her one imperfection—her broken stride—I knew her as Gautier's mummy princess, whose foot he had temporarily possessed. It had reattached itself imperfectly; but like an exquisite Japanese vase with a single, half-intended flaw, the princess's limp made her all the more inhumanly beautiful.

"You are the Princess Hermonthis," I said, as she stopped before me.

Her musical voice was that of a child's, but weighted with the wisdom of centuries of entombment. She said, "Only those who are apt to recognize me have ever found this path."

Her dainty hand reached forth and took from me the flashlight. She said, "Nothing of your world is allowed here." She held it with two fingers, far away from her side, as though it were a loathsome slimy animal, and dropped it. To my amazement, it did not clatter to the stone floor, but fell and fell and fell. I could see it oh-so-vaguely glinting as it whirled and whirled into the black depths beneath my feet.

"Come," said Princess Hermonthis, the gentlest of commands. "Others await thee."

I followed the Princess through sable darkness, through caverns the vastness of which was hinted by the hollow resonance of our passing footsteps. I followed her down and down treacherous, uneven stairways, deeper and deeper into the world, or the unworld. At one point I was forced to walk in an awkward crouch, the ceiling came so low, and elsewhere to move sideways through narrow confines.

Now and then I heard the rustle of wings, the whisper of sorrow, but always far away, as though it issued from an unseen world outside these walls. They were lost souls struggling weakly for ingress, pleading at the edge of my awareness. I strained to hear their petitions, as God must struggle to hear ours, but the more attentive I became, the more distant were the cries.

I heard instead a pleasant tinkling that by slow degrees grew more and more melodic and insinuating. My nostrils were assailed by the pleasant musk of Princess Hermonthis's perfume: resinous, sublime, and sweet. In my fist, grown pale from tightness, I felt the bottle, its stopper forming painful indentations in my palm, reminding me of the world I'd so recently quitted, and might still regain, if fear should send me fleeing.

Then I heard laughter, rough and bold. In the tunnel far ahead was a wan, green light. The

music of tiny cymbals and hand drums and silver-
stringed lutes was now unquestionably seducing
my senses. The Princess Hermonthis kept before
me, never once looking back, sure as she was
that I would not draw away. The back of her
head, the swaying braids of her hair, periodically
blocked my view of the green glow. Each time I
saw the light anew, it seemed no nearer. Yet it
was nearer, and by degrees I understood that the
light was all around me; that the Princess Hermonthis, and myself, were the source of this wan
gleaming.

We had gone down and down, it seemed to me,
for a very long time, for thousands of years for all I
could tell, down into what should have been the
very center of the womb of the world. Then we had
risen but briefly along a smooth gentle slope—
insufficient, it seemed to me, to have returned to
any surface. Yet what, here, was a great depth, or a
great height? For now the Princess stood beside a
yawning gate, where the smooth stone walkway
ended and finely sifted sand began. She turned to
face me with her placid, copper face revealing no
emotion. Beyond her, I could see an indigo sky that
had not one star in it, but only a marvelously fat
white moon, or perhaps it was the sun grown dim
at the edge of time.

I stood beside the princess in that entryway and

gazed out into a stark but lovely place. I saw sil-houetted against indigo six great pyramids, and knew that I was standing in the seventh. A caravan palely shining in the orb-light was winding its way between the dunes in my general direction.

"You must now choose," said the Princess Her-monthis, who held her small, perfect hand toward me.

Upon an albino camel at the head of the cara-van was a woman clad in the robes of a sheik, or perhaps a Levite, and I knew that young, heroic face.

"Is it the land of death, or of perpetuity?" I asked the girl at my side. She gave me the sibilant reply, "Yes," her palm still upraised. My own hand was shaking as I reached out to her, giving her the bot-tle and the stopper. I said, "Will you see that Helen receives this?" The dark eyes of the Princess flashed mystery, but no reply, before she turned away and returned to the deeper darkness of the pyramid. I knew I would not see her again, and lamented it. Nor would I ever see my comfortable urban apartment or any other place that had been known to me before this moment. I did not regret that.

A vitality rose from out of my heart that I had not known since youth, if ever I had known it. The amazon caravaneer caught sight of me, then threw back her head, laughing into the indigo sky. I ran swift and wild into that weird bright darkness filled with Virginia's mirthful greeting. My hair was Lilith's rising in a gale of laughter, and my lithe, young arms were open to the night.

ROADSIDE MEMORIALS

Joseph Nassise

A DRUNK DRIVER KILLED MY FRIENDS!

So read the sign now standing at the corner of Thunderbird and Main. It stood in almost the exact spot where Martin had pulled the bodies of two teenagers from the smashed wreckage of their yellow Nissan Xterra just two days before, shouting its message out to any and all who passed by. Around it was a haphazard collection of candles, flowers and photographs, laid out in commemoration of the lives that had ended so abruptly there.

"Freakin' morbid, that," his partner, Giles, said, but Martin barely noticed. He couldn't take his eyes off the memorial, stunned by the size of it. It had to be six feet square and the accident wasn't even forty-eight hours old yet. *Where the hell had all this stuff come from?* It was disturbing, uncanny even, how swiftly such memorials could appear. Back home in Philadelphia, he'd never heard of the practice, had never laid eyes on even one such marker, but here in the Southwest they were practically guaranteed to show up whenever there was a fatal accident. They sprang up overnight like ravenous weeds. He wasn't certain where the tradition had come from or what those who created the memorials hoped to achieve, he just knew that being around them made him uncomfortable. It didn't matter where the accident had taken place—back roads, city streets or the long stretches of road bisecting the desert—time and time again he would see them there, like soldiers standing solitary vigil in the darkness.

". . . don't see what good it does."

"What?" he asked, as the marker swept behind them in the distance and he belatedly realized his partner was still speaking.

Giles waved a hand toward the rear of the ambulance. "Those stupid memorials. Those folks are dead, right? What good do those things do them?" He snorted in disgust. "Besides, I'd rather have folks visiting me in the cemetery than in the middle of nowhere. Who wants to be reminded they'd died in the middle of a freakin' car wreck?"

Martin nodded, turning away from the window as the memorial slipped away behind them in the distance, but he wasn't really listening. It had been a long night; three car accidents, a knife fight, and two heart attacks, the most activity they'd had in one night in weeks. *And we aren't even halfway through our shift.* All he wanted to do was get back to the hospital and crash out for awhile before the next call came in.

At thirty-six, Martin Jones was already tired of his so-called life. He spent his days sleeping, his nights cleaning up the messes left behind by other people's mistakes. Gone was the idealism that had gotten him into the EMT business in the first place, washed away by too many stupid accidents, too many senseless beatings, and more than his fair share of horrible car wrecks. It didn't help that his days were other people's nights.

Tonight was worse than usual, however. He'd felt an odd sense of unease all evening and the weirdness surrounding that roadside shrine didn't help. It was almost as if he could sense something, something looming just beyond the horizon; at any moment he knew it was going to come charging in to swallow everything whole.

It wasn't a comfortable feeling.

As Giles droned on, Martin leaned back in his seat and wearily closed his eyes. Tonight's shift couldn't end fast enough as far as he was concerned.

*   *   *

The call came in around two a.m. A tractor trailer rig had jackknifed out on I-17, taking out three vehicles before colliding with a bridge embankment. Traffic was stopped in both directions for miles. Ambulances from three different hospitals had been called in, including their own.

Martin was behind the wheel for this trip. Switching back and forth halfway through their shift kept them both from going crazy with the redundancy of the job, and tonight he was glad for the change. He couldn't seem to get his mind off all the roadside memorials they passed, especially that large one he'd seen back at the beginning of their shift, and staring out the passenger window as they drove around all night wasn't helping. He'd never really paid much attention to the things before now, but tonight they haunted him. It was simply amazing how many of the damn things were out there. One hell of a lot of people where dying on these streets, that was for sure. At least driving would keep his attention focused on the road and not on those weird little shrines and the deaths they represented.

When they arrived at the crash site, they were updated on the casualty list. Eight dead, three wounded and a truck driver with nothing but a scratch. Martin had long since stopped being surprised at the vagaries of life. It was just the way things were. Still, he couldn't help but feel sorry for the lives that had ended so abruptly there. All those unrealized dreams.

Giles chatted up the female driver next to them while they all waited for the firefighters to cut the bodies loose from the wrecks and call them in. Judging from the condition of some of the vehicles, it was going to be awhile.

Three cups of coffee and two hours later, they were finished. Having been the last to arrive, they were the last to be loaded, and most of the crews at the scene had already left by the time they got the body stowed away in the back, ready for transport to the morgue.

As they pulled onto the main drag a repetitive thumping could be heard from the right rear side of the ambulance. When Giles got out to investigate, he found a six-inch piece of steel sticking out of the rear passenger tire. Cursing a blue streak, Giles prepared to change it while Martin went to tell the remaining officers they were going to be a few more minutes.

It shouldn't have been a big deal; after all, the guy in the back didn't have any place to be anytime soon. But something about the evening, something about the call, had Martin spooked. He found himself nervously drumming his fingers on the dashboard and gritting his teeth the way he did when he knew he'd screwed up. It was totally unlike him and that's what made him nervous. Something was wrong.

He could feel it, taste in the air.

That sense of impending doom.

He felt like he had a hundred pairs of eyes on him and several times he found himself searching the darkness around them, looking for persons unknown.

More than once he snarled at Giles to hurry up, only to receive blistering waves of swearing in return. Finally he couldn't take it any more. He jumped out of the truck, pushed his partner aside and finished tightening the bolts on the tire himself. He didn't know what was wrong; all he knew was that he wanted to be out of there as quickly as possible.

Unwilling to even take the extra time to properly stow the spare, Martin simply threw it in back next to the body. Climbing back into the driver's seat, he gunned the engine and pulled onto the road.

He made the mistake of looking back, however, as they left the scene.

Behind them, in the gray light of the early morning, he saw a figure dash out of the woods near the crash site, drop something on the spot where the tractor trailer had been, and then disappear back the way it had come.

Without understanding what he had just seen,

Martin knew that the strange figure had been the cause of his unease.

And suddenly he desperately wanted to understand.

Without another thought he slammed on the brakes.

Giles bounced off the dashboard as the ambulance skidded to a stop, not yet having had a chance to buckle in. "What the fuck?" he swore, but his question was left unanswered as Martin threw open the door and ran back toward the scene.

"Martin? What are you doing, Martin?" Giles called after him.

But Martin only had eyes for what was ahead. Even before he could see it clearly, he knew what it was.

A small white cross.

This one was of the Celtic variety, with the center point wrapped in a large circle. It was still swaying slightly from the force that had been used to plant it in the ground.

The sight of it sent the hairs on the back of his neck crawling.

The body hasn't even left the scene and someone is already erecting a marker on the spot?

What the hell is that all about?

He walked over and squatted beside it. It appeared to be fashioned of a couple of thin, wooden slats, like the kind that made up packing crates.

The circle appeared to have been cut from similar material. The whole thing was painted white and from the looks of it, it had probably been done with a cheap can of spray paint.

In other words, it was perfectly normal looking.

So why did it creep him out so much?

He didn't know.

He reached out a hand to touch it, but stopped short of doing so.

Very slowly, he stood up and backed away from the cross, in the same manner one would move away from a suddenly snarling dog.

When he was several feet away, he turned and jogged back to the truck, feeling like he'd just narrowly escaped a danger he didn't understand.

Behind him, the eyes of the living and the dead watched him leave.

Martin couldn't get the events of the previous night out of his thoughts, so he called in sick, determined to get to the bottom of what he'd seen. He'd made arrangements to borrow his brother's black Trans Am and the car was waiting for him in the driveway a little after nine. Like the car, he, too, was dressed in black, hoping the dark clothing would help him blend in better and avoid being seen.

He spent an hour hanging around in the local Safeway parking lot, listening to the battery-operated police scanner he'd bought earlier that afternoon, and then he got lucky. A two-car accident on highway 60. An elderly lady had lost control and smashed into another vehicle driven by a young woman. The girl was in critical condition and was being removed from the wreckage; the older woman was already dead.

That was all Martin needed.to hear. The Trans Am's tires smoked as he peeled out of the parking lot and raced for the scene.

Traffic was stopped a quarter mile from the wreck, a police officer rerouting traffic to the nearest off-ramp. Martin pulled over to the side of the road, parked the car in the breakdown lane and approached the officer on foot. He flashed his identification, saying he'd been called in to fill the right-hand seat on an ambulance that had gone out with only the driver, and managed to scam his way through.

As he neared the crash scene, he slowed and looked around. Several emergency vehicles were parked nearby, but no one seemed to be looking at him. When he was sure he wouldn't be seen, he jogged up the embankment and pushed his way into the scrub brush lining the noise barrier at the top. Once out of site, he continued moving until he was immediately above the scene itself.

From here, he could keep watch on everything going on.

And he could get a better look at the mysterious crossbearers.

If they show up.

Scratch that. When they show up.

They'll be here.

Martin settled in for a long wait.

From his position on the hill, he watched the ambulance load up the injured girl and the older woman's body and then drive off just shy of an hour later. The tow trucks and the police were there for another half hour and then they, too, left. Seeing their blue flashers fade into the distance, Martin moved into a crouch, ready to make his way down the hill to confront anyone who arrived.

It was good that he did. Only a few moments passed before a figure scuttled out of the ditch slightly farther down the road, near the spot where the elderly woman had died.

Martin burst out of the shrubs and charged down the hill, intent on catching whoever it was and discovering just what was going on.

He closed the distance swiftly and the other didn't hear him coming. As he drew closer he could see that the figure was clothed in dirty robes and in its hand it held a white cross, like the one he'd seen at the accident site last night. As it raised the cross over its head, preparing to sink it into the earth, Martin snatched it out of its hands.

"What the hell are you doing?" he cried.

The other whirled around and Martin had his first good look.

What he saw sent his heart stuttering in his chest.

The thing had no face.

Only the slightest sense of features existed, as if it were an unfinished canvas given life before its time. Its eyes were shadowed indentations beside the nub of a nose, and where its mouth should have been was only a flat expanse of gray flesh.

"Holy shit!" Martin yelped, stepping back. He couldn't believe what he was seeing.

The creature rose to its full height, an odd tittering sound emanating from it. Martin had the disturbing notion that the thing was laughing at him and maybe it was. But where was the laughter coming from if the thing had no mouth?

Beyond a doubt, Martin knew he'd made a mistake.

Some things were best left alone.

This, *this thing*, was certainly one of them.

He had no idea what he had stumbled into, but he knew it was time he got the hell out of there. He turned to run and found a second, similar creature standing a few feet behind him, blocking his escape back up the hill.

Martin hadn't even heard it approach.

From the darkness around it, several more of the creatures suddenly appeared.

Martin stumbled away from them, out into the road, his hands held out defensively before him, praying they wouldn't follow.

A weird, haunting cry rose on the wind and the leader took a step toward him, causing Martin to back up even farther.

That was when the delivery van roared around the corner, silhouetting Martin in its headlights where he stood by the side of the road. The driver slammed on the brakes, but it was too late. His rearview mirror clipped Martin on the shoulder and tossed him aside like a rag doll.

Martin never took his eyes off the creatures watching him. Their odd, featureless faces were the last things he saw as he slammed against the ground and the darkness closed in around him.

He woke up in a hospital bed, a swath of bandages wrapped around his skull. His doctor told him it was only a minor concussion, but he'd have to stay a few days while they made certain there was no internal damage. Martin had no recollection of the events leading up to the accident and the doctor said it was unlikely he would ever recover more than bits and pieces of those few hours, but if that was the worst of it, Martin felt he couldn't complain.

Late in the afternoon of the third day they discharged him with a prescription for some codeine and orders to get more rest before trying anything strenuous. His boss gave him the week off without argument and he spent it lying around the house, recuperating.

The ride into the office went without incident and it wasn't long before he was down in the locker room, joking around with the other EMTs. Giles insisted on driving for the night, something Martin didn't blame him for, and the two of them settled back into their easy routine.

Their first call came in fairly quickly: an elderly man over at the Northside Rest Home had breathed his last. Martin and Giles were dispatched to pick him up and bring him in.

Northside was on the other side of town, but since they weren't in any hurry Giles took the scenic route. He wound his way through the city streets, taking as many of the back roads as he could to avoid the traffic that had fled the construction on the expressway.

Martin glanced out the window and froze as they drove by the scene of an accident they had worked the month before.

A white memorial cross now stood on the spot, draped with ribbons and flowers.

The sight of it terrified him.

The light turned green and Giles drove off, but Martin couldn't rid himself of the haunting image of that cross and the unexplained fear it stirred within him. As they passed others, his fear, unease and disgust only seemed to grow. By the time they reached the nursing home, Martin was all but useless, cowering in the corner by the door, refusing to look anywhere but at the floorboards beneath his feet. He would not get out of the truck and so Giles was forced to handle the call on his own.

On the ride back to the hospital, Martin chose to sit in the back with the corpse, preferring the company of the dead to having to lay eyes on another of those crosses.

When they returned to base, Martin excused himself, apologized to Giles and his supervisor, and went home sick for the rest of the evening.

Martin spent the next day turning the events of the previous evening over and over again in his mind. He'd seen such roadside shrines more times than he could count. They'd never bothered him before.

What had changed?

He didn't know.

What he did know was that the crosses unnerved him. They frightened him. He sensed instinctively that they were dangerous, but wasn't able to put just why into words. All he knew was that they shouldn't, *couldn't*, remain.

Despite his fear, he felt driven to get rid of them.

Called to, even.

Doing so proved much harder than he expected, however, when he tried to do just that later that night. The crosses were sunk deep into the ground—so deep that it was impossible to pull them loose no matter how hard he tried. He was forced to resort to cutting them off at the base, but even this wasn't easy. The wood seemed to have been treated with some kid of special chemical. An ordinary saw wouldn't even dent them and the hacksaw he resorted to using went through blades like they were butter. The need to do it all at night, when there was less a chance of getting caught, did not make things any simpler. Yet he persevered. Martin was on the road almost constantly once the sun went down, roaming the city streets, tearing down as many of the makeshift shrines as he could find, scattering far and wide the objects visitors had left behind.

He had no idea if destroying the memorials was actually doing any good, but the physical action made him feel like he was doing something, *anything*, and so he kept it up as long as he could each night, only stumbling home after the sun had risen in the east and the danger of being seen became too great.

The nights began to blur together as Martin pushed himself to the limit.

He was at the Mobil station at the corner of Thunderbird and Main early one morning, only feet away from the makeshift memorial that had started it all, when he finally cracked beneath the strain. He had finished filling his tank and was turning to replace the gas hose into the pump when he caught sight of a young girl adding a wreath made of photographs and flowers to the memorial on the corner.

Exhausted, dismayed, appalled at the seemingly endless array of these roadside shrines, Martin couldn't take seeing another person build them up any higher. He dropped the hose, ignored the splash of gasoline across his sandaled feet, and rushed the young woman, screaming at her to stop what she was doing. Snatching up a wooden sign that made up part of the memorial, he brought it cracking down across the woman's skull when she turned to see what the commotion was about.

By the time the police were able to tear him away from the victim ten minutes later, it was hard to tell just what she had once looked like. Blood ran thick in the gutter, coating her long blond hair and the face of the nearest of the flower wreaths like some kind of organic spray paint.

Martin had begun screaming in tandem with the trapped souls standing in the midst of the memorial behind him when he'd begun striking the woman, and did not stop until the responding officers shocked him into unconsciousness with their Tasers.

* * *

"All rise. The Honorable Judge Prentiss Wilson presiding," cried the bailiff, as the judge returned to the room.

Martin dutifully rose to his feet beside his attorney, but he was barely aware of the proceedings. His trial had been swift, the jury's decision even swifter. Five weeks after the incident and here he was waiting to be sentenced. The public had wanted swift justice for the brutal and unprovoked attack and the district attorney had given it to them on a silver platter. Truth be told, Martin didn't care what happened to him any longer. He just wanted it to be over with so that he could go back to his bunk and curl up again, safe from those faceless thieves that had haunted his every waking minute since the accident. He'd been running ever since that night and he hadn't stopped until they'd locked him up inside.

The judge had been speaking for more than ten minutes when Martin's public defender nudged him in the side, telling him to pay attention. The judge was going to deliver the sentence.

"Mr. Jones, based on the testimony at your trial, it would appear that your behavior has been uncontrolled for quite a while. You've been physically violent, eccentrically erratic at best. Your attorney may have requested leniency due to the fact that this is your first such offense, but if I were to release you back into the public in your present condition, I'm afraid I would be remiss in my duty to the people. Never mind to that young lady still languishing in critical condition. Based on the findings of this court, I sentence you to five years' confinement.

"For the time being, I'm remanding you into the custody of Mount Holy Oak Hospital for a thirty-day psychological evaluation, the results of which will determine where you will spend your sentence.

"Questions?"

Neither side had any, so with a crack of his gavel the judge rendered his sentence. Martin barely noticed. He'd drifted past the point of caring these last few weeks, knowing as he did what lay beyond these cement and steel walls. All of those crosses gleaming in the darkness . . . it had become too much for him to think about. At least inside the walls of the courthouse and its adjacent jail facility, he did not have to see them standing there, mocking his impotence.

No, as far as he was concerned, they could keep him locked up forever.

They put him in irons with the other prisoners for the walk out to the transport vehicle. Hands chained to the waist, feet chained together, prisoner after prisoner chained to each other. He shuffled along with the rest. At the door to the bus they checked his ID once again, matching his photo to his face, and then they were loaded up, the guards pushing them gently into seats in every other row, the shorter length of chain that had tied them to one another now used to secure them to a large ring in the floor of the bus in front of each seat.

The windows were covered with a thick steel mesh and a guard rode on either side in the front seat, their shotguns out and ready. The driver, too, was armed; Martin could see the butt of his pistol from where he sat a few rows away. Martin was relieved; he'd been dreading the move from the jail to the hospital facility. Fifteen, maybe twenty minutes and he'd be safely inside the hospital walls with enough dopamine coursing through his veins to get him to forget he'd ever seen such things.

As the bus pulled away from the curb and merged with the traffic around it, Martin, his head down, kept his gaze focused on the floorboards in between his feet, determined not to see another of those damned crosses if he could help it. So earnest was his concentration that he wasn't aware there was a problem until the guard a few seats ahead of him began cursing and shouting out the window.

"Hey, asshole! Get the fuck away from us. This is a government vehicle."

Martin looked up. The sun had set. They were out in the middle of the desert, halfway to their destination, nothing to be seen in the harsh glow of the street lamps ahead of them but four lanes of blacktop and an occasional cactus that dotted the dirty landscape around them. Martin followed the guard's gaze to the left and turned just in time to see a black El Camino come swerving back across three lanes of traffic to hang directly off the driver's side of the bus. The car's passenger side window was open. Martin watched as a long, dark muzzle appeared from within its depths. Before he could shout a warning, the gunman fired.

Three quick shots, one immediately after another.

The bus driver's skull exploded, showering the windshield with a smattering of blood, brains and gore.

The El Camino swerved in one direction.

The transport bus went in the other.

One moment they were traveling sedately down the road, the next the driver was dead, the guards were bouncing around the front seats, a shotgun went off, accidentally or otherwise, and by then the bus had left the blacktop. It jolted over an irrigation ditch, careened off a large outcropping of rock, and soared off the edge of a deep canyon before smashing roof down into the desert floor some hundred feet below.

* * *

When Martin opened his eyes the first time, he had a moment to glimpse the crumpled wreckage of the bus around him and then a wave of pain washed over him, pain so intense that it stripped him of his ability to breathe, to see, and he was quickly drowned in its wake.

When he regained consciousness a second time, he pain was less intense, enough so that he could move slightly without blacking out. At first he was disoriented, confused, uncertain of where he was or how he had gotten there. But as the minutes passed he began to remember: the trial, the prison bus, the shotgun blast, everything.

The moon was high in the sky and nearly full. By its silvery light he could see that he was trapped in a narrow opening formed when the roof of the bus had collapsed down upon the seats around him. The tightness at his midsection let him know that he was still chained to the floor beneath him by his restraints.

He was resting in a pool of something sticky and viscous; it sucked at his skin as he braced himself up on his right arm and pulled his face away from the floor. His thoughts were slow, jumbled, as if he was seeing everything from behind a veil of thick fog, and it took him several moments to realize that his left arm was hanging limply at his side.

He could barely feel the pain emanating from his dislocated shoulder.

It took him even longer to realize that he couldn't feel his legs at all, but he wasn't able move his head enough to see them beneath all of the wreckage.

He wasn't going anywhere.

His heart sank at the realization.

A sound caught his attention.

It was a familiar sound, yet one he couldn't place.

A rhythmic thumping, like sheets snapping in the wind.

The sound grew louder, closer.

Something's coming.

The sound nagged at him, teasing him with its identity.

He turned his head to the left, so that he was looking out the window of the bus to the desert landscape beyond, searching for the source. The floor of the arroyo in which they had landed was dotted with outcroppings of rock and the occasional piece of wreckage from the accident.

Martin barely had eyes for the landscape, however.

He was too busy staring at the seven white crosses arrayed in a semi-circle just a few feet away from where he was trapped, their shadows stretching across the desert sand behind them in the stark moonlight.

One cross for each of the other men that had been traveling in the bus with him.

Martin's scream was drowned out as the thumping sound grew near, louder.

Abruptly, silence descended.

The night seemed to hold its breath.

Out of the shadows behind the crosses a lone figure emerged.

Darkness seemed to cling to the newcomer, hugging him, like a large cloak draped about his form, preventing Martin from getting a good look. All he could tell was that it was a man.

For a moment Martin even wondered if the figure was simply a figment of his imagination, a phantom brought on by the shock and blood loss he knew he must be experiencing, but then the figure began to walk toward him. As he did, the shadows surrounding him slowly dripped away, pooling at his feet.

Now Martin could see the newcomer more clearly. The stranger was tall, somewhere over six feet, and dressed in a pair of dark jeans and a matching shirt. Despite the summer heat he wore a long trenchcoat over his clothing. Perhaps it was the sound of the trenchcoat flapping behind him that he had heard, Martin thought. Maybe he would be getting out of this after all.

Then the shadows at the feet of the stranger re-formed into man-sized shapes dressed in loosely flowing robes and wearing featureless faces.

The dam inside Martin's mind burst and the memories flowed like sudden rain.

Any hope of rescue swiftly fled.

The stranger spoke. "My, my, my. What a predicament you've gotten yourself into, Martin. Stuck like a rabbit in a hole. What a damn shame, that." The man's voice oozed with sarcasm and the threat of violence. Behind him, the creatures tittered and swayed, predators waiting to rush their prey.

Martin couldn't speak. His lips trembled, his mouth gaped, but no sound came out. The fear he felt at the others' presence had swept the fog away from his mind, however. His heart beat faster, harder. The blood around his body flowed anew.

"What's the matter?" the stranger asked. "Cat got your tongue? You had to know we would be coming for you, didn't you?"

At last, Martin found his voice.

"Who are you? What do you want?"

The stranger cocked his head to one side. "Who am I? What do I want?" he mimicked. "I'm surprised you haven't figured it out yet. What is the line from that stupid book? 'His tail swept a third of the stars out of the sky and flung them to the earth'? The stranger grinned—a horrible, leering grin that split the night like the rasp of a chainsaw. "I'm nothing more than a fallen star, you stupid monkey. But unfortunate for you, even fallen stars need to feed. And I'm tired of you messing with my dinner."

He snapped his fingers and the creatures rushed forward, charging into the confined space around him. His flesh burned where they touched him and he thought for certain he was finished, but seconds later he found himself dragged free of the wreckage and dumped to the ground in front of the stranger, his chains now severed and loose.

Before he could do more than gather his wits, his arms and legs were quickly seized by several more of the things, holding him down. Another held his head in a viselike grip, preventing him from turning away.

The stranger stepped closer, scooping up a handful of dirt as he did so. He spat into his hands, mixed the saliva in with the dirt, and then smeared the mixture over Martin's eyes.

Cold.

Intense, burning cold, the likes of which he'd never experienced.

Martin clawed at his eyes, wiping the muck off of his skin, relieving the pain.

The sight that met his eyes when he opened them again forced another ragged scream from his already weary vocal cords.

The crosses were gone. In their place were seven wraithlike forms, writhing in pain. Though hazy and indistinct, they were still recognizable as the men who had occupied the bus with him. Their lower bodies were encased in a cobwebby substance that pulsed and glowed with an eerie greenish purple cast and kept them rooted where they stood. Within its depths, Martin could see hundreds of tiny mouths opening and closing. Each time they did, the wraiths would scream in pain.

Horrified, Martin tore his gaze away from the dead, only to find himself looking at the stranger again. The man's shirt was now hanging open. Across the gray skin of his chest were hundreds of similar mouths, opening and closing in unison with the others. The stranger's head was thrown back in pleasure and his eyes shone with joy.

Martin's recoiled in fear.

Looking down, the stranger grinned once more. "Should have left things well enough alone."

He reached for something behind him, outside of Martin's view. A moment passed and then he thrust the same arm toward the earth with breathtaking force.

When he pulled away, another white wooden roadside cross stood stark in the moonlight, still swaying slightly.

Martin jerked his head back, stunned. "But . . . but I'm not dead yet," he sputtered, his mind trying hard to come to grips with the situation as his body continued to bleed out its lifeblood into the desert sands beneath him.

The stranger leaned in close, so that the injured man could smell the stink and feel the heat of the breath on his cheek. "Don't worry." The grin again. "You will be soon."

The faceless creatures faded into the darkness. The stranger stood and stepped back a few feet from Martin, giving him a good look. The man's coat billowed out behind him like a great sheet caught in the wind and then split in two. Seconds later he leaped up into the moonlit sky and disappeared.

In his wake, a single dark feather drifted to the earth and came to rest just inches from Martin's face.

Seeing it, Martin finally understood the oddly familiar sound he had heard just before the stranger had appeared.

It had been the sound of wings.

Large, powerful wings.

Angel's wings.

As his life left him and his body went cold and silent, Martin's soul found itself trapped there with the others and it began to scream.

It would continue screaming for a long time to come.

COMFORTS OF HOME

Michael Laimo

WILL WORK FOR FOOD, the sign read, or so he was
told. He'd never learned to write, or read, so he had
to trust one of the men at the gathering: a leather-
skinned, long-bearded drifter who'd called himself
Jyro. He'd thought, *Who names themselves after a frig-
gin' sandwich?* It wasn't as though the guy's mother
gave him that name. But who knew for certain? Not
Charlie. Not anyone else at the Squat.

South Miami didn't offer much in the way of
shelter, so the Squat remained overly popular, and
overpopulated. Each night a lone police vehicle sat
like a sentry across the street at the burned-out
pawn shop, replaced every two hours by its twin.
Inside, the driver and his partner ate subs and
sipped coffee so they wouldn't die from all the excitement.

It'd been only six months on the streets for Charlie. His cash ran out along with his luck, and the

room rental was offered to someone with deeper pockets. He hadn't really earned his keep at the Squat yet (as in the real world), but the streets welcomed him anyway, as did the strays that duped him out of half his earnings with their pining eyes and covetous mews. Better to give than to receive, he reasoned, believing that those who pay with their goodwill shall earn their fair keep in the end. Contemplating the crowd about him, with its abusive disposition and makeshift hierarchy, he wondered if anyone mired at this level could ever rise to taste the cream at the top. Probably not.

So why not make the best of any situation? The sign had seen better days, now swelled with rain and furled at the edges. C-shaped indentations approached the words on the front, his grip now limited to cramping fingertips campaigning to get his message across. It'd worked, the sign, depending on location of course, supplying him with just enough money to get by on: food for him, and Shitty-Kitty for the cats.

Charlie knew the others at the Squat sniggered at the weird guy who slept with the cats, making it known that he was one of the "Squat freaks." Thankfully these self-appointed leaders never followed through with their cat-mashing threats. Or so he thought. After all, many different cats showed up every night.

Of course, they weren't really *his* cats. The city

had quite a problem with the strays, and made a not-so-grand effort to eliminate their presence by trapping them and bringing them to the downtown shelter where they'd be gracefully put to sleep, thanks to the taxpayers who insisted on a rabies-free park. But they bred faster than they were caught, so there were always one or two more to add to the evening mix, and soon enough cat-man Charlie had himself at least two dozen nightly visitors to contend with, which was just good and fine by him. Thank the good Lord for Shitty-Kitty, which cost only a dollar eighty-nine for a five-pound bag. That left him with about five to seven bucks a day to feed himself. If he found work.

The jobs were few and far between, and paid ten bucks on a good day, but only if he put in ten hours. He'd gotten work from the landscapers who at times were unwilling to shell out minimum wage to the Rent-A-Ricans who worked their day-labor asses off to support eighteen-year-old pregnant wives and malnourished kids. The deal was always made ahead of time, and if Charlie wanted the promise of work the next day, he'd have to abide by their agreement. Yeah, ten bucks was just fine, so long as he could eat and feed his cats.

The Lauderdale Road exit off I-95 was always a safe bet. He'd stand on the grass shoulder, holding up the sign (WILL WORK FOR FOOD), and wait for the landscapers to pull in from Boca or Jupiter or Delray with their side-slat pickups and a spot for Charlie in the back alongside the mowers and the Rent-A-Ricans, who always cowered at the foul odor of the homeless guy. Of course, Charlie was never paid in food—that might cost even more than the ten bucks he was usually offered.

The only problem, really, was getting to Lauderdale Road, which was a good mile and a half from the Squat. His sneakers had long ago shown the signs of age, soles worn through to threadbare socks, the laces stolen one night while he slept. His feet bled daily, even before the day's work began, and he remained mindful of the pain, doing his best to shove it aside until he returned to the Squat.

It'd been three days since he last ventured out, and neither he nor the cats had eaten in nearly forty-eight hours. They'd begun to climb on him, twenty, maybe thirty altogether if you included the kittens, kneading their paws all over his stagnant form. *They're hungry, they're hungry*, Charlie thought over and over again, knowing he was the only one who'd ever feed them. And if he didn't, well, then fairly soon they'd give up on him and leave him alone in the world that had been so damn cruel to him.

He took his sign (WILL WORK FOR FOOD) and began the long, arduous trek to the interstate exit where traffic would be high and a passing pickup might just have an extra spot in the back for him to crawl into. He left the Squat early in the morning while it was still too dark to attract attention from those on their way to determine their net worths in life. He'd never begged for money like so many of the others at the Squat routinely did, yet still, those he crossed paths with eyed him suspisciously and diverted their determined paths to avoid any possible confrontation, whether it be physical or simply olfactory.

The rising sun loomed surreptitiously behind a veil of clouds, casting gray light across the early morning bustle of southern Florida. The threat of drizzle loomed, but would soon be defeated by another 98 degree day. By the time he made it to the Lauderdale Road exit, sweat doused his body and dehydration threatened to take him down.

He held up the sign (WILL WORK FOR FOOD) as cars and trucks came to rest at the traffic light. Those behind the windows peered at him until he attempted to lock their gazes. The drivers, shock-value urges fulfilled, quickly returned their sight to the road only to press onward as the traffic light switched from red to green.

The thin cloud cover burned away as the sun beat its maddened rays down on Charlie's head. He began to smell himself again, and did his damndest to ignore the stench. The early morning hours quickly segued into rush hour. A tremendous thirst sapped his energy. His vision began to fade. Charlie had to dig deep for the strength to simply hold the sign up.

In a moment of thin traffic, a lone truck advanced from the interstate and came to rest at the traffic light, its motor idling like the purr of a great tiger. In the back, wood slats running nine feet high corralled thousands of navels on their way to be crated and shipped off to supermarkets across the state. The aroma of freshly picked oranges doused Charlie like a deluge of sweet water.

Charlie held up his sign: WILL WORK FOR FOOD.

The driver rolled down the window. Middle-aged. Marlins cap. In need of a shave.

Charlie pinned his gaze.

The driver did not turn away. He grinned pitifully. "Hungry?" he asked.

Charlie nodded.

"Thirsty?"

"Yes sir," he answered timidly, lowering the sign.

"I just might have a job for you," the driver said. "Get in."

Charlie looked up at the thousands of oranges packing the rear of the truck. How was he supposed to get up there? Was this some kind of cruel joke?

The traffic light turned green. Charlie half expected the truck to take off, but it didn't move.

"In the cab," the driver said. "Hurry it up. Light's green."

Charlie scurried around the front of the truck, the sharp pain in his feet lost to the thrill of the moment. He opened the door and hopped into the cab, wedging his sign between his legs. Cool air covered his body like a blanket. The driver handed him a plastic grocery bag filled with oranges. "Help yourself."

In silence, Charlie peeled and ate four oranges, paying no attention to the roads they traveled. His body tingled with uncanny delight as the cool juice seeped down his throat, as the rich pulp settled in his stomach. Only afterward did he wonder how many hours he'd have to put in for this ten minutes of ecstasy.

"There's plenty more where they came from," the driver said. "As many as you can carry home."

"Thank you."

"Plus, say, fifty bucks."

Fifty bucks? There is a God after all.

He eyed the driver, only somewhat suspiciously. Desperation made every opportunity seem reasonable. So far there seemed nothing to be concerned about. The man was nice, although quiet, driving with a purposeful direction in mind.

"Where're we headin'?" Charlie asked.

"Capshaw. Just south of the city. There's some warehouses there. Gotta drop off this load."

"You need help boxing them?"

The driver turned left, then shook his head. "No,

we got employees that do that. Union guys. And, well . . . they don't do no dirty work."

"Dirty work?"

"I . . . I need your help cleaning up a bit of a mess."

Charlie nodded. "For fifty bucks, I'll clean up any mess you got."

"It's an overnight job."

Charlie hesitated, then said, "That's okay."

Twenty minutes later they pulled onto a dirt road leading away from an industrial park filled with cement warehouses. From the thickly sweet aroma filling the air, Charlie figured that a citrus juice plant operated somewhere nearby, and right here along this road were the warehouses where the oranges and grapefruits were temporarily stored before they went off to the nearby factories for juicing. When the factory quotas were filled, many of the fruits were either crated for the super-markets or roadside stands, or simply donated to charities.

At the end of the dirt road sat a warehouse smaller than the rest. It was clearly less kept up than the others, this one nothing more than a wooden structure, perhaps a single-unit home in the past whose wood beams lay inescapably caught in the webs of decay. White paint curled away from the pitted facing like a peeling sunburn. High weeds burst from the base of the building in scattered clumps. Horseflies the size of bumblebees hovered about in droves.

"Here we are," the driver said, jumping down from the cab. A small cloud of dust rose around him. Charlie followed, eyeing the place with skeptical curiosity. The smell of something rotten filled the air.

"What's this building for?"

"I'll play it straight with ya," the man said, removing his hat and swiping his sweaty brow. "This here's where all the rotten fruits go. Been more than a few bad batches of late, and with the surplus and all, we've been working overtime trying to find places to ship our regular stock. So, what you have here is about three months' worth of dead fruit. It's been accumulating—still is—and with business being as bad as it's been, well, we can't really afford to pay the union clean-up crews. Which means we gotta do it ourselves. So I guess this is where you come in."

Charlie peered at the man, then back at the small warehouse. *Three months' worth of oranges baking in a hot warehouse. . . .*

"There's a Dumpster out back, next to the door. There's also a few good shovels and a cooler filled with food and water. All you gotta do is fill up the Dumpster with the bad oranges. Should be able to fit 'em all. I figure that with a few rests for food and sleep, you should be able to wrap it all up by tomorrow morning. I'll be back then with your money. Sound good?"

Charlie nodded, somewhat tentatively. The cooler filled with food and drink was the clincher, really, otherwise he might've walked away from it all. Not that hiking back to the Squat would be a better alternative. *Well . . . his friends were there. And tonight they'll be sniffing around for him, wondering where he's gone.*

The man returned to his truck, waved, then drove off, leaving Charlie alone to face the elements. He took a deep breath, then circled around to the rear of the warehouse, feet crunching over dried reed stems and burned crabgrass. The waft of putrefaction grew thicker, and by the time he reached the closed door of the building, the smell was so bad a nausea rose up in him that completely wiped out his appetite. *Smells worse than the Squat*, he thought, trying to amuse himself. *Smells like dead bodies*.

He eyed the cooler—a rather small one at that—then stepped to the door.

He opened it. Went inside.

The baking stench assaulted him like a fist, punching its way deep into his lungs. The oranges he ate twisted against the walls of his stomach, threatening to leap from his trembling body in a streaming acidic mass. Jutting crookedly from the eight-foot ceiling, a single bulb dimly illuminated the sea of decay before him, a gray, pulpy mound wholly unrecognizable as the pile of citrus fruits they used to be. Seven feet high and perhaps twenty feet across, the bulging mass glistened in spots with mold patches still freshly festering. Thousands—no, *millions*—of flies, most of them as large as the ones he'd spotted out front, covered the swelling mountain like sprinkles on a dishful of soft-serve yogurt.

And goddamn, the thing was *moving*. Not as a whole mass, but in spots, pulsing as though amphibious things twisted uncomfortably beneath the membranous skin. Of course, nothing really moved beneath the surface. It festered on top: oversized patches of writhing maggots, unsettling the mound's coating with their collective movement. And . . . there was a *sound*, the white noise of the flies buzzing about in a mad chorus, emulating a barber's electric clippers approaching the fine hairs around your ears.

Oranges and grapefruits, Charlie thought incredulously, *definitely past the sell-by.*

Charlie spun away and staggered outside, leaning himself against the rough steel surface of the Dumpster. The 98 degree weather felt welcomely cool against his soaked skin, and helped to suppress his gorge. Pacing his breath, he waited a few minutes, then located a bottle of water in the cooler and sucked it down.

For one man, Charlie thought, it *would* take all day and night to clean up this mess, as the driver so indicated. He wondered if he should just blow the job off, take the food and slip away back into the obscurity of the real world. But then what? Hell, it'd take him at least thirty minutes to walk out of the industrial park, and a homeless man carrying a small cooler in a private park might raise suspicions.

Fifty dollars.

That's a lot of Shitty-Kitty.

"The cats," he said. "They need me."

So he grabbed a shovel and went back into the warehouse, determined to get the job done. At once the oppressive heat whacked him, sending putrid air back into his body like a blast from a furnace whose coals had been replaced with human flesh. The mound loomed, like a giant squid on an ocean's bottom, he the ancient sailor aboard Captain Nemo's *Nautilus*, harpoon readied for attack. He circled around the left side, three feet of space allowing him passage to the rear of the structure; the mound sloped upward to near-ceiling height on the right, surprisingly retaining its orange color, looking like some odd spread of woodland fungus.

Using the shovel's blade, he poked at the heaving mass, testing its resiliency. It sank down to the brace and parted the sludge, making a farting sound. With two hands, he pulled on the handle.

Like a drift of snow, a green-gray-orange slab separated from the mass and plopped to the cement foundation in a gelatinous heap. A foul-smelling odor burst up. The heap farted again. Peering at the cutaway, he could see that some of the oranges beneath the surface had retained their round shape, looking like sickly tumors. The flies, seemingly unhappy with this disturbance, soared about his head like fighter planes.

Jesus, how am I gonna do this? he thought, looking back out toward the bright slice of light in the doorway. Feeling sick again, he paced back toward the front of the warehouse.

His foot caught a puddle of slime near the base of the mound. With only three feet of space between it and the wall, he had no room to fall on solid ground and, like a football player leaping into the end zone, landed facedown in the heap. He struggled to free himself, arching his neck in order to gasp for air, arms attempting to push his body up, but succeeding in only plunging bicep-deep into the muck. He twisted his torso around, keeping his face above the mass, which seemed to want to swallow him like quicksand. The mound shifted, miring him, securing its hold. He kicked his legs, which still remained free but found no purchase as they slid on the greasy surface. Soon, they too began to settle into the muck.

Charlie was stuck.

He twisted and turned and dug and grasped, tiring himself to the point of exhaustion. Eventually Charlie could do nothing but lay helplessly and wait.

And wait.

The hours slid by. In due time the maggots and slugs found him. They crawled on his slime-coated skin, delighted with their find. Horseflies and mosquitoes and palmetto bugs buzzed freely about, like helicopters around a disaster.

Time passed on. He slept periodically, only to be awakened by a bee sting or the hardened flutter of a palmetto bug's wings. Darkness loomed, the light from outside fading to gray, the room barely illuminated by the pallid glare of the single bulb from above.

Just enough light.

To see the rats.

It reflected off their eyes, beady oil drops glistening as they contemplated the warm breathing flesh before them. They scurried along the edge of the structure where the wall met the floor, only feet away, climbing over one another, squeaking euphorically as they came closer to him, closer, their twitching whiskers dappled in gray sludge, sharp claws scratching the cement, teeth bared in anticipation.

Charlie had been here for a long time, he knew, and the hours of inaction numbed his muscles,

making it difficult to even flinch. The rats accumu-
lated as if word had been dispatched of found
treasure. Their bodies were pulsing lumps of black
hair, amassing, fidgeting, squeaking. Soon, they became uncountable, a throbbing wave disappearing
into the darkness. Charlie thought it best to stay
still, to play dead and pray they'd soon move on to
the sweeter source of decay surrounding him.

Two rats separated from the crowd, large ones
tottering back and forth, each of them the size of
footballs, sniffing toward him with wet pink noses.
Their tails wriggled against the concrete, helping
them to rise on their haunches and peer at him with
their eyes ... their eyes that now glowed red beneath the dull glare of light. The crowd pressed in
behind them, pushing the two forward, and then
there were three and four and five, and soon they
multiplied even further as they fell over one another, screeching and scratching amidst the tide of
muck reaching out from the mound. Thick, foul
hairs rubbed up against the exposed skin of his ankles.

Then, a bite. One the rats at the lead of the pack
took a nip from his calf. He could feel the warm
flow of blood against his skin. He cried out. Another came at him, quick and determined, tearing
away at his ankle, then sitting up and staring at
him, its teeth stained with blood.

Soon there were rats at his face, climbing adeptly

through the sludge, and even here with all the sour decay surrounding him, he could still smell the sewage on their hides—the fouler odor of garbage and excrement. One climbed through the tangled mess that was his hair, getting caught up in it like a fly in a web, pulling and squeaking frantically in an effort to escape. Another crawled across his neck, taking a quick nibble then scrambling away over the mound as if afraid of getting caught in the act. Blood trickled down, drawing more rats toward him. He could feel them covering his legs, his waist, his chest. One sniffed at his mouth and he spit and screamed, chasing it away, the horrible taste of it left behind on his lips.

Charlie yelled and cried, his echoes unanswered in the dank warehouse. Those that worked in the park (*union workers*, he heard in the driver's voice) had gone home hours ago, leaving the area vacant save for the mandatory security guard who was probably watching television in some glass booth near the gated entrance a half mile away.

More rats crawled. Scratched. Bit. Lapped.

Charlie screamed, thinking, *This is it. My time has come. Life on the streets wasn't so good to me after all. . . .*

There was a loud squeal. Then another, and then the rats began to scramble away, crawling over one another in a mad frenzy. Some crossed over his body, many more tumbling away, down the mound. He could hear them trying to flee, *hundreds* of little clawed feet scraping madly against the wall. In a minute's time, they were gone. A few were still within eyeshot, moored in the pile and unable to escape. More rats squealed, seemingly meeting some kind of terrible fate.

Someone had come to save him! Had heard his screams!

"Hello!" he cried. "Please, help me!"

But there was no answer, none that he could hear.

The rats kept on squealing. Amid the fray, he felt the light patter of feet on his torso. He shuddered, looked down, expecting another rat.

Standing on his chest was a cat, a gray tabby with a brown spot on its pink nose. It mewed loudly at him, saying, *Don't worry, Charlie. We'll help you.* The cat's mouth moved along with the words in Charlie's mind.

Charlie smiled. "Hello there Mr. Puddy Tat," he said, giggling like an idiot, realizing clearly that he'd, quite suddenly, lost his mind. *Cat's don't talk.*

They do to you, Charlie.

"Who said that?"

I did. Over here!

Charlie looked in the direction from where the voice came, and saw another cat, this one black with white paws, standing on the mound a foot away from his head. It had an injured rat in its paws, a bubble of guts purling from its mouth. The cat seemed to be grinning. *We're here now, Charlie. All of us. We need you to come back to the Squat.*

"The Squat . . ." Charlie uttered, his voice weak and scratchy.

Yes, the Squat. It's where you belong. It's your home.

The cat leaned down and sank its teeth into the rat's gut, ripping away a hunk of hairy flesh. Blood came out in a spurt.

Charlie did his best to peer about the warehouse, despite the bad angle and poor lighting. The cats from the Squat *were* here, at least fifty of them, some of them he recognized too. Many of them had dead rats in their mouths; others darted around trying to decide which ones to attack next. The rats squealed, but soon their cries for mercy were replaced by the victorious mewls of the cats. In a few minutes, the rats were defeated, and the cats lay basking in the bloody aftermath, licking their paws and purring in post-clash respites.

Again Charlie tried to move, but could not. So he closed his eyes and fell back into a slumber, dreaming of the cats, of how they managed to get here. It didn't matter, really. He only hoped they would dig him free of his imprisonment so he could rush to the store and buy them bags and bags of Shitty-Kitty.

"Hey. . . ."

Charlie felt a nudge on his shoulder.

"Hey, you okay? Wake up, man."

Charlie opened his eyes. A figure came into view. Marlins cap. Grubby beard. Tan. The driver. "Uh . . ." he managed to say.

"Jesus, you okay? Let me help you up." The driver grabbed Charlie by the arms and pulled him free of the mound. There was a horrible squelching sound as Charlie ripped free of the mess.

Charlie blinked. As the room came into focus, he saw, and remembered.

It looked like a bloodbath. Hundreds of dead rats, everywhere. All of them severely mutilated.

"What the hell happened here?" the driver asked.

Charlie kept looking at the rats, wondering where his friends had gone. "I don't remember," he answered.

"Well . . . we need to get you to a hospital."

"No. . . ."

The man looked at Charlie with dismay. "But you're injured."

"No . . . they need me."

"They need you? Who needs you?"

Charlie looked around. "Sorry I didn't get the job done."

The man waved him off. "No, don't worry about it. As long as you're okay."

Charlie nodded. "I need a bit of money," he said. "For food."

The man reached into his pocket, handed Charlie the fifty dollars he promised. "Don't worry about the job."

Charlie nodded his thanks.

The man helped Charlie to rise. "Where can I take you?"

Charlie looked at the man. "Please take me back to the Squat. Back home."

"You're bleeding. You need to go to a hospital. Or a shelter."

Charlie shook his head. "They'll protect me."

"Who?"

"Please . . . just take me back to the Squat."

The man nodded. "That's your home, huh? The Squat?"

Charlie nodded. "Yep. They're waiting for me there," he said. "They need me."

"I'm sure they do," the man answered, stepping over the dead rats. "I'm sure they do."

THE CALL OF
FARTHER SHORES

David Niall Wilson

The barber shop in Cedar Falls was more than just a gathering spot for tired old men with nothing better to do than to trim the few remaining wisps of gray from their temples and pass on the latest fish stories. Brown's small shop sported two chairs, three barbers off and on, and the memorabilia of dozens of lives. Terry Brown was the sixth generation of Browns to run the small shop. His father had come back from the war, honored and decorated, just in time to take the reins from Jeremiah Brown, who'd cut hair in Cedar Falls for nearly forty years. There were sighs of relief when that torch was passed. More than a few heads of hair had borne the mark of a slight palsy and unattended cataracts, but it hadn't been enough to keep them away.

Jeremy stood on the steps, taking in the changes

time and weather had etched across the face of the old building. He hadn't stepped foot in Cedar Falls in nearly ten years, but he remembered the last time he'd mounted the steps to Brown's Barber Shop with a clarity that ran like cold rain down his spine. Small details surfaced—details with more clarity than those he could have brought to mind from the breakfast barely cool in his stomach. The aroma of his father's cigarette-scented flannel shirt, the rustle of leaves, rolling and scurrying down the sidewalks as he'd stepped up onto the curb. Cars had been larger in those days, and Jeremy smaller. The scents of gas and oil had carried on the wind, blending with wood smoke and the acrid scent of burning leaves.

There had been chairs outside the shop in those days, metal chairs that bounced if you hit them just right, and leaned back nearly to the sidewalk behind if you had the proper size and age. They were usually full, pulled close in beside the sand-filled ashtray and flanked by a Thermos cooler.

Now antismoking laws and open-container fines had ended all that, and what remained of the chairs themselves were deep scrapes in the wooden planks of the Main Street boardwalk. Jeremy hesitated outside the door. The exterior changes had done nothing to still the *presence* of the place. He closed his eyes, and years melted away in an instant.

There were animals of all sorts lining the walls, some heads, fish so large they had seemed surreal and improbable to a young boy whose fishing experience extended to bluegill and catfish. There were the heads of deer, a bear, a wild pig, and, in the corner, Jeremy's favorite, a stuffed mongoose poised in eternal battle with a coiled, moth-eaten snake. There were tools of unknown use and origin, black-and-white photos so yellowed and dusty you had to stand with your nose pressed to the glass of their frames to make out the images. Squat figures in black pants, black shoes and white shirts, standing in front of buildings that only peripherally resembled those on the city streets Jeremy had walked as a child.

And the wooden figurehead. Jeremy stood, leaning against the frame of the doorway, and shook as the memory of that worm-eaten chunk of wood invaded and took over. Dark wood—so dark it seemed soaked with seawater—damp and rotting, the thing glittered with coat after coat of varnish. Jeremy's father had told him it was to fight off the rot, but Jeremy had never believed it. The varnish—so thick it clogged the lines of the original sculpture—had seemed more a prison, holding that rot *in* so it couldn't escape and infect those standing too near.

It was a woman, or had been at some point in history. Carved from a single log, it had long angular features, huge, mournful eyes that stretched down and down to high cheekbones and a slender, pointed nose—almost Roman, he'd heard others say. You could tell the woman the piece had been modeled after had been beautiful. Even the ravages of the ocean, the weather and the years hadn't been able to mask it. There was an eerie sense of something hovering just beneath the surface of the wood, staring back at you if you studied it too closely and watching you move about the room if you pretended not to notice. Always.

In his pocket, sharp page folds pressing through the worn denim of his jeans to scrape his thigh, was the letter that had dragged him home. The type had smeared from sweat, too many folds, and too many readings. The return address was one he'd never seen before, and would likely never see again. Probst and Palmer, Attorneys at Law. The address wasn't local to Cedar Falls. Jeremy's father had left him with two standard rules. Never do business with friends, and even if you break rule number one, never do business in your own backyard. The less people knew about what lay behind your smile, or your frown, the less likely they were to be able to find a chink in your armor and take you down.

Jeremy had never understood who in Cedar Falls would want to take him down, or his father, for that matter, but he understood the rules. Probst and Palmer's offices were in Kingston, a hundred miles to the north, and Jeremy had stopped by on his way, to pick up paperwork and keys. His father had left things in good order. The house was paid for, the taxes good for the year and the insurance caught up both on the property and the ancient Chevrolet sedan he'd left behind.

All of it was ordered and neat, empty, and far too bizarre to be handled all at once. Jeremy had driven to the house, parked out front and stared at the door and the windows for about fifteen minutes, then driven away. He knew he should have gone in, checked the place over and unpacked. There were more papers to sign, and the utility companies would have to be notified that services should be restored. Jeremy knew, but he just couldn't face it.

So here he was, head against the wooden frame of Brown's Barber Shop, sweat trickling under the collar of his flannel shirt as he fought for balance against suddenly weak knees and a whirling panorama of memory and pain. He didn't need a haircut, but he very suddenly needed to sit down, so Jeremy twisted away from the wall and slipped inside with a deep breath.

There were two bright overhead lamps, one hanging over each chair on a single stainless steel chain, the light funneled toward the floor by aluminum shades. The edges of each were yellowed and dusty, and Jeremy wondered, just for a moment, if some of that stain wasn't tobacco from his father's cigars.

Some things hadn't changed at all, except in perspective. The once-giant sailfish, while still huge, seemed possible through adult eyes, the mongoose and snake seedy and dusty rather than mysterious and dark.

The room was empty, and though the lights were on, there was a sensation of . . . emptiness. Deep, dark emptiness that matched the hollow ache in the pit of Jeremy's gut. He stepped in and let the door swing closed behind him with a squeak.

For a moment, he just stood there, taking in the room, the scent of old leather chairs and hair tonic, the slightly acrid scent of oil burned in the gears of chrome- and Bakelite-handled clippers that should have been retired in the sixties. Whispered voices from his past spoke of presidents and congressmen long dead, bake sales, and sea stories. Dust motes danced beneath the hanging lamps, and Jeremy turned to the wall at the back, taking a step deeper into the gloom.

She was there, just as he remembered. There were a few more photographs lining the wall to either side, some in color, which didn't fit his memory at all, but Jeremy's gaze was focused. The wood seemed to grow from the wall, curving and taking shape slowly as it built up to the deep-set holes that were her eyes. Long, flowing hair, deeply etched into the wood, each line darker in the center and lightening as it neared the surface of the wood. The longer Jeremy stared, the more real she became, the room fading around her until all he could see was a woman, gazing back at him in quiet desperation. He stepped closer, one foot hesitantly sliding through the dust, then the other. Just as he reached out his hand to trace her cheek with one finger a voice cut through the shadows.

"Can I help you?"

Jeremy spun, eyes wide and his mouth dropping open. The man who'd spoken leaned against the second barber chair on one elbow, watching Jeremy with interest. The cheeks had grown heavier, and wrinkles lined the skin beneath his eyes, but Jeremy recognized Terry Brown instantly. It had to be Terry. He was the spitting image of his father, and in that instant the echo of Jeremy's father's voice, and the scent of smoke and leather nearly overwhelmed him.

"I . . ." His words caught in his throat for a second, then he turned, stepped forward, and offered his hand shakily. "I'm Jeremy Lyons," he said. "I used to come here with my father."

In that moment, the other man's face shifted through a series of emotions—surprise, a deep, impressive smile, a quick flash of insight—and ended in a sympathetic frown. "Jack Lyons' boy?"

Jeremy nodded. "The last time you cut my hair," he said softly, "was for my high school graduation."

"Flattop," Terry nodded, "high and tight, just like always."

Jeremy turned back to the wooden woman mounted on the wall for just a second, then stepped away and walked toward the barber's chair, extending his hand.

"I'm guessing you aren't here for a trim?"

Jeremy grinned wryly. "I don't know why I'm here, exactly. I went by the house . . . just wasn't quite ready for it. When I came back into town, it just seemed natural. I don't know how many afternoons and evenings I spent in here—reading, drawing, listening. Guess I thought it would be a little more like home than that empty house."

"Not a lot of action these days," Terry smiled. "I get busy about one or so, but by three or four it thins out. Only a few old-timers remember the way things were, and mostly they come around on the weekends. Not a one of them has needed a real haircut in years, but they come, and they pay, regular as clockwork."

Jeremy smiled. "Just like always."

The two laughed comfortably, and Terry moved away from the chair toward the front door.

"Let me lock up," he said. "I've got a few bottles of beer in back. No one waiting up for either of us."

Jeremy almost bowed out. He had no right imposing his depression on someone else. The more he thought about it, the less sense it made that he'd come to the old barber shop at all. It was a place to get your hair cut, and all the magic, if there'd truly been any, had long departed. He turned to the wall a final time. Almost all.

Jeremy had never been in the back room of Brown's Barber Shop. He'd seen his father disappear through those doors countless times, but he'd never been allowed past the entrance. Even now, as Terry slipped in ahead of him and flicked on the dim light, he hesitated. It was like violating his father's will beyond the grave.

"We had to move most of the social activities back here as the years passed," Terry said conversationally, pulling open an aged refrigerator and grabbing two longnecks from the frosty interior. "Health inspectors were cracking down, mothers dragging their children in where fathers had always done so before, complaining about the cigarette smoke and threatening to close us down.

"Hell," Terry chuckled, plopping into one of the old leather chairs lining the wall of the back room and twisting the top off his beer, "we even had animal-rights activists protesting the animals on the walls."

"I don't know how you survived it all," Jeremy

said, shaking his head and taking a seat a few feet away. "I don't know how you stayed here at all."

"Well, the staying is in my blood." Terry smiled. "Been a Brown in this shop almost as long as there's been a Cedar Falls. Wouldn't want to be the one to break a streak like that. The rest was easier than it seemed. They opened a new shop in the mall out Whitewall way. It's got a big clown chair for the kids and a playroom with Nintendo. That left us the regulars and the few too lazy to drive that far. It's enough for a living, and that's all a man can rightly ask of life, I think."

Jeremy thought about that for a moment, taking a long pull from the beer bottle.

"I wish I could have thought that way," he said at last. "I wish I'd've been happy to come here every week, get a trim and hear the old stories. I wish I could have been more like my father—at least a little. I feel like it's all been lost, and all I have to show for the years is an empty house and dreams I have no one to share with."

"Never married, huh?" Terry turned away for a moment, then took another long drink, draining his bottle and rising for a second, glancing at Jeremy, who shook his head. "I never settled either. Never could find anyone I felt comfortable with, not after Dad passed on. There's been a couple of times I thought I might be on the right track, but . . ." He shrugged and opened his second beer. "Some men are meant to be alone."

Jeremy nodded.

"I miss those days, sometimes," he said softly. "I miss the stories. I miss hearing old Mulligan talk about catching that marlin out there. I knew, even then, that he never set foot on the deck of a fishing boat in his life, but the words were magic. It wasn't the truth, but the story, you know?"

Terry nodded. "I do. Don't get much of that anymore. Mulligan passed on about seven years ago, Billy Jensen shortly after that. Mostly they come and talk about those who've died, now, and wait for their own turn."

"There's one story I never heard," Jeremy said suddenly. "I know there's a story, because my father used to let bits and pieces slip. That figurehead on the wall out there, the woman. He said your father brought her back from the war. . . ."

Terry grew suddenly stiff, and for a moment Jeremy thought the man would chase him out of the shop and lock the doors behind him forever. Tension rippled through the air and tingled along the hairs on Jeremy's arm. His hand shook, and he forced it to steady.

"Some stories are best left to the dead, and their memory," Terry muttered, downing his second beer and rising quickly.

"Did I say something wrong?" Jeremy asked

quickly, taken aback by the sudden reaction his words had brought.

"Not at all," Brown said brusquely, "but it's getting late. I know you need to get settled in. Maybe you could stop in during regular hours for a trim."

Jeremy sat, stunned, staring at the bigger man and trying to figure out whether he was kidding. There was no humor in the barber's slate gray eyes, so Jeremy rose slowly, downing the beer and handing over the empty bottle.

"Nice to see you again, then," he said, turning. "Nice to be back."

Terry's features trembled, as if he were fighting some inner battle. Maybe he wanted to say something, take something back, but in the end, he held to his silence, only nodding as Jeremy slipped out of that forbidden room and into the shadowed barbershop once again. Jeremy glanced at the wall, and in the darkness, shadow cloaking the carved wood, it seemed a woman stood, watching him. He could have sworn her eyes glittered brightly and that a slender arm reached out, fingers beckoning.

Then Brown was at his side, ushering him toward the door with a firm hand on his back, mumbling something about the good old days. The air was cool, and the streets were deserted. Jeremy stood on the walk outside in confusion, then shrugged and turned to the road, and his car. Might as well get to some memories of his own.

*   *   *

The old home was full of stale air and dim memory. Jeremy had had vague ideas of cleaning up, arranging things and putting them back in order, but he should have known that his father would leave no such satisfaction. Everything was in its place. A very light sheen of dust coated everything, but beneath it the floors gleamed. The glass glittered— even the silver had only the faintest tinge of tarnish. The power was alive and waiting. There was a yellow note, hanging from the knob of the front door, to let him know they'd stopped and cut it on. "Just as your father had asked."

Jeremy's room was much as he'd left it last visit home. He'd been in his senior year of college, and the remnants of that time littered the desk and the walls. His bed was turned down, as if expecting him. Too much. Jeremy closed the door on that particular set of nightmares and moved down the hall. He pushed, and the door to his parents' room swung open easily, hinges oiled. No sound. There had never been a sound. Jeremy had listened and listened, but he'd never been able to tell when they came and went. The room beckoned, dark and . . . inviting. It was a strange, exhilarating invitation, but an invitation nonetheless. For the first time since driving into the tiny, dirt-water town, Jeremy felt as if he were home.

The switch beside the door didn't operate a ceiling

fixture as he'd expected. A single, dim light pooled yellow illumination over the floor from the dresser to his right. Rather than cutting the deeper shadows, the lamp's glow accentuated them. The bed was an expanse of darkness, flanked by low-slung night-stands of still darker wood. The windows were hung with heavy drapes of indeterminate color, pulled tight across closed blinds.

Odd shapes hung from the walls, and a huge old mirror glittered across the back of the dresser. Je-remy stared at that mirror. He couldn't make out anything in the silvered surface, but he stood, still and quiet, and watched the reflected glow of the lamp.

His mother had sat there, right in front of that mirror, brushing her long hair for hours. Jeremy had never actually set foot in his parents' room, but he'd watched her from the doorway, when she didn't know he was looking. He wondered if a part of her might be captured there. If he stared long enough, would her face appear? Would he feel the soft stroke of the brush through his hair? And where had his father been when . . . ?

Shaking his head, Jeremy turned from the mirror quickly. Again, too much.

Moving to the bed, he laid his suitcase out and unsnapped it quickly. He needed to get his mind out of the past. There were a lot of things to accom-plish: clearing out the house, gathering his parents' papers and belongings, the lawyers. All of it loomed over him like the specter of his father, leering and poking, tugging him first one direction, then another, and the last thing he needed in the midst of it all was more illusion and memory. Illusions and memories had haunted him for too many years.

Before he could think of his father's accusing gaze, he opened the drawers of the old dresser and shoved his clothes hurriedly inside. It was nearly comical, the way the finality of the gesture washed through him in a wave of sudden relief. He was in. The dresser was his, not his father's, not a thing he would be punished for violating. The room—the house—everything in it—was his.

With a sigh he pushed the drawer shut and turned, seating himself on the edge of the bed. The woman stared down at him, smoother than he remembered, and darker, her hair seeming to drip from the polished wood surface.

Jeremy grew very still. His heart pulsed, slowing with his breath painfully until it felt as if it might stop altogether. The moment was identical to a hundred acid-tripping moments in his youth, pulsing with the neon beat of bar lights and the sultry backbeat of strip clubs, pounding with the rhythms of a thousand songs. Still and silent.

Beside the window, sliding out from the edge of the heavy curtains, was the wooden figurehead from the barbershop. He knew it couldn't be the same one. He had just seen it—had reached out his hand to touch it—but the sensation it was there— that it was real and identical and *watching* him was undeniable.

Mesmerized, Jeremy rose, stepping forward. He heard the soft echo of Terry's words in his ear. "Some stories are best left to the dead, and their memory," but the words flitted through his mind and away, as if whispered across a great distance.

Jeremy reached out one hand, letting his fingers come to rest on the smooth, polished wood, and his stomach lurched. The scent of hair tonic and musty leather assaulted his senses violently. His vision blurred, then focused. The wall had changed. Lengthened. For just an instant, the floor pitched beneath his feet, and he clutched the wooden carving tightly for support.

"No," he whispered.

Everything had shifted, and the pungent scent of tobacco smoke hung in the air. To his left, dim, yellow light flickered, and he could hear the scrape of feet, the groan and squeal of old springs as heavy bodies settled into aged chairs. The shadow-forms of dead, mounted animals surrounded him, their glass-eyed stares too high. As if he were shorter. As if he were younger.

As if time had rewound its tape.

A heavy cough, then laughter, deep and guttural.

Jeremy's heart lurched. He knew that cough, and that laugh. He pressed into the wall, nearly collapsing, and closed his eyes so tightly that they squeezed shut on the heavy smoke, burning and tingling. He thought about the bed behind him. He thought about the door, still ajar, less than three feet away, and the hallway beyond. He thought about his father's liquor cabinet, and with a sudden shove he pushed away from the wall and spun.

His knee banged into something hard, and he cried out. His eyes opened to flickering shadows, and a huge, dark shape silhouetted against yellowed light.

"Who is it?"

The words hung in the smoky air, mocking Jeremy's sanity.

Jeremy held his breath, pressing back to the wall.

"That you, boy?"

Jeremy tried to remain silent, but it was too much. That voice, a voice he'd been conditioned from birth to obey, was irresistible.

"Dad?"

The world shifted again. Jeremy felt his mind whirl, saw the lights shift and heard heavy footsteps approaching like the beating of primal drums, timed with his heartbeat. He knew he was falling, but somehow he couldn't react to it. Strong hands clasped him under his arms, hands too

large, covering his shoulders, fingers gripping and
lifting.

Then—mercifully—it was dark.

Jeremy woke next to the scent and cool caress of
leather. He was curled in a chair. How was that
possible? A single chair, club style, with brown
leather and metal rivets. Voices droned, the sound
shifting and growing more clear with each beat of
his heart. He smelled smoke, thick in the air above
him, and he saw that a single dim bulb hung from
a bare wire in the center of the room.

Jeremy curled tighter. He wanted to know what
was being said, to put it into perspective before he
sat up. It was all a mistake, obviously. He shouldn't
be there. Not like this, not small and vulnerable,
shivering in a chair shrouded in shadow, but alone
and brooding in his father's room. It would all fade
if he sat up. He would be passed out across that
bed, nothing on the wall behind him at all. Nothing
but a mirror to stare into that would stare back and
mock his meaningless life—that would show him
the younger face of the father he'd lost.

"She's hung there nearly ten years," a deep, guttural voice cut through Jeremy's thoughts. "Hung
her there myself. The nail is a square one; drew it
by hand from the very wood of that ship."

There were murmurs, but no words, in reply,
and the voice continued until an image twisted into

shape in Jeremy's mind. It was Terry, but not exactly Terry. It was an aged, too-squat Terry with a beard gone gray down the center and gnarled, liver-spotted hands. It was a Terry two generations back, when the barbershop had been so much more than a barbershop, and the back room had been sacred.

"She'd ridden the waves so long it took a good hour's work just to wipe away the salt scum that held her to the prow. She was bolted down, of course, but those bolts had long since surrendered to salt and wind. They crumbled like dust when I tried to pry them loose. For all that, it was no easy task. That ship clung to her like a lover, green mossy slime stretching like some godforsaken glue. Two more days and she'd have dined with Davy Jones himself. The plan was to scuttle her over the far side of the reef, where her bones could blend with the coral and not be a hazard."

"Seems a shame," a softer voice replied, floating out from the far corner of the room. "I mean, that ship was a beauty. Shame to see her go down."

The silence that followed grew heavy, and despite the ludicrous notion of cowering in a chair much too big to be real, Jeremy felt himself shiver as the weight of it settled over the room. Someone coughed, and a glass hit the table with a heavy clunk.

"Maybe you should have let her go, too." The

words echoed. Jeremy recognized his father's voice. For some reason this was more comforting than disturbing in that moment.

There was a quick grating sound as a chair pushed away from the table. Heavy footsteps followed, and then Terry Brown's grandfather's rough voice continued.

"I couldn't bear to see her go. Not that way. Not after all I knew. She didn't belong to the sea—not then, not ever, though the barnacles and the weather had done their best to disguise her as one of their own." He paused again, then added more softly. "I couldn't send her back to him. Not that."

"Tell us," the soft voice Jeremy didn't recognize cut in. "Tell us again."

Jeremy dared to uncoil his small frame slightly, peeking just over the arm of the old leather chair. He saw a tall, broad-shouldered man with his back to the table, one hand gently caressing the cheek of the figurehead on the wall. The woman's eyes returned that gaze with more emotion than was possible, and Jeremy ducked back into the tentative safety of the chair.

"They said she was beautiful," the elder Brown's voice rose, a practiced storyteller practicing his art. "So beautiful that men would travel miles just for the chance to see her face, or hear her voice. They say she had the beauty that starts wars, or ends a dynasty. They say . . . she was loved . . ."

Jeremy felt the world shift again, and he started from the leather seat. His balance failed, and he teetered to the side, clutching at the arm of the chair. It wasn't there. He grabbed an armful of air and toppled, crying out softly and striking the floor hard. His senses reeled, and he felt the soft brush of something on his cheek. The acrid scent of moth-balls filled his nostrils and he coughed violently, rolling to his back.

The silence of his parents' room surrounded him. The ceiling—lowered tiles he remembered his father laying in place, one at a time on the rickety, dangling framework that held them suspended over the room—shimmered.

"Makes the room look longer and wider."

Jeremy heard the voice clearly. His father's voice. Staring at the tiles, the room in the back of the bar-bershop fading from his mind slowly, he could still hear the words as clearly as the day they'd first been spoken. He remembered the skeptical frown in his mother's eyes, and the silent nod. He remembered thinking that the tiles did nothing but make the room short and squat. He remembered saying nothing.

Rising slowly, he reached to the bed for support and levered himself to his feet. The wall was bare. Nothing. Not even a photograph, or a gilt-framed mirror to fill the space. The mirror he might have understood, because then the face he'd touched could have been his own.

On the nightstand beside the bed, a framed photograph of his parents watched him.

"Not this time, old man," Jeremy whispered.

He grabbed the pillows from the head of the bed and yanked free the down comforter, heading for the hall. Moments later, without a backward glance, he slipped through the doorway into his old room. He didn't flip on the light. He sprawled out over the bed and wrapped himself in the comforter, sliding his head between two down pillows and closing his eyes, drifting off to sleep before the dreams could descend and trap him in that netherworld between rest and reality.

Autumn in Cedar Falls was a quiet time. Things were ending and beginning, school in session and the football season in full swing. Churches were gearing up for the final bake sale before Thanksgiving, and the road crews were oiling and winterizing their equipment for the annual war with the weather. Despite the comfortable familiarity of it all, Jeremy couldn't shake free the cold knot of ice from his chest.

He could still hear his father's voice, and every time he closed his eyes, the scents of leather and tobacco permeated his world. He drove straight through the center of town, skipping the market and passing the general store, still in operation despite the competition of the new Super Wal-Mart down by the highway. There was only one place he was likely to get his answers.

He parked right in front of the barbershop, waiting until the dust had settled before he stepped out and closed the door behind himself. There was no light inside, but he knew Terry was open. The barbershop had always been open—Jeremy couldn't remember a time when it had not been. Of course, most of those memories were of visits with his father, and there was no clarity of time, or space. Jeremy had been more of an accessory than a companion, brought along because it was what fathers in Cedar Falls did.

Now there was no father, and the town was slowly dying around the edges. So little remained of what had seemed so huge and imposing those many years in the past that the town hung against the sky like a tattered and torn postcard. Not many people were up and about on a Saturday morning, at least not in town. There were a couple of kids playing in the park out front of the post office, and just before Jeremy reached the barbershop door, a police cruiser rolled slowly past behind him, moving on to other pockets of inactivity en route to the diner by Route 12.

Jeremy wondered fleetingly why he hadn't noticed the general decline the day before. Everything had seemed so . . . quaint. So rural and down-home comfortable. Now it looked like a too-old prop in a bad horror movie. The buildings leaned, seemed ready to fall over backward at the slightest provocation, nothing more than propped up plywood silhouettes.

The barbershop was dark—even more so than before—and though the door was open, there was no sign that Terry was open for business. There was no sign of any activity at all, in fact. Dust covered the chairs and the walls were dingy. Jeremy released the door and it swung to with a squeal of old metal in need of oil. The only illumination came through the slats of the blinds to his rear, and from beneath the crack of the door to the back room. From there a soft, yellowish light trickled, slipping to puddle just beyond the base of the door, which was closed.

"Terry?" Jeremy didn't call out too loudly. Something held him back. There was no answer.

He called out again, a bit more insistently, and stepped closer to the door in back. "Terry? Are you there?"

Nothing again, and moments later he stood, ear to the wooden frame of the door, trying to press his eye to the crack that was releasing the light. The sound of shuffling feet reached him, and the soft murmur of voices.

Hesitantly, Jeremy reached out and rapped on

the door. At first he thought no one had heard him, and he was toying with the desire to knock louder, pounding until they let him in and told him what the hell was going on, when the door swung wide. The floor beneath him lurched sickeningly, tumbling him forward, and Jeremy reached out with a cry that drowned quickly in the roar of . . .

Waves. Crashing, rolling high above and tumbling toward him, foam-tipped and peppering his face and eyes with hard, stinging salt-slaps of spray. His stumble brought him up abruptly against a wooden rail, and he clutched the slimy surface tightly as his chest slammed into the solid wood and his knees threatened to buckle from the impact.

The water hit then, and everything else disappeared. Jeremy pressed himself tightly to the wood, clutching with his hands and gripping with his knees, fighting the crushing weight of the cold, relentless pull of the seawater as it pounded, then receded with a sickening sucking sound over the side, and the world tilted backward as quickly as it had leaned forward. Closing his eyes, Jeremy clung more tightly still to the rail, fingers slipping and groping along the wet wood for purchase, feet threatening to slip off behind him and down.

For an eternity of deafening sound and flashing lightning, he hung nearly perpendicular to the sea, then he rushed back the other way, compressed tightly to the wooden rail and his breath left him. Voices cried out, nearly lost in the gale, and Jeremy's mind swam with the words, trying to order them so they made sense, trying to find the courage to release the rail, turn, and step back through the door and into the barbershop—the world.

The same world that chose that moment to lurch again—not so violently this time—and Jeremy felt the ship turning beneath him, felt the prow coming about, just in time, slicing the next of the monstrous waves that had threatened moments before to wash him from the deck into a sea of insanity. The voices grew clearer, and Jeremy risked releasing the rail with one hand to brush the soaked hair from his eyes.

It was dark—too dark to make out anything much farther than the length of his arm from his face, but the lightning flashes gave a strobed pseudolight just visible through the stinging salt. Jeremy could make out the prow of the ship, dropping down with a stomach-stealing lurch to shimmy at the base of a huge swelling wave, then rising, so high that only the sky and the angry face of the storm—creased in deep green, blue-black, and silver by the searing crackles of lightning— filled his vision. There was a shape, solid and un- moving, like a body leading the ship through the storm. A woman. Droplets of water washed back and off, giving the illusion of silver hair in each lightning burst.

From behind, strong fingers gripped suddenly beneath Jeremy's arms, and he was jerked from the rail and hauled up and back. The ship was no more steady than before, but the danger of slipping from side to side had passed, and moments later Jeremy crashed to the wall of what must have been the ship's cabin.

"Get inside!" The words screamed through his eardrums, blocking out the storm, just for an instant, and Jeremy turned, wild-eyed. Terry stood there. Not Terry—taller with similar features. The man's hair waved wildly about his head and his eyes smoldered with barely controlled anger . . . and strength.

"Get below, damn you!" The man repeated, cuffing Jeremy on the side of the head. "I've not enough men to make it without you."

Other hands groped from the shadowed doorway of the cabin and Jeremy was jerked inside, just as another wave crashed across the deck and threatened to drag him back to the railing, or farther. As he tumbled backward into the shadows, Jeremy caught a last lightning flash. The woman's figure stared out over the waves stoically.

His foot caught on the top stair, and he tumbled, ignoring the loud cursing of whoever it was that had dragged him to safety. He felt the contact as the two of them slammed into the wall, then continued back and down, banging one knee painfully and twisting midair trying to get his hands beneath him. There was nothing. Nothing but shadow, and as he passed to darkness, he felt damp wood as his hands struck first, chin following, in a jarring tangle of tar-soaked hemp and salt-soaked planks. The darkness that followed was sudden, and complete.

Jeremy returned to consciousness amid the scents of leather and tobacco. His head pounded painfully, and his eyes refused to focus. The room was adrift in smoke—tobacco smoke, pungent and overpowering. He coughed, hand rising to cover his mouth and body convulsing until he bent nearly double from the effort to draw clean air into his lungs. His eyes stung, and he could barely focus through the pain, so he closed them tightly.

"Quite a tumble."

The words hung in the air, making no sense coming from the direction and voice that they did. Jeremy brushed his fingers gingerly over the growing knot on his head and forced his eyes open once more.

He was in the back room of the barbershop. The old refrigerator hummed too loudly against the wall. Terry sat across the table from him, an open beer resting between cupped palms.

"I was wrong," Terry went on. "Been here by

myself so long, I'd started to think things would come full circle and end. Seemed right. Now I see she's been callin' you back all along."

"She?" Jeremy coughed the word out.

Terry just watched him, raising his beer and taking a long drink.

"You know who I mean," he said at last. "Now I have a story—*the* story. You just sit there and try to concentrate."

Terry rose slowly, moving to the refrigerator and drawing forth a second cold beer, which he carried across the room and placed in front of Jeremy on the table. The barber untwisted the cap with a quick jerk of his wrist and left the bottle to stand, tiny wisps of steam rising from the neck that reminded Jeremy of the ship—the waves. The throbbing in his head subsided to a dull ache, and he rose, moving the leather chair he'd been leaning back in closer to the table and grabbing the beer tightly. He raised the cold bottle to press it against his temple for a moment, then took a drink and met Terry's gaze.

"Tell me."

"It started in Scotland," Terry began slowly. His eyes, and his voice, took on a distance and a depth they'd not seemed to possess previously. "None of our fathers were even gleams in their own fathers' eyes at the time, but one thing was the same: the ocean. Even then, when women waited by the fires and wars were fought hand to hand, enemies staring one another in the eye and defying death, she called to us. There was one who answered.

"Angus was his name, and he took to the sea so young they say he was sailing from near the day he was born. The son of a son of a sea captain, bred to the ocean—the far shore. Born with the burning need to see what lay beyond the next wave. Angus Griswold belonged to the sea.

"Until he met her," Terry stopped, nodding toward the door, and the barbershop beyond—the woman hanging on the wall—the world that seemed so distant Jeremy could scarcely grant it credence.

"She was the daughter of a merchant he met in his travels. Angus wasn't one to settle in one place, but the day he met her, he found that an anchor had been cast that would not dislodge. She was beautiful. Beyond anything he'd seen, rivaling even the blue of the deepest lagoons and the scent of the islands after a storm, she drew him. At night, on the deck of his ship, he would think of her, writing letters long into the night, only to crumple them and toss them aside in anger, drowning his imagination in rum and dark thoughts, until even his men began to talk.

"He returned to Scotland soon after, and erected a keep overlooking the waves, tall and strong, of stone dragged from the very edge of the sea. All that time, he kept her face in his heart. He wrote more letters, and eventually, a few of them weren't crumpled. He sent the first, then the second, and when she replied to his third, he wrote again, until at last he found himself before her father, a tall, thin man with piercing eyes. You've seen those eyes, mirrored in the countenance of his daughter.

"They were wed, soon after, and settled into that keep. That prison."

"Prison?" Jeremy asked, finally finding the courage and strength to take the beer in a shaky hand and draw deep. "You said it was a keep."

"It was that," Terry said softly. "It kept him from his other love—his oldest love. It kept him from the sea, while holding it out before him like a carrot dangled before an ass. She loved him, Jeremy. She loved him with all her heart, mind, soul. She loved him, and in the end, it wasn't enough.

"Ten years to the day after he brought her home, Angus bought a boat. He told her it would be for short trips—jaunts up the coast and back—but she knew. In his eyes, the waves danced, and the sun set over shores with unknown coastlines.

"He sailed within the year."

"Sailors have always sailed away," Jeremy said, lifting his eyes to meet the barber's. "They come home."

"Not Angus," Terry shook his head and sipped his beer. "Not that time.

"He was gone a year before she began to really worry, sending letters home to her father, who was less than sympathetic. He'd received her dowry, and she was aging—still beautiful, but not of marrying age—and still married, in any case, to Angus. The year stretched into another, and another—ten years, Jeremy. She lived alone in that keep for ten years, spending the money Angus had amassed in a life of sailing and trade, and pining for the one thing that had drawn her to the ocean's side. The one thing she couldn't have.

"Every night, she watched at the balcony outside her room until the sun set and the moon rose high above the waves. Every night she prayed. Some say, near the end, when the loneliness had started to make her crazy, that she prayed to others than the God we know. There were books found in her towers, books none could place or translate—some written by hand, others printed in faraway lands. Angus must have brought them home, but it was obvious that his lover was the one to find their use.

"Then one day, the ship returned."

"You said he never came back."

"And he did not. The ship came back. Most of his men came back. Angus died of a fever, wasted away to nothing in the cabin of that ship. They buried him at sea, but before he died, he set them to bring his boat home. To bring her the treasures and secrets of the world he'd found. To tell her he loved her.

"None of it mattered. They pulled in and she flew to that shore a woman possessed, to find no man, but only wealth. Only salt-soaked board and men too long away from home. Only more loneliness washed ashore.

"They brought it all to her, and she held a feast such as had not been seen in those parts since Angus himself was alive. They drowned themselves in the food they'd missed and the local girls, washed it all down with barrels of wine. She watched, smiling all the while as if she was sharing their good humor.

"When they woke, every man jack was locked in that ballroom. She'd had men come in during the night and bar the doors with stout planks. They were left to rot with what remained of the food and the wine, even the women who'd joined them. They carried on and wailed at her, even tried to set the place on fire. None of it worked. They were trapped, and she was going to go and let them stay, leave and never come back."

Jeremy shuddered, casting a glance at the door—toward what lay beyond. "What happened?" he asked softly.

"That night, she stood on her balcony as always," Terry replied. "As she stood, staring into the waves, he came to her. Moss was matted and woven into the long hairs of his beard, and his eyes were half eaten by fish, but he came, staggering from the waves. She just watched him come, no effort to help him or to hinder. She watched as he staggered to the walls of the keep and beat his rotting hands against the stone walls.

"'Let them go,' he cried. 'Let them go, my love. I've come back.'

"No one knows for certain if she listened," Terry said at last. "She released the men the next day, giving them back enough of what they'd brought her to build a new ship. She made certain that everything was perfect—every board, every sail handpicked. And she sent for an artist. A young man, some say a eunuch. He brought the wood with him from Egypt, a solid block of it, taking up half his cart. As the ship was built, the man worked."

"She sailed with that ship?" Jeremy asked, breaking the silence.

"No. She died. She died, alone in her tower, leaning on the wall that overlooked the waves below, but the work was finished, and when they saw what she'd commissioned, the work the eunuch had left, the men would not leave her behind."

Both men stared at the doorway now. Beyond it, they could feel the draw of the wood, dark and curving tightly to the wall behind, eye sockets of something darker than shadow. In their heads, a voice, calling out softly.

"Your great-grandfather found that ship," Jeremy breathed. "He brought her here."

Terry rose, turning toward the refrigerator again without a word, and the lights flickered suddenly, threatened to die, then steadied. They were dimmer, their radiance more yellow, and Jeremy staggered half to his feet, bracing himself on the arms of the chair as the floor lurched sickeningly.

"Damn," Terry cursed. He turned back, a brown longneck bottle in his hand. Tipping it up, he took a long swig and strode across the deck to where Jeremy now stood, wild-eyed and staring at the doorway, now a stairway once more. Beyond the walls, the waves crashed, and Terry—not Terry—handed over the bottle with a wild-eyed stare.

"We can't let her go down," the man whispered softly, almost plaintively. "We must keep her afloat. She . . . she loves me."

Jeremy took the bottle, turned to the stairs, and staggered through—into the clear night air beneath the stars. His car stood just to his right, and the moon was bright and full. He downed the beer in a single gulp and fell heavily over the hood of his car. In the shadows behind him, he felt the weight of eyes, and the call of farther shores.

It was good to be home.

OUR WORLD, HOW FRAGILE

Paul Melniczek

Robert blinked, and his head felt strange. He didn't feel . . . right.

He looked down the aisle from the checkout, where he held a small paper bag filled with . . . stuff? He didn't even know what he'd purchased. But that mattered little.

What really mattered were the two men in dark jackets and wraparound black sunglasses who watched him from the back of the grocery store, near the fruit stand, which was filled to overflowing with piles of apples. Robert froze, feeling cool metal—coins in his hand—and hearing someone mumbling words to him that he couldn't quite catch. . . .

There was a store clerk, a woman by her clothing, her head looking away in the other direction.

The lighting was poor, trickling in from the ceiling bulbs, and things appeared distorted. Robert ignored the clerk, closing his hand around the change and automatically placing it in his trouser pocket. Robert sensed danger coming from the two men staring him down. Two men whom he *knew* beyond any doubt were after him, and would kill him once they managed to corner him somewhere.

No, he definitely wasn't all right. . . .

Robert turned away and headed for the entrance, stepping onto a large mat as mechanical glass doors opened before him. Outside, he was surrounded by the buzz and hum of a sprawling urban sidewalk, filled with countless men and women with nondescript faces parading in every direction as they went toward their individual destinations.

Instinctively, Robert pivoted to his left, hurrying directly for a large gray bus with door yawning wide open as it swallowed a number of pedestrians within its dark maw. Time was running out for him, and his only thought was to reach the bus. He knew the men were now leaving the store and would catch him if he slowed. This was an escape from those pursuing, and without hesitation Robert scurried ahead, leaping in before the doors could fully close. Breathing hard, he fed the change into the metal container. Even though it was the exact amount, he didn't question the fact, only accepted it as what was needed. The bus driver's face was hidden beneath the hood of a large, bulky overcoat.

Robert passed down the aisle, glancing across the dim interior at the nonentities—faces shrouded by newspapers, faces turned to windows, hats pulled low over faces, and gloom obscuring faces. Unsettled by the bus and its anonymous occupants, Robert ignored these things, melting into the shadows himself as he pushed and tripped his way into the very back, flopping down onto a ripped seat.

Fear held him tightly within its grip, and he felt the restless flutter of his heart in his chest. Sweat poured across his brow, clammy fingers pattered along his back, unpleasantly finding a spot in the middle that made him feel cold and uncomfortable. Robert heard the doors slam shut as the bus churned forward, the engine laboring in protest. The acrid smell of exhaust was strong, and he nearly choked from the bitter fumes. Peering outside, he looked onto a dismal world, the tainted bus windows making everything appear drab and lonely.

He looked for a sign of his pursuers, but couldn't spot them as the bus scudded away, leaving the grocery store behind. Robert backed deeper into his seat, relieved that there was no one else sharing the section. He peered forward, staring at the backs of heads, and the sides of faces, all of them shadowed and indistinct. There was an undercurrent of unease flowing silently along the seats and aisles that Robert couldn't directly identify but keenly felt. His inner senses were more vivid than the outer ones, blazing with conviction that *something* was terribly wrong. The passengers seemed almost like mannequins to him, breathing and living, but not really alive. Not like he was.

It was a horrifying and frustrating notion, but one which he had no explanation for—that, and his lack of knowledge concerning the men who followed him. He possessed no knowledge of the reasons, only the actuality. *They* were after him, and would not rest until he was killed.

Robert stared ahead, such chilling thoughts plaguing his mind. He realized that he still held the grocery bag, and he probed inside, fishing out a round object. A piece of fruit, an apple. He bit into the red skin and chewed, the flavor dull, somehow incomplete. Robert continued eating until the apple was reduced to a thin core, and then he tossed it onto the floor of the bus, knowing that this careless action would go unnoticed.

The bus rumbled onward, and he glimpsed cement and brick buildings plummeting upward, behemoths expanding beyond his limited vision, vanishing into gray oblivion. Cars and trucks bellowed past, and at times he caught a chance glimpse of the driver, or occupant, featureless and cold. But he was different from them all.

For he *felt*.

He was alive and aware, his emotions whirling in confusion. Foremost was fear—a steady, growing dread of the men following him and what they would do when they reached him. Even now, Robert wondered where they were. Who they were. He couldn't recall when they started after him, or even what he'd done to rouse their hatred. But there could be no doubt as to their intent. Escape was the only thing he could do. To where, he didn't know, but he was confident that he would make the right decision.

The bus stuttered, bouncing over something in the road, and Robert fixed his attention on the passengers again. The front of the vehicle was shrouded in murkiness, the driver existing only in his memory, seemingly a world away. Despite the separation of scant feet, Robert felt as though the other riders were unreachable. He sat there in his own cosmos, a lonely, frightened man, hunted by a determined enemy who only wanted him dead. The heads twitched and jerked, arms moved to turn a page, legs shifted to balance weight. A cough, a murmur, a low voice speaking words, like a toneless, flat instrument too weary to play a melody anymore, spent and used up. There was activity around him, but it was distant and merely served as background to the greater setting—the one focused on *him*.

How he understood this, Robert had no idea. But it was as certain as the breath exuded from his lungs, the agitated drum of his heartbeat, the sticky drops of sweat on the palms of his hands. He had the ghastly feeling that they were all just puppets, performing in a hopeless and tragic event, one that featured him as the main character. Their parts were inconsequential but necessary, if only to add validity to Robert's dilemma. And he could not go to them for help, as it would prove futile. For a moment, he thought about tapping the shoulder of the man who sat in front of him, even reaching out with one wavering hand, briefly, before withdrawing it again. It was no good. There was nothing for him there. A prop, a filler. A body with fixed, and limited purpose.

His mind wandered to the pursuers, and he suddenly had a terrible notion. What if the two men had boarded the bus without him knowing it? He couldn't even see the front, as the dim lights made the vehicle look more like a murky cave than anything else.

His anxiety mounted, pausing at a new level of terror. He felt all the physical signs, cowered from the mental ones. His right eye trembled; there was a tic beneath it. A fresh coating of sweat bathed him in cool waves. Robert strained to pierce the obscurity and see if the men were lurking somewhere along the dusty aisle—creeping slowly, steadily ahead, with circumspect movement, until they had their prey cornered. Robert felt a scream lodged deep within his throat, but he knew it would go unanswered. The world was deaf to the danger which threatened him, and he was alone to fend for himself.

Then something moved, a larger shadow detached itself from the haze. Two shadows. *They* were on the bus, and coming for him. . . .

His throat parched, he gasped, his body tingling with adrenaline and fear. Reflexively, he backed up further into the seat, knowing it would do no good. They knew where he was, had sprung onboard without his knowledge. Robert turned, automatically grabbing the emergency handle. There was no other way. . . .

He lurched to the side and flung the panel open. The bus was moving along at a brisk pace, and he knew there was great danger in such action. But there was danger in every move for him.

Without hesitation he kicked it open all the way, dropping down in an attempt to land on his feet and roll to the side. He felt the air rush by in a *whoosh*, and he was weightless for a long moment. Then the impact came as he fell heavily on the dirty road, the stench of oil, tar, and exhaust blending together into one noxious assault. His sense of balance was fragmented, and the gray world spun around in a vortex of colorless stone and shrieking metal. There was pain in his leg and side, and he tasted the coppery warmth of his own blood in his mouth.

The world finally slowed, then paused, and he knew he'd stopped rolling. Breathless, he lay still for a while, hearing the background noise of the city toiling through its automation. A city that could not help him.

Robert pushed himself up with a bruised arm and he looked around. It was amazing that a car had not struck him. Impossibly lucky.

He stared to his left at an alley strangled by shadows. Able to walk, he limped along, heading for the corridor. People passed him by, but like all the others, took no notice of him, the faces vague, always turned at an angle that prevented him from seeing their features.

Robert had no answers, and no time to pursue them at the moment.

The alley was littered with piles of filth, the residue of a heartless metropolis. Dented aluminum cans, ripped garbage bags, and heaps of newspapers all hugged the sides of the corridor, as if trying to remain obscure. Robert felt there was something very important about his observation, but couldn't pin it down. He hurried forward, keeping his head bowed. His entire body ached, but at least he could still move.

A shuffling figure appeared from the gloom—a

derelict wearing an oversize trench coat. The bum staggered about, but in a peculiar manner, as if following a carefully laid out path. Robert paused, despite his fear of pursuit, to watch the bizarre spectacle. He wanted to grab the man, stare into his face and scream at him, *What's going on! What's the matter with you?*

Instead he let the vagrant pass him by, meandering to either side, tripping here, stuttering there, but always advancing toward an unknown destination. Like he was merely playing a part in something much larger. . . .

Robert's boots clicked along the rough stone, and he hurried down the alley. Several yards later, something loomed dark and massive before him, stopping him where he stood. Squinting, he saw the outline of a huge brick wall, windowless and as final as a verdict. Dead end.

He needed to go back. Before . . .

But it was too late. Footsteps echoed from somewhere behind him. The game was over.

Robert looked desperately for a way out, and immediately spotted a fire escape several feet to the right; he lunged forward. The metal was moist to his touch, rusted and dirty. Ignoring the fresh burst of pain searing his limbs, he pulled himself up, gaining the bottom platform. The sounds of pursuit quickened, and Robert felt his heart pounding in his chest. The fire escape was slippery, only adding to his difficulty. He clambered higher, at times using his hands on the steps, like an animal climbing a staircase.

Time was of no consequence. The only thing he knew was to flee.

Up he went; one level, another. His hunters were relentless, and he heard furtive movement below, but he tried not to think about it. Several times he slipped, adding more bruises to his legs. Once he struck his chin, the impact nearly knocking him unconscious. He passed a number of doorways, finally hesitating at one on the fifth floor. He reached for the handle and found the door was open. Entering quickly, he slammed it shut behind him, turning the lock with a loud *snap*, which disturbed the silence inside. Scanning his surroundings, he saw that he was in a narrow hallway, dimly illuminated by a scattering of lightbulbs which flickered off and on, as if in some undefinable pattern.

Robert plunged ahead, running along the hallway, which smelled of must and spoiled food. He came to a stairway and paused for a moment. Behind him nothing moved. The quiet lay upon the building like an invisible blanket, smothering everything. He went up, knowing only one thing—keep moving. His boots thudded on the tired wood, the echoes swallowed up by the damp walls. He passed several levels, ignoring the closed panels. He needed to go higher. Put as much distance between himself and the pursuers as possible. He didn't know where they were, but they would certainly not give up.

The certainty of this knowledge bothered him, but he dared not pause to question the fact.

Robert soon gained the top stair, which ended at a large metal door. He pushed it open and found himself standing on a black rooftop, vents and pipes jutting outward in several places, a number of rusted barrels standing upright like mute sentinels. The sky above was a veil of gray, murky and lifeless. Like everything else, he thought . . .

A backdrop. Inanimate.

What's going on here?

Trotting forward, he searched for another door, one which would lead him back again to another part of the structure. But this seemed to be a poor choice, he thought to himself. Would there be another exit? He looked around frantically, realizing that he'd used the only entrance.

He had to retrace his steps—there was no other way. Why had he not considered this before? Completely frustrated at his own irrationality, Robert returned to the doorway, noticing that the sky had darkened. And the door was closed.

Hadn't he left it open? He thought so, and as he stood there, two shadows slunk from the side of the barrels, materializing into the forms of his grim pursuers.

Without hesitation, he pivoted and ran for the other end of the building. Footsteps followed, slow and firm, mocking his own panic with their deliberate pace. He reached the other side, knowing that he only had seconds until the men would have him cornered.

Peering over a wall that lined the roof's edge, he spotted a narrow ledge, a catwalk at least a dozen feet down from the brink. Robert lifted himself up, groaning at the renewed agony burning in his limbs, and dropped over. He landed hard, and he felt a twinge in his left ankle. Stumbling, he nearly fell over the side. Balancing himself, he crawled to his right, staying close to the cold brick. Long moments passed as he moved ahead in this fashion, the air gusting in his face, gripping his bones with nasty, icy fingers. There was no part of him that didn't hurt. He chanced a glimpse over the edge and felt a brief flash of vertigo, both alluring and alarming. He failed to see the street below, instead only seeing haze and angles. Continuing, something solid loomed before him, directly on the catwalk.

Someone stood there, and he knew one of his pursuers had somehow blocked his escape. There was a scraping sound behind him, and he turned his neck. The other man had scrambled down as well. He was trapped, from the front and back now. The roof was out of reach, and no windows were open nearby.

Trembling with fright, he noticed something sticking out from below—a drainspout descending into oblivion. In an incredibly hazardous move, he lowered himself to the edge, feet first, one hand clinging desperately to the stone, the other hand pawing at the air for purchase. The men moved in closer, and Robert felt himself slipping. His fingers were rubbed raw, and he grabbed for the elusive spouting. Terrible seconds passed, and then he felt the slickness of the drainspout in his grasp. Gambling that it would hold, he dropped farther, placing all his hope in its not cracking from his weight.

Leaving go entirely of the ledge, he placed both hands on the spouting and wrapped his legs around as well. He began lowering himself as the structure buckled, and every inch felt like an eternity, drowning him with the fear of falling. He closed his eyes, willing his hands and feet to retain their hold. Robert felt himself moving downward, and the absolute futility of his situation blazed forth within the blackness of his mind.

What's going on? Why am I even here?

There were no answers to comfort his torment. He couldn't even recall what he'd been doing before entering the store. For that matter, Robert didn't remember *anything* prior to seeing his pursuers inside the grocery, almost as if his mind had been completely wiped clean, and only the present existed. The past was like a massive, impregnable wall. The future was a shadow of uncertainty. When he tried to think ahead, his mind went blank, as if something prevented him from even *pursuing* thought in this direction.

And the present seemed to be just a sequence of terrible, sporadic events, the only purpose being to thrust him from one dire situation into another. . . .

Robert had the hideous feeling that he was caught up in something much larger than he could ever understand, with reasons beyond his comprehension, ones that he could never possibly know the truth about.

Daring to open his eyes a crack, he realized that he now was completely alone, hovering over air and not moving anymore. Robert wasn't sure if he even still clung to the spouting or not. . . . It was as if he were the only one allowed to exist, with every other vague detail withered into nothingness. The grayness surrounded him, consumed all, and he felt numb to all his senses.

No sound reached his hearing.

No smell or taste.

His pain was now gone, and all he saw was gray. But even his vision began to fade, and he felt weightless, his thoughts leaking out into oblivion.

Why . . . ?

This question was all that was left of Robert,

and it held him together for one more brief moment. In that small period of time, his last dim recollection was of something being ripped apart—the entire world, *his* world, being crushed into nonexistence.

And then even that was gone.

Slowly crumbling. . . .

In his hand, he hefted the paper for a moment, and then tossed it into a circular trash can. He looked over as a figure entered the office; his wife.

"What, didn't like that one?"

He shook his head. "No, just couldn't find direction. I wandered and got lost somewhere. So I threw it away."

She slowly approached. "Doesn't that bother you, though?"

"Hmm?" A curious look.

"Creating something, and then abandoning it. You gave birth to an idea, people, and then tossed it all away. Doesn't that make you sad, even just a little?"

"Maybe," he answered. "But that's just part of it all. Visualizing, forming, and starting again from scratch if it doesn't work out. You deal with the inanimate. Put them through the motions, try to make it all come alive. Sometimes you're successful, other times you're not."

His wife reached inside the trash, pulling out the discarded paper. "Do you like the feeling of being a creator? There's a certain power in such creation. And destruction. . . ."

"I know," he answered quietly, moving to the single window and gazing outside. "With a simple magic wave of the hand, placing pen on paper, I've given birth to a unique world. And then once dissatisfied with my product, I cast it aside, like dust in the air."

"I wonder if the characters become more than what you intended."

"What do you mean?" He remained staring outside, the sky dull and flat.

"Formed from your mind, they're given a small dose of life, even if it's just in your thought, and maybe for only a fraction of time. That's almost like a taste of life, isn't it?"

"Strange idea." He almost laughed, then his face turned serious. "Never really thought of it like that, though." He paused for a moment. "Do you actually *believe* it might be possible?"

His wife joined him, standing at his side.

"Who knows?" She whispered. "Do any of us have answers to *anything*, or do we only have questions? Maybe we're all just going through the motions, with everything decided for us already."

He coughed. "That's a disturbing thought."

They both looked outside, watching in disbelief as vast cracks materialized like veins across the heavens, consuming the sky and swallowing all into nothingness.

THE CRAWL

Gerard Houarner

When Dylan Shiel woke up, he was belly-down on cold concrete, the early morning sun golden in his eyes and warm on his face, shining through an alley across the street. The morning chill raised goose bumps along his back and exposed arms.

The bones were loud in his head, and they were calling him back to the cave.

Birds sang. Weeds peeked through a crack in the sidewalk a hand's length from his nose. Buds were growing on the dipping branches of a magnolia by the curb. From somewhere nearby, cutlery clinked, plates and cups clattered. The smell of bacon spiced the breeze blowing from the river. Clouds skidded across a lightening slate dotted with fading stars looking over the town of Tomerance.

The last thing he remembered was looking up at the full moon at the mouth of the cave, and feeling as big and empty and dead inside as that bright disk, his fear as dark and endless as the space between the stars, right before going down into the earth to answer to the bones.

He had to get back to them.

Someone came running around the corner. Dylan turned his face to the ground. Steps skittered to a halt. Harsh, ragged breathing reminded him of when he'd had to run hard and long to get away from unpleasant things.

Unlike whoever had come up on him so quickly, so desperate to be first.

The kick exploded in Dylan's lower-right ribs, and he grunted, gritting his teeth against anything louder. One shot. All that was allowed. Whoever had kicked him sobbed, shuffled, but didn't leave. Dylan caught a glimpse of the shoes—a pair of basketball sneakers, familiar, but they were a popular style—and braced for another blow. That wasn't allowed, but neither was taking a second shot.

The second kick never came. The assailant ran off, satisfied at last. Dylan took it as a good omen.

A van drove by, side panel marked with a contractor's name. Dylan had done work for that man. The van kept going. Dylan didn't know if the driver hadn't seen him, didn't want to see him, or was hurrying to pick up the best of the day laborers lining the intersection just outside of town. Maybe he'd bring the whole gang over later.

The sun brightened, blinding him with its glare.

It was time to move. He had a long day ahead of him.

He started crawling down Central Avenue.

He'd heard changes in the way the bones sang, low and subtle at the back of his mind like a guilty conscience, all of the past week. At first he'd thought he should be getting ready for another carry. Only six had answered the call last time, and one of them had crawled, so that left five bound to the bones. If no one new showed up, the forced fellowship would be down to four and closer to extinction. If he lasted until there was no one left but him, who'd carry him out for the crawl?

That would have been a way to get out of his obligation.

But then the call grew louder: a steady drumbeat in his skull, a heart echo, accompanied by a low moan and a rumbling chant, punctuated by cutting shrieks. Day and night, even when he managed to fall asleep, the bones called in this new way. When he couldn't sleep, or hold down food, when liquor or smoke or even pills couldn't dull the impact, and he forgot the day of the week he was in, and didn't care about work or money or taking care of his family or himself, he understood he was the one.

Crying and prayer never worked before, and they didn't again. Going up to the cave before he was supposed to, with a stick of dynamite, only made him so sick he passed out in the woods. The bones wouldn't let him light the fuse to do himself in, either, though they let the flame burn down to his fingertips.

In the middle of the night, he got into the pickup and headed out of town. He woke up in a ditch and, worse, still alive. He tried using the shotgun, taking the barrel in his mouth and rigging a lever to pull the trigger, but lost the use of his limbs when it came time to kick and blast his brains out.

He stopped trying options that he'd already discovered didn't work long ago, when the bones first began calling to him. There was no point in adding to the suffering. So he went back home and began practicing the crawl, working his way across the living room floor the way he'd been taught long ago in basic training, then through the whole house, between the dining room chairs and under the table, as far as he could get into the space around the toilet bowl, behind the couch and in every closet. If the bones wanted him to crawl, he'd give them their goddam crawl.

Renee left then, and took their boys, Tom and Jake. She grew up in Tomerance, as he did. She'd seen the crawl and knew what was coming, though nothing about the mechanics behind the events, or his involvement in them. She'd never done anything to make the bones call to her, but given his reputation, she'd probably had suspicions about him.

A good thing she left, too, since he thought to rig traps with the iron, a few hammers, and hand weights, to simulate sudden and unexpected blows, so he could practice giving in to the pain. The boys didn't need to see their father in that condition. Maybe Tom had been old enough to sneak out and catch the last crawl on his own, but Jake hadn't been born yet. Tom would've enjoyed watching his father train as if for a torture olympiad, but for Jake, the display would've been too much. That one would make it out of town someday.

In the real crawl, with the bones singing in his head, Dylan used his arms and legs, kept his ass low, his head down. The rehearsal had toughened his joints and left him with bruises, but concrete was tougher than wood, tile and certainly carpet. Just like the first kick had been harder than anything he'd handled at home. After half a block, he was already aching. But that pain, or anything else he'd endured from his gang days to military duty in a desert of burning oil wells, was nothing compared to what was coming.

His mother was next.

He'd reached the front of the diner when she came out. The smell of bacon and fresh bread was thick in the air, making him hungry. She'd been waiting, watching, knowing the offering was usually dumped along Central Avenue, which is what locals called Route 491A coming through town. In the old days, he might have been dropped off at the Gitten Bridge, or on the old river dock, or even in the thickest part of the woods across the river, which was now protected parkland. In those days, the crawl might have taken days, with people riding or even walking to town from miles around. In these days of cars and instant gratification, those who needed to could make the trip in no more than half an hour. The crawl usually barely lasted the day.

He could tell it was Mom by the boots—the black ones he'd bought for her last Mother's Day. "I'm the first, aren't I?" she asked, coming through the glass diner door. She didn't offer anything to eat. Helping wasn't against the rules. It was even encouraged, as it made the offering last longer and gave more people a chance to come around. "I'm so proud," she said.

"Mom, I'm not supposed to talk about who comes or what happens."

"Oh, that's not right."

"Yes, it is. If I do, it ruins the sacrifice—"

"Nothing's ruined, dear," his mother said, crouching beside him and tousling his thick red hair. For a moment, he was embarrassed that he hadn't showered or shaved in days. "Your aunt Sandy, when she offered herself before you were born, she told me what everybody she could remember did to her, every last one. It was kind of a warning, I think, as some of them were angling to marry me and she didn't want me to suffer with any of the ones who were really bad."

His dad, before he left Mom, and the town and the county and even the country, had said something different: Mom should have been the one to give herself. For what she'd done. There'd been a couple of black boys passing through, staying well out of town. His mother had said some things about them, made her younger sister Sandy say she saw what was supposed to have happened. The boys were never seen again.

They'd both been young back then. They'd grown to play more tricks, like the way Sandy made a man marry her, and what Dylan's mom did to drive the one she loved but who didn't love her back to jump off the Gitten Bridge. They'd settled into calmer ways, and his father said he'd never believed all the stories about the sisters, which is why he married one of them.

Aunt Sandy had heard the bones. His mother should have heard them, too. But she was never involved in Tomerance's stranger traditions when he was growing up. And he'd never spotted anyone who might be her, under the disguises people affected to hide their shame at being called, in all the time he'd been coming to the cave. He was sure, as hazy as his memory was, that she hadn't been there last night to drag him out of the cave and dump him into the street for the crawl.

Mom never answered the bones. She probably didn't even hear them. Maybe she'd forgotten what she'd done, or never let the past wear at her like wind and rain until the skeletal remains of her wrongs were exposed. Whatever the reason, she never had the need to crawl.

Aunt Sandy had done the deed in her sister's place.

Dylan wanted to tell his mother that maybe Aunt Sandy had passed along the secrets as a way to share the burden with the person who should have carried it. That's how the bones might have forgiven spilling secrets to her sister.

He wanted to point out how easy it might have been to use her as an excuse for what he'd done, to say that all the harm she'd committed had somehow tainted him. He wished he'd had her smallness, her lack of awareness and imagination, so he could say that he'd been born bad and that all the things that had happened, in this county and in others, weren't his fault. If he'd said that long and loud enough to himself, through the haze of enough booze and drugs, maybe he would also have been able to shut the bones out of his head when they called. Of course, he didn't have her constitution. And there weren't enough drugs or alcohol to keep out the bones for very long.

He needed to say she didn't have to give him any of what she was carrying, because people claimed by the bones couldn't get any use out of the crawl. The meaning of the bones was clear on that point.

But he kept quiet because it wasn't his place to give. He was the one receiving.

"Mom, what are you carrying for me?" he asked. He glanced into the diner. There were no other customers, though one of the waitresses stood by the counter in her polished white running shoes, busy doing nothing with paper and pencil.

His mother rummaged in her handbag, and for a moment he thought she had brought him something to eat after all. But then sunlight glinted off of metal and her arm went up and came back down with something flashing in her hand and a sharp pain erupted in the flabby meat where his right shoulder joined his arm.

He had to crane his neck to see the knife sticking out of his T-shirt, light blue staining dark from blood leaking out around the blade. He hoped he wasn't going to lose the use of an arm so soon. That would be a bad omen.

Crying, she raised her arms to hit him with both fists closed, but stopped herself when she met his upturned gaze. "You have your father's eyes," she whispered, then collapsed on top of him with enough force to have qualified as a blow. She sobbed into his back.

The waitress came out and jabbed his left calf with a pencil. The cook followed and dribbled hot grease from a still-sizzling frying pan onto the exposed skin of his right ankle, where his jeans had rolled up and the athletic sock had slid down. The cook watched Dylan's skin burn, as if studying the effect of a change in a secret recipe. Then he left, and his Mom seemed to notice the smell of cooking flesh, and she left, too.

Dylan went on with the crawl, the knife still sticking up out of his back. Nothing major had been hit, so he was good to go for more.

Traffic along Central Avenue picked up with the morning commute and commercial delivery runs. Everyone had reason to pass through the middle of town today, it seemed. The bones had a different call for the townspeople. Dylan could almost remember what it sounded like—a faint wail, like a baby crying, that made people come out and release what they'd held in for so long.

The chief of police stopped by in his cruiser. The town's second cruiser pulled up behind him. Tomerance's entire police force of three full-time and three part-time officers came out and delivered one short, sharp blow each to Dylan's legs with their batons, as if they wanted to make sure he couldn't change his mind and run away. He'd played on the county high school football team with one of the officers. The father of another had arrested Dylan several times, though none of the charges ever led to a conviction. He'd never gotten along with the chief.

Someone laughed while playing with the knife handle sticking out of his back, though Dylan couldn't tell who through the blazing agony shooting up his legs. A knee was broken, that was for sure. Maybe both ankles. It was going to be a slow crawl.

After taking their one blow each, the officers left. They always did, even when it was one of theirs on the ground. Especially when it was one of theirs. They'd stayed away for three days ten years ago, when the old chief showed up, crawling.

Once the police were gone, the townspeople came out. The few outsiders present watched in horror, but the manifestation of the sacred and the savage worked its mystery and unlocked doors to their hidden natures. As Dylan had always seen it happen, strangers surrendered as easily as residents to the deeper-running currents of guilt, violence and enigma passing suddenly through their lives.

Most people punched, leaning over him and even getting down on one or both knees. Their blows were weak. They didn't have much to give. A few had practiced, thinking through the technical difficulties of effectively hitting a man on the ground. They'd performed the ritual at least once in their lifetimes, maybe several times, and been disappointed, perhaps frustrated. This time, they had vulnerable targets picked out. They knew they could turn him over, if they wanted to. They dropped with their punches, adding the weight of their falling bodies to the strength of their arms. Some even held a roll of quarters in their fists.

The ones who ran on instinct knew to kick, and where.

The contractor came back and promoted his business with the crowd by offering the use of tools: a hammer, a wrench, screwdrivers. After a while, Dylan couldn't tell what was being used. An argument broke out when someone pulled out his mother's knife to use on him again. At times like this, not everyone understood the bones in the same way. Some said it was against the rules, others said it was just fine, since they'd shared the hammer. The knife was lost in the argument and people moved on.

By midmorning, the early rush was done and Dylan had crawled three blocks. Pain, the blinding arc through the morning's time and the broken space of his body, subsided into a buzzing in his head, a steady, driving current through his body. His bones.

Dylan didn't need to crawl. He didn't want to

die. He'd been born with an engine of destruction in his heart, and he'd gone far and hurt many with its power. It had taken a long time for the bones to work the flaws in that engine so that, at last, it could be driven to its own annihilation. In the end, he'd never had a choice in what he'd done, or in paying the price for coming into the world.

The bones let him know it was time to come, their call rising over his denials and then his rehearsals of the past week to the crescendo of an unbearable keening vibration in every part of his body. He'd gone out at last to answer them, wishing he was more like his mother, immune to burdens. Or that there was someone like Aunt Sandy to take his place. Or that, in the court of bones, there was a way to hide evidence or intimidate witnesses, summon legal tricks out of lawyers or appeal decisions.

But there was no escape or reprieve. He moved on to the final turn of the journey he'd been on all his life. The darkness at the back of the cave, thick as night between the stars beyond the moon, embraced him. And delivered him into the wilderness of pain. His own, and all that grew and festered and spoiled in places only the bones could feel.

Pain, the blaze consuming every part of his body, let him go on. That fire was the fuel to the engine, forged by character and transformed by consequence, driving him along this last, terrible passage to the cave and whatever waited beyond.

Dylan turned on Poplar Street, went past Academia and Industry Avenues. The bones were drawing him back to the cave, and he was taking the shorter route, which took him through some rough countryside. Some folks didn't let things like being in town stop them, but a lot of people felt freer out of sight of everyone else. Dylan wanted to give the shy ones, the ones who needed it most, the chance to give what they had in themselves. That was a part of what the crawl was about, after all.

Dylan went on crawling.

The woman came up on him after he'd crossed the train tracks. She looked old enough to be his grandmother, with her white hair and thin, tremulous hands. But he recognized her as the mother of someone he'd known in school. A freshman, when he'd been a junior.

There'd been an accident, the kind resulting in being in the wrong place, time, and company. Dylan still remembered the boy's cries for help. He couldn't say for sure if he'd laughed.

"You're forgiven," she said, keeping her distance. Clasping her hands together over her belly, she continued, "I forgive you. You killed my baby boy. They couldn't prove it, but I know you did. He wasn't the first, either. Or the last. And you've done worse." She bowed her head as if in prayer. "But this isn't worth it," she continued. "Nothing's worth this. I don't want to see you go through what you put good people through. I don't want to see what happened to my baby."

She went away. Dylan bit back a shout to bring her back. He wanted to say thank you, to tell her that now, after years of the bones calling to him, he regretted what he'd done, wished he'd never committed the act that had hurt her and killed her son, longed to have never been born.

But saying those things wouldn't change anything, wouldn't make her turn around and let him see real forgiveness in her eyes, the kind with no pain from the loss he'd made her suffer, nor would speaking take away the joy he'd felt, still remembered feeling, and even, in the secret heart of certain nights, yearned to feel again, when he'd done those terrible things to other people.

The bones called. Dylan kept crawling.

In the hard scrabble, under the noon sun, a slim, long-haired blonde came out from a cluster of factory storage containers where homeless frequently sought shelter. She was dressed in baggy castoffs that made her look young, but beneath the grime covering her pitted faced she was closer to his age. He remembered a cleaner, youthful version of that face, twisted with pain underneath him. He turned his face to the earth, shut his eyes. Pebbles pressed against his flesh and smelled faintly of acrid chemicals.

"I'm sorry," she said. "Don't look."

He didn't. But he heard her gag and choke, felt blood splatter across his back. She collapsed, throwing an arm across one of his smashed legs and sending new shoots of pain up his spine.

He was at the tree line to the woods when his wife reached him. She was wearing her worn green sweats and the old, dirty running shoes he'd yelled at her last week for keeping. She'd said she didn't want to mess up her new sneakers, and he'd asked why'd she bother buying them, and the argument had spun out of control from there.

"What do you have?" he asked her.

"I don't have a thing for you, Dylan. I just stopped to see . . . to see how you were doing. There's nothing I could ever add to what you're going through."

Already, she was sounding like an ex-wife.

"Tom left the house early this morning, before I was up," she continued. "Didn't go to school. Jake cried, said Tom was running away because he couldn't take this small town, and he couldn't take you anymore. Jake had a hard time understanding. You know how sensitive he is." She waited for a response.

Dylan placed to whom that first set of sneakers that had run up on him belonged. But he followed the rules and didn't tell her what he knew. For once, he appreciated the cruelty in the compulsion directing him. And an instant later, knew that enjoyment was wrong.

"Are you going to stop this bullshit and help me look for our son?"

He kept crawling.

"That boy will never forgive you," she said. "Neither of them will." She left, her pace faster than when she'd approached him.

Pain spiked in his joints as he went through the woods, climbing the gradual incline. The earth was damp and teeming with bugs. Half-buried stones and fallen branches were like teeth gnawing on Dylan's flesh.

From the shadows, someone whispered, "It should have been me. I should be the one crawling to the cave. I'm sorry."

It wasn't either of his sons. The voice might have belonged to one of the people who came to the cave. Or it might have been someone pretending to be a member of their priesthood of the damned.

"I don't care," Dylan replied. He waited, feeling murder grow from the shadows. But the rage hadn't ripened yet, like his. Whoever was talking was only a beginner.

"I went down with some of the others last night," the stranger said. "We dumped you in town, but all the while, I knew I should have been the one. I need to be stopped."

Leaves rustled. Steel scrapped against rock. Then, quieter than the woods, someone wept.

Dylan moved on.

A woman came and kissed him, and he wished that had been his wife, but it was probably only someone who's heart he'd broken when he was young, or maybe she'd only loved him from afar. She was gone before he could ask if she had anything for him.

Dylan needed to rest. To die in the woods, letting the pain consume him until his engine broke down and caves and bones didn't matter. But there was no stopping, except for those who came looking for him. The bones wouldn't let him.

The incline grew steeper as he got into hill country.

School let out, and local teenagers returned from the county high school by car and bus. Dylan could tell because of the wild cries echoing under the trees. The kids had found out about the crawl, and the curious ones, and the wild ones, and the children who were like he'd been at their age, were out hunting for him.

A girl found him first. Dressed in loose black pants and a top, silver studs and jewelry decorating her pale flesh, she had the look of one of those outsider kids who people assumed had run away when they disappeared. Dylan knew the type well. But instead of taking a swing, or pounding him with a rock or a branch, she knelt beside him and wiped the blood from his face, pushed hair out of his eyes.

"I'll take your place," she said, with gentle gravity. "Get up. I'll lay down where you are. Beat me so I'll look like I'm the one that's been crawling."

Gratitude overwhelmed Dylan. He didn't know what to say to hope.

"I know where the cave is," she said. "I've been there, though the bones never called. I'll go to them, and I'll die there, and you'll be saved."

Yes was on Dylan's tongue. The word tasted sweet. But he could no more get up and let her have the crawl than beat and rape her. The bones called him, not her, and she had no stake in what he had committed.

Her offer struck the deepest of any hit he'd taken so far. He kept going, not answering her, not even asking if she had anything to give.

The kids caught up to him. They laughed and danced around him, keeping their distance and throwing rocks at first. Then the bold ones came close and used what they'd brought on him. Some of the bats and tools still had blood on them, from when their fathers and mothers had used them on Dylan earlier in the day. A giggling teenager taped M-80 firecrackers to his hands and lit the fuses. The explosions stunned Dylan for a moment. The stumps at the ends of his arms shocked him. The crowd of kids thinned suddenly, as if they, too, had seen too much. Dylan threw up, but the bones kept calling, and he kept going.

Evening closed off the woods to everyone except those who needed the cover of night to forget the rules and do what they had to do to him. He was stripped, and later, the chill breeze ran over his naked body and cooled the blood and other fluids sprayed over his wounds.

Someone threatened him with an axe, singing, "Here comes the chopper to chop off your head," while playing a flashlight beam first across the axe blade, then into his eyes. Dylan stretched his neck to offer him a good target, but didn't think the bones would let him get away with being murdered. The axe blade bit into his throat. His head lolled to the side. Pain ran through him, liquid and hotter than the sun, and the engine that drove him screamed.

He kept going.

The last to come set him on fire. Dylan wondered if he'd done anything personal to that one, or if gasoline and flame lived inside that spirit. But at least his burning body parted the pitch-black night and showed him that the cave wasn't far.

At last, he lay at the cave mouth, like a shaman, or a fool, come out of the wilderness to his home.

The bones fell silent. The cave became just a cave. The night, only the night. Pain fell away like worn-out clothing, and the engine that had taken him this far shut down, disintegrated. He was empty again, except perhaps for the dust of what he'd been.

Dylan thought he'd finally gone numb. He pushed himself forward. Discovered he had fingers again, and hands. Breathing hard, he ran those hands over his body. The cuts and bruises, the broken bones and crisped flesh were gone. He was whole again.

He had to be hallucinating. The pain had driven him insane. Or maybe he'd died, and his soul was set loose on the world as a ghost in punishment for escaping the bones.

Dylan sat up, back against the cave wall at the mouth, and carefully inventoried his senses and body. He heard himself breathing, tasted dirt. His flesh was solid. He was cold, even though his clothes had miraculously been reconstructed right on him. He was alive. He could walk down the hill and back into town as if nothing had happened, and go home and look for his oldest son, and hold the younger close, and when they were a family again he could go to sleep in his bed next to his wife and the next day go to work.

And then he thought, I'm free.

The bones no longer ruled him; the burden of his

guilt had been taken away. He'd never have to crawl again. He'd never have to show up at the cave when the bones called, and help someone else crawl. Was it possible he'd been forgiven, that the people he'd hurt had been made whole, and those he'd killed had returned to life?

Dylan didn't know he was going to cry until the tears burned his eyes. The relief was too much. After believing that the crawl and going down into the cave was his destiny, he didn't know what to do. There was a moment when he thought he'd been robbed of his birthright, that something precious had been taken away from him at the last instant.

When he'd caught his breath and gathered his thoughts, stopped his crying and accepted the healing, he discovered a simple truth in the quiet night, in the peace with the bones: he'd always had a choice.

He'd discovered the engine of destruction inside him, and he'd liked it. He'd picked that engine over the one rumbling with creation because it was fast and easy and because it made him feel good, better than everyone else. He'd rebuilt it, made it stronger, kept it oiled and running smooth, fueled by other people's pain, and never thought to count the cost of his appetite. He was happy, which was all that mattered. School, coaches, his father when he'd still been around, even his mother, all did their best to guide the shape of what he was becoming. The military worked hard to harness and refine the thing that made him work. But Dylan resisted, wanting the engine tuned only to his needs. Even as he cursed his father for leaving and his mother for being what she was, he'd picked what he wanted to be. At every crossroad, he'd turned away from the world around him and lived for what was inside, even after he'd started hearing the bones. He'd never been doomed or destined to do what he'd done.

That was all the bones ever wanted from him: to know he had a choice.

Dylan sat for a while at the mouth of the cave, in the darkness, listening to the rustling underbrush as forest life moved around him. He considered again the reality of going back into town. No one had ever done that, after a crawl. He'd be the first. Maybe that was all it would take for nobody to ever have to crawl again.

He stood up on two strong legs, supported by two good feet. He breathed the woodland air deeply, taking in the richness of its life, and its death.

And then he went down into the cave.

Because maybe that was the right thing to do. Or maybe not. But it was his choice to let everything in the past go, and it was his choice to throw his weight on a scale that might not even exist to help balance out some of things he'd done, and it was his choice to see what the bones had for him after calling for so long. He didn't think anyone would miss him back in that other world, even if the dead had come back, the broken been made whole, his son returned home, and forgiveness was bright in their eyes.

And he was afraid that he might find that engine of destruction inside him once again, and tinker with it, and see how fast and far it could run. He didn't know, even after the crawl, if he'd turn away from that path, and the terror of going back to what he'd once been loomed larger, cut deeper, than any fear of the bones and the cave.

So Dylan went down for the last time to the bones, which were gathered in a great pile that covered the wound far below, still bleeding, forever bleeding, never healing, no matter how many bones were offered, and he lay down on top of them and fell asleep.

He slept forever, but he dreamed he belonged to a choir of bone, and sang of pain, and called others to the cave. No matter how many came, he always called, even when no one answered, even when there was no one left to answer.

Because the wound—the first one, far below—still bled, bled forever, never healed, no matter how many bones of the dead were given, no matter how many were called to answer.

A Bram Stoker Award nominee, **John Pelan** is a prolific editor of horror anthologies and coauthor of several novels, short stories, and film and comic scripts, and he is an active member of the Horror Writers Association. One of the founders of the northwest alternative publishing revolution of the eighties, he also founded Silver Salamander Press, an imprint with a reputation for uncompromising dark fiction. he lives with his wife in Seattle.

Roc Science Fiction & Fantasy
COMING IN OCTOBER 2005

Penguin Group (USA) Online

What will you be reading tomorrow?

Tom Clancy, Patricia Cornwell, W.E.B. Griffin,
Nora Roberts, William Gibson, Robin Cook,
Brian Jacques, Catherine Coulter, Stephen King,
Dean Koontz, Ken Follett, Clive Cussler,
Eric Jerome Dickey, John Sandford,
Terry McMillan…

You'll find them all at
penguin.com

Read excerpts and newsletters,
find tour schedules and reading group guides,
and enter contests.

Subscribe to Penguin Group (USA) newsletters
and get an exclusive inside look
at exciting new titles and the authors you love
long before everyone else does.

PENGUIN GROUP (USA)
penguin.com/news